BEN MALLORY THREW OPEN HIS COAT AND GRABBED FOR A PISTOL.

His brother Wake did likewise, and I froze in my tracks. Shea's hands had rested in his pockets for a good five minutes. Now I knew why. His right held a new Colt, and it exploded three times before I even knew what was happening.

Wake Mallory fell backward, a neat round hole in his right cheek. Shea's second and third shots ripped through Ben Mallory's chest seconds after the taller gunman discharged a single shot.

Later, after he'd dragged the Mallorys off and buried them past the trail, Shea said, "It troubles you some, the killin'?"

"Yes," I confessed. "Happened so sudden."

"That's how it come out here, Illinois," he said. "This is hard country, and it's full of graves. Won't be the last death you'll see, son."

210

PRESCOTT'S TRAIL

G. CLIFTON WISLER

ZEBRA BOOKS
KENSINGTON PUBLISHING CORP.

ZEBRA BOOKS

are published by

Kensington Publishing Corp.
475 Park Avenue South
New York, NY 10016

First printing: January, 1989

Printed in the United States of America

for Melanie

Chapter 1

I remember the farm that rainy August of '50 as a golden sea of corn. The tall rows of maturing plants waved gently in the summer breezes, and I often gazed out from the porch imagining myself aboard a brave ship sailing across the Pacific. It was, I suppose, too fanciful a dream for a farm boy. But after all, it had been scarcely two years since I'd made the great crossing up the Oregon Trail, leaving behind fourteen years of childhood in Pike County, Illinois, to embark on the greatest adventure of any boy's life.

Just then that adventure was much on my mind. When no one was watching, I would dig out old journals from my leather chest, noting the faint pen scratches that attested to one adventure or another. The sketch of a buffalo south of the North Platte near Chimney Rock recalled to mind the first great hunt of my lifetime. An ill-shaped rose beside Fort Hall denoted my sister Mary's wedding to Mitch Crawford. The delicate crosses marked the burial spots of friends . . . and family.

"Darby, there's work waiting!" Papa called whenever my daydreams took me too long from my labors.

"Sure, Papa," I always replied. I would then scramble to my feet and set out upon whatever task had been assigned me that day.

Papa was a farmer, you see, a man who believed in planting things, in sinking roots deep in the warm earth. He was happiest marching behind a plow, turning up fresh furrows for new crops. His brightest smiles came when he tore open husks and touched the sweet yellow kernels of

7

corn at harvest. I could always tell that the apples and peaches from his orchards delighted his taste in a way no others ever would.

"It's the fruit of a year's labor, Darby," he would tell me.

It disappointed him some that I never found the same affection for the products of my long months of back-breaking effort, ceaseless sweat, and endless toil. I was more apt to smile at a hawk passing high overhead or look longingly at the distant snow-crowned peaks of the Cascades. Some folks, you see, aren't born to the land. To them fields and plows and roofs are chains that confine the spirit and smother the wayward soul.

I'd tried to explain it.

"Papa, don't you remember how you felt when you crossed the Appalachians as a boy?" I asked. "Can't you recall first seeing the Ohio River, rolling along in a wagon with your brothers?"

"I only remember chopping wood and watching out for bears," he answered.

"And what about heading west two years ago, climbing the Rockies, fording all the great rivers, seeing wild Indians and buffalo and . . ."

"I recall burying your mama," he grumbled.

I asked nothing more. I remembered that, too.

We had a good farm, near six hundred prime acres nestling alongside the Willamette River just south of Oregon City. We'd given most of it to corn that year, though the bordering hills featured an orchard of apple and peach trees. Papa was fond of fruit, and he had the orchards planted our first spring on the Willamette.

Elizabeth's Wood, papa named the larger of the orchards, for that same spring Mary welcomed into the world her first child, my little niece more commonly called Bessy. Elizabeth was Mama's name, also, and I always thought the orchard more fittingly belonged to her. What did a baby know of trees? Mama loved the springtime blossoms, and no one was her equal at baking tarts and pies.

"Trees are a blessing," Papa often told me. "They provide a man shade in summer and firewood come winter. Their fruit can sustain him, and the lumber cut from their trunks offers shelter from the cold and the damp."

"They're pleasing to look at, too," I remarked once.

"True enough, though so's a killing frost. A farmer has little love of such things. His life's a hard one, and it's best he doesn't lose himself in dreams."

I could never explain to him that for me, the dream offered a temporary escape from my prison. Papa glowed when holding a ripe apple or walking between bulging corncribs. I saw only the close of a season's work and a taste of what another planting moon would too soon bring.

"A man does his best to grow a proper crop," Papa once told our neighbor, Mr. Kershaw. "Some plants, though, don't take to the soil. Their seed's a bit too wild, maybe, or the land's too arid or too moist."

They'd been talking about the stunted peas Mr. Kershaw had raised, but I couldn't help thinking the same might have been said of me. John Henry Prescott had seen four of his five sons live to see their sixteenth summer now. Evan and Andrew were married and prospering back in Illinois, and Jeff, by the tone of his letters, was headed in the same direction. Me, I was the rogue seed, the dreamer of the crop.

Papa never said it, of course. There was no need. His eyes told me daily of his disappointment. I'd be seventeen come spring now, and still I was scarcely a hair over five-feet-six. Hard work had done little to square my shoulders. Jeff had daily used a razor when fifteen. My chin remained free of all but the finest white hairs. If Mary allowed my hair to go long between clippings, people tended to mistake my sandy-brown head for one of the Peters girls.

"I was a bit of a runt myself," Mitch liked to say by way of offering comfort.

"Mama was smallish," Mary added. "You've always had her eyes, Darby, and her hands."

Yes, and Papa thought me delicate as well. In all my life none but a handful of men thought me up to a task, and they'd all shared the long months crossing the mountains. Maybe it was because they knew of my wayward heart, listened to the temptress wind beckon them into the high

9

country.

"I'm a farm boy," I always answered when that wind whined through my window and seduced my heart.

The last week of August Papa seemed to take on an oddly serious face. Oh, he was dour enough most times, but he devoted his evenings to walking the fields with Mary or Mitch or myself. He would pass whole hours sharing family tales with the baby, who if she made any sense of the words, offered no evidence of the fact. Bessy could make sounds, true enough, but r's were past her. She called me Doddy and chewed on my fingers.

So it was that when Papa led me to the hills south of the house, I thought little of it. We passed through the fields, and he examined the greening stalks and nodded his satisfaction. If only he'd offered me such a nod!

"Son, what's that yonder?" he asked as we came to a low hill crowned by a solitary apple tree.

"An apple tree," I told him. "Growing all alone."

"Why's that?"

"Don't know," I confessed. "The ground there's good for planting. I guess we could move some seedlings over there once harvest's finished."

"Ever give that tree a good look?"

"No, Papa," I said, growing confused. "Is it somehow special?"

"Yes," he said, waving me along as he started up the hill. When we reached the tree, he pointed to its bare, though green branches.

"It's got no apples," I observed. "Seems mature enough. Why's that, Papa?"

"Even an apple tree wants company," he explained. "Takes a mixing of sorts for a tree to bear fruit. You might think of it as a mate."

"Like a wife, you mean?"

"Yes, son," he said, sitting beneath the tree and touching its trunk with a tenderness I much envied. "There are people like this tree, Darby, men who wander far from home like the seed that gave life to this tree. Maybe the wind carried it along for a time, but it came to nothing till it was planted in the ground. Even so, alone as it is, it will bear no fruit. For that it wants company."

10

"Sir?"

"Your mama used to fret about you, Darby," he continued. "She said you had a wandering soul. You've never taken to the land like your brothers, especially since we set off for Oregon. I thought it your age at first, but you're close to as old as Mary was when she took a husband. It's time you left those old journals in their proper place, saved your memories of the Rockies for telling to grandchildren. This is a good farm, and it will make you a good living."

"It's a good farm, Papa," I agreed.

"It'd be a comfort for me to know you'd be here reaping and sowing after I'm gone, Darby."

"This is your place, Papa," I told him. "Not mine. You're right when you talk about my wandering soul. I've got the itch to climb mountains, to set off here and there till I've seen all there is to see."

"It sounds like a great adventure, I'll admit, but you've got yourself moonstruck, Darby. That kind of life's as barren and hopeless as this lone apple tree."

I wanted to explain how my heart ached and my feet itched, but the words wouldn't come. Instead I sat beside him, staring silently toward Mt. Hood's great hulking shoulders and knowing he would never understand.

That night after everyone else had taken to bed, I lit a candle and spread out the journals on the wooden floor of my room. Papa and I had built it behind the kitchen after our first harvest had brought in enough of a price to buy the needed lumber. As I recalled the satisfaction we'd shared in seeing the walls rise, I knew it was that same feeling Papa hoped I'd come to have at harvest time.

I knew it wouldn't happen. There, on a rough sheet of letter paper, was a map of my own, sketched from memory and by studying the charts in the back of the journals. Included were places I'd been . . . and places I hoped to visit. It was a map of dreams, I suppose. And if the small crosses chilled me to the bone, then the mountain ranges built fresh fires inside my soul.

I stared out the window. The wind caused the linen curtains to fill, and their phantom shapes reminded me of people left behind.

11

"Mama, I miss you," I whispered as my mother's face seemed to appear atop the first shape. "You'd understand, wouldn't you? I'm bound to go."

The second shape was a grizzled face lit by a pair of dazzling eyes. Dirty strings of oily hair leaked from beneath a weathered leather hat, and one shoulder seemed to dip a bit as if to reflect the burdens life had set upon him. One hand reached out to me with but three fingers, and I recalled the tale of how he'd cut two digits from the hand to mourn a wife and child swept off by plague.

"Shea," I whispered.

That was his name. Three Fingers, the old trappers and Indians at the Green River ferry had called him. His Christian name was Tom, I'd learned, though I'd never heard anyone call him by it. Trapper, hunter, mountain man, and wagon train scout, he'd led us from Independence to the Platte, across the flatlands of the Sweetwater country, into and out of the Rockies, and along to Oregon. From pity, or loneliness, or perhaps because he saw in my eyes the same wayward spirit, he'd offered me his company and counsel. We'd ridden out ahead of the train more than once, had hunted buffalo and stalked grizzly.

If Papa'd been less alone, I might have ridden with Tom Shea into the high country two winters before. Or maybe if I'd been taller and less likely to take fever with the first snowfall, he would have invited me along. Things being as they were, he'd insisted I stay.

"You will come back?" I'd asked.

"In two winters," he'd promised.

Two winters? That time had passed so very slowly. Shea would soon reappear, though, likely riding at the head of an emigrant train, bellowing out a greeting and expecting me taller and stouter, no doubt.

"You'll take me this time," I spoke to the phantom Shea. "We'll winter in the high country, and you can teach me to trap beaver and work the pelts. You'll . . ."

The door cracked open, and Papa's troubled face peered down at me.

"Morning comes early, Darby," he said sternly. "Candles cost money, you know."

I nodded, then set about gathering up my journals and

maps. In no time they were again safely packed away, the candle was snuffed, and I rested beneath a light blanket appropriate for the cool August eve.

Papa spoke little more of the lone apple tree, and he said nothing at all of catching me with the journals. Instead he talked about digging a well so I wouldn't need to carry water from the spring to the house.

"You're good at digging wells, I recall," he said, resting a hand on my shoulder for the first time in months. "I know it seems a hard life, living on a farm, and lacks the adventure of some other pursuits. You always know where you are, though. And where you'll be next year."

"Sure Papa," I muttered.

"That's a fine thing, Darby."

"For some," I said, mustering my courage. "Papa, the thing is that not all people are alike. Shea told me once it's the not knowing that's the best part of life."

"What's a wayfarer like that know of life?"

"Something,' I answered. "Papa, you remember how Mr. Kershaw found that red-tailed hawk last spring, the one that broke its wing?"

"I remember."

"Mr. Kershaw mended the wing so it was close to new, and he built a cage so the hawk wouldn't fly off. It was to be a pet of sorts. What happened to that hawk?"

"You know full well it died, Darby."

"Did all right at first, though. Wasn't till it began to see the rest of the birds flying that it lost heart and started to wither away."

"You recall I warned Kershaw against keeping it caged."

"Papa, you said some things are born to fly. It's true. They can't be tied to the earth, planted firm like apple trees and cornstalks. They have to set their sights on the clouds. I'm like that, Papa."

"You're not old enough to know what you are," he objected.

"I've walked pretty much two-thirds of the way across the American continent. I've shot game for my table. I've stood up to danger, known sorrow, and worked hard. Is there something else to manhood I don't know?"

"Son, don't rush yourself."

13

"I've been rushed, Papa. You worked most of the softness out yourself, and life's wrung out the rest. It's time I made my own way."

His eyes died a little when I said that, and his shoulders seemed to lose their old straight-as-an-arrow stiffness. He didn't argue with me, just dropped his chin to his chest. Afterward he went off alone more and more.

"It's your doing," Mary complained to me. "You're breaking his heart, Darby Prescott. What heartless creatures boys can be!"

"All I said was that I'd be heading out on my own by and by. He's known that a long time, Mary. Shea will be through soon, and then . . ."

"Shea!" she cried. "That old goat? Darby, that man was kind to you, I realize, but you don't really imagine he's coming back here to take you off to the mountains, do you? It's been two years since you laid eyes on him, and even if the Indians haven't scalped him and some buffalo hasn't trampled him, it's clearly unlikely he'll ever come through here."

"He promised," I insisted.

"What's a promise to a man like that? Darby, he's a gypsy wind, that one. You can't build your life on one of his promises."

"Yes, I can," I assured her. "You don't know him. Unless some Cheyenne's scalped him like you say, he'll be through here. Soon, too."

"You're a hopeless dreamer," she said, throwing her arms into the air. "Hopeless! And you've hurt Papa. Best make amends, Darby Prescott."

"I'm sorry it hurts Papa to think of me leaving," I told her, "but I'll never make even a middling farmer. You know it. Papa does, too, deep down in his heart."

"In his broken heart, you mean?"

"Wasn't me that broke it," I argued. "I can't help being who I am, Mary."

"Nor can he."

"Guess not," I confessed, stumbling out the door and wandering out to the barn.

Long ago we'd fenced in a section of pasture for the horses. We had five of them, a team for hauling a small

14

open-bed wagon, two plow horses, and a graceful white stallion given me by some generous Nez Perce Indians when our wagon train passed through the Blue Valley.

"Here, boy," I called to the horse, and he trotted over eagerly. Papa had called him Hercules on the papers he filed with the county, but I always called him Snow. He, too, was one of those things born to fly, and there wasn't a swifter pony for miles around.

"Shame your papa don't hold with betting," Mr. Kershaw once told me. "You could make a fair profit racing a horse like that!"

Well, Papa wouldn't hear of making wagers, but he didn't hold against riding, and whenever my mind troubled me especially, I climbed atop Snow and raced around the meadow a few times.

Usually I took the time to saddle him proper, but something about the wind sweeping off the mountains sent me clambering onto Snow's bare back instead. I grabbed a bit of mane with one hand and rested the side of my face against his great strong neck.

"You feel it, don't you?" I asked as the horse anxiously stomped about. "That wayward wind wants to blow us out onto the plain!"

Snow responded by racing off at full gallop. When we reached the fence, I took a deep breath and pressed my knees together. Snow leaped over the three foot rails, and we raced on along the muddy creekbed that separated our farm from the Kershaw place.

I rode close to an hour. A week before, Papa would have scolded me for taking so much time from my chores, but when I returned, my shirt open and my hair swept back from my forehead, he seemed almost to laugh.

"Have a good ride, son?" he asked.

"Like waltzing with the wind," I answered.

"Well, there's work waiting."

"Yes, sir," I said, climbing down from Snow's back and leading the animal through the gate. I saw him brushed and watered before joining Papa at the woodpile. Without speaking, he handed me an ax and set off toward the house.

As I split lengths of pine and spruce into stove wood, I

couldn't help watching the sun glistening on the distant peaks. A silent voice seemed to call out, enticing me toward that distant unknown.

"I'm a wayfarer," Tom Shea once told me. "Just a seed blowin' in the wind."

I recalled the lone apple tree and frowned. The wind rose up out of the east then, sweeping the accumulated perspiration from my forehead. I slipped off my soggy shirt and set to work on the logs.

"Just a wayfarer," the wind seemed to whisper.

"Yes, I agreed. "Bound to roam."

Chapter 2

It wasn't long thereafter that Papa took to coughing. He never let on to anyone that he was sick, of course. There was harvesting to do, and no one would ever accuse John Henry Prescott of taking to his bed when work awaited his hands.

The rest of us were busy, too. Mary gathered in the cornhusks with little Bessy strapped to her back Indian-fashion. Mitch and I walked between rows, filling our baskets, then emptying them in the wagon. The work started at daybreak and went on past dusk, leaving us all spent by the time we returned to the house. Otherwise Papa's drawn face and sunken eyes wouldn't have taken me by surprise that first week of September.

"Papa, you best leave the work to us today," I told him as he recovered from a violent spasm of coughing.

"I'm not dead yet," he barked at me.

"You will be if you keep on," I complained. "Stay with the wagon today. It's not so damp there."

"You turning farmer on me, Darby?" he asked. "I can still snap husks faster than the lot of you."

"I'll not argue that," I said, resting my hands on my hips. "But if you don't stay on the wagon, I'll bind you head to foot. I swear, Papa."

"I'll help him do it, too," Mary added.

Papa reluctantly surrendered, but it accomplished little. He continued to grow paler, and he barely touched his food. At night he'd wheeze and cough so that little Bessy would wake. Between the two of them, I could hardly sleep.

17

"I think he's bad sick," Mary told me when I helped her scrub the breakfast plates the next morn. "Maybe we should fetch a doctor."

I nodded, then raced off to saddle Snow. In an hour I was in Oregon City, and by noon I had a Dr. Josiah Nettleton back at the farm.

Though I was old enough to ride to town, I wasn't thought of an age to share the results of the doctor's examination. Dr. Nettleton gave me a grim nod in leaving, and a post rider appeared that afternoon with a cough mixture which eased Papa's discomfort considerably.

There was no longer much thought of Papa helping with harvest. He left his bed only to tend to his bodily functions or join us for meals. He'd grown painfully thin, and his hair seemed to whiten overnight.

"Walk with me a bit, Darby?" he asked one eve.

"Sure, Papa," I agreed.

We stepped out to the porch, but he was too weak to walk far. Instead we sat together on the pasture fence, watching Snow's ivory flanks dance by in the moonlight.

"That's a fine animal, old Hercules," he told me. "Those Indians know horses."

"Sure," I said, feeling uneasy as he ran his fingers along my arm, then gripped my shoulders.

"You've grown some since we left Pike County," he declared. "Bess said you would. She always was a bit puny, you know, too frail for hard living. I blame myself for it."

"Sir?" I asked, confused.

"Your mama," he said. "She never was strong enough to take to the trail. When Matthew died, I suppose her heart just left her. Pitiful hard, losing a boy so young."

"Yes, sir," I agreed. My brother Matthew had been three when a fever swept him away from us.

"I see her in you, Darby," he told me. "Your Mama, that is. You had her eyes from the day you were born. Her gift for music, too. Wish we had a piano. I miss the music."

"There's one at the church in town," I reminded him. "They let me play whenever I want. I'll take you in tomorrow and play you some hymns."

"Got harvest to finish," he muttered.

"Then come Sunday," I suggested. "Can't work on the

18

Lord's day."

"Yes, Sunday," he whispered. "May not be able come Sunday."

"Papa?"

"I heard your mama calling to me last night, son. She said it's a clear trail set before me."

"Papa, we need you here."

"No, Darby, you're ready to head off on your own. Told me so yourself, remember? Mary's got Mitch. He's a good man, and he'll welcome you to stay or go as you choose."

"Papa, you're talking crazy."

"The doctor said it clear enough, son. I knew it even before, of course. A man can't live with the land, watch the seasons come and go, crops ripen, leaves fall, without knowing when death's calling. Truth is, I miss your mama. It'll be good to have her at my side again. I've got just one regret."

"Sir?"

"I'll never get to see you full grown. I wish I could tell your ma you'd filled out, turned tall and fine like she always expected."

"You'll be around to see my kids grow tall."

"No, son, the sun's setting. I feel it. You walk proud wherever it is you choose to go, Darby. It's a Prescott trait, you know. Find old Shea if that's what you will. But when the loneliness sets in, don't forget that lone apple tree. Pair yourself up with a good woman and sink roots. It's the only way a man ever makes himself happy."

"Yes, sir," I said, rubbing the moisture from my eyes as he rested his head on my shoulder. He'd always seemed like such a large, solid man. Now he was a mere shadow. I had to help him back into the house.

"Why don't you see if you can snag a trout for supper, Darby?" Mary asked.

"Has everybody gone and gotten daft?" I asked. "Mary, we've had dinner, and it's pitch dark. I don't know if I could even find the creek."

"Go check the horses then," she pleaded. "Darby, I need to talk to Papa, understand?"

There was an urgency in her eyes, and I left. My arms and legs ached from the long day in the fields, and I would rather have taken to my bed. Instead I sat alone on the fence and softly sang one of Mama's favorite ballads. I looked overhead and imagined her delicate features etched into the brilliant face of the moon.

"Mama, you know Papa and me never really understood each other much," I told her. "But you don't have to understand somebody to love them, do you?"

She didn't need to respond. I knew the answer. Instantly I jumped down and raced back to the house, eager to share with Papa that sentiment. Mary's forlorn face outlined in the doorway told me something was dreadfully wrong.

"Papa's gone," she whispered. I was too late.

We laid Papa to rest just before Sunday services. Being harvest time, Reverend Sibney thought it unfair to take folks away from their fields. As a result, most everyone for miles around was there. Folks who came out from Independence with our company recalled how Papa had ridden at the head of the train, Captain Prescott, as steady a man as any you'd hope to meet.

The Kershaws offered us help should we need it to gather in our crops, but Mitch shook his head.

"Papa took pride in our standing on our own feet," Mary declared. "Besides, Darby's here."

I eased my own grief some by playing hymns on the piano. I tried to think of some especially favored by Papa, but it was Mama most enjoyed music.

"He loved any she enjoyed," Mary told me. "And though you didn't always notice, he boasted most pridefully on your playing."

I hadn't noticed, and the words stung.

"This was a good man," Reverend Sibney proclaimed as he told of Papa's life, of his often-told exploits in the Black Hawk War and his two great journeys across the continent. I found myself listening as if hearing it all for the first time. And afterward, I knelt beside the grave and silently told Papa in death what I wished with all my heart I'd been able to tell him in life.

The next day, as we labored in the fields, a lawyer arrived with a stack of papers.

"Mrs. Crawford," he told Mary, "you're to hold joint

title with your brother. Most unusual. Generally hereabouts, property passes directly along the male lineage."

"I guess Papa thought Darby might need a hand working the farm," Mary said, forcing a smile on her face. "Where do we sign?"

The lawyer pointed to the appropriate lines, then brought the papers to me.

"Isn't any point to me signing," I declared. "I'm no farmer."

"The property is worth a good deal of money," the lawyer whispered. "The orchards especially. I'm certain you could get a good price, especially with all the new emigrants arriving."

"This is the Prescott farm," I said, glancing at Mary. "You'll still call it that, won't you?"

"Darby, sign the papers," Mitch argued. "You may come to want the place later on. Shoot, you're only . . ."

"A boy?" I asked. "A poor orphan? Papa'd never abide such talk. All I want's my horse and my clothes. You two'll likely have a houseful of kids before long, and you'll need every acre and tree."

"Darby, what will you do?" Mary asked.

"I'll put myself on Snow's back and ride out into the high country with Shea. He'll be along."

"That's foolish talk, Darby," she grumbled. "He's probably dead and buried by now. You've gotten no letters, no word of . . ."

"None's needed," I said, handing the papers over to her. "He promised. He'll come."

I had little chance to consider the matter those next days, though. There was no time for mourning when corn cribs needed filling, and hard work was a better tonic for heartache than any other I'd discovered. It wasn't until the last of the corn was brought in that I had a chance to catch my breath. The following morning while Mitch and Mary and little Bessy went into town to see about having the crop sold when dried, I set off for the small pond I'd built by damming up run-off from a spring.

"You're older, Darby Prescott," I said, gazing at the somber reflection in the placid water. "No beard yet, but you're sour as a lemon."

I might have added a few other observations had not a wagon rumbled up the trail. Suspecting Mitch and Mary had reconsidered leaving me alone, I rose to my feet and set off to assure them I would not vanish into the mountains without saying farewell. But the wagon proved to be Mr. Hogan, boss of a logging camp on the far side of Mt. Hood, together with his pretty wife and three of their sons.

"I'm sorry we missed the service for your papa, Darby," Mr. Hogan said, climbing down from the wagon and gripping my shoulders in his huge hands. "He was a fine man. I heard you played. I've missed the sound of your music."

I sighed. Mr. Hogan had been in Oregon for years, but he'd come along with us back in '48 to bring a piano for his wife. That piano had boosted our spirits a hundred times. Then we'd lost it on a treacherous stretch of the trail.

"The piano at the church doesn't have half the tone as that one," I said, remembering the delicate notes the instrument provided. "But I guess it suited Papa all right. He wasn't much on fancy ways."

"I finally got one to my house, you know," Mr. Hogan told me. "Came 'round the Horn to San Francisco, then up the coast, on up the Columbia and the Willamette, and cross country to my door. You'll have to come try it sometime."

"If I ever get up your way," I told him.

"That's what came across my mind," he said, gazing to his wife, then the boys. "You know I've got a rather large collection of boys at my place. Five of my own now, and three girls to boot. There are also a few nephews, one cousin, and such odd camp orphans as I can't seem to get shed of. I don't know what your plans are, but I never knew you to favor farming much. A lumber camp's not an easy place to make your way, but the work's honest, and the company would be fair."

"You could stay with us at the house," Mrs. Hogan said, her eyes coming alive as the boys nodded their agreement. "You might even help me teach the little ones to play a note or two. Well?"

I couldn't help returning their smiles. A warmth seemed

22

to flow out of that wagon, and it grabbed at me with a grip as solid as Mr. Hogan's.

"I can't," I said, gazing at my toes. "It's a kind and generous offer, and I'll always be grateful for it. But Shea's promised to come for me. I'll be heading for the high country soon."

"Shea?" Mr. Hogan asked, grinning. "I didn't know that old cuss was anywhere nearby. We'll have to have a talk or two. Where is he, son?"

"Most likely nudging a line of emigrant wagons up the Barlow Road," I said, turning toward the trail that wound its way from the Columbia through the Cascades to Oregon City.

"You mean you haven't seen him?"

"Not for two years now," I confessed. "But he promised to come by in case I still had a wandering spirit."

"And you do?"

"Was born with it," I said, grinning for the first time since Papa died.

Mr. Hogan exchanged an uneasy glance with his wife, then frowned.

"Darby, I wouldn't get my hopes up too much. Most of the trains have already come through. There've been big gold strikes in California, and many a train bound for Oregon turned south. Two years is a long time. A thousand things could've happened to Shea in all that time."

"I know," I confessed. "But I figure he's too ornery to get himself killed. He never broke his word that I saw. He'll come."

"Well, I hope he appears soon then," Mr. Hogan said. "Winter in the high country's not to be taken lightly. And if he doesn't, the offer's still there, Darby."

I nodded, then showed them around my pond. The boys, being a bit hot and dusty from the trail, availed themselves of the chance to enjoy a brief swim. I sat on the dam, watching them splash their father, each wave of laughter reminding me how I'd rarely shared such a moment with Papa.

An hour or so later the boys hopped out of the pond, and Mr. Hogan resumed his journey.

"Don't forget what I said," Mr. Hogan called as he left.

"And take care, Darby."

"I will," I promised.

When Mary returned, I shared Mr. Hogan's offer with her.

"My brother in a logging camp?" she cried. "Mama would turn over in her grave! I've heard tales of the language and such in those camps. Bunch of heathens, the whole lot. I'll not have it."

"You know Mr. Hogan," I argued. "I'd stay in his house. It's just a passing thought, anyway. I'm heading off with Shea anyway."

"Oh, yes, the phantom Shea. Darby, I wish you'd forget that nonsense."

"He'll come," I insisted for what seemed the hundredth time.

"Wishing it so won't make it happen," she whispered, not angrily but with a gentleness that told me she understood. She drew me to her side, hugged me tightly, then led me over to little Bess.

"Watch her a minute, will you, Darby?" Mary asked. "I've got a few things to tend."

If I hadn't been tending Bessy, I might have noticed the dust rising from the distant mountainside. It's possible I could even have spotted the tiny white canvas covers of wagons rising and falling like sailing ships amidst the traildust. As it was, I wasn't freed from my duty for close to an hour. By then a line of wagons seemed to stretch for miles across the far slope.

"I guess all the trains weren't through after all," I said, recalling Mr. Hogan's words. Shea was apt to be with that bunch, or perhaps the next. I hurried inside the house and packed up my belongings. But when I reemerged, no tall rider appeared to whisk me off to the high country.

"Don't hope too hard," Mary warned. "It'll break your heart."

No, that had happened too often already. Papa had taught me to be hard, and life had seasoned me to expect disappointment. Besides, I knew Shea would come.

I was down at the pond, swimming, when he arrived. He rode a gray horse peppered with brown splotches, and his buckskin clothes were near black with dirt and dust. A

24

great beard flowed down his face onto his chest, and a necklace of beads and eagle claws danced around his neck.

"Sure don't look like a man ready to winter in the mountains!" he bellowed.

"Do you?" I answered, slapping water up at him.

The dust and fatigue etched lines across his forehead, and his exhausted eyes hinted of a hard and eventful journey.

"Know anybody hereabouts calls himself Illinois Prescott?" the scout asked.

I did, of course. Being from Pike County, Illinois, Shea had named me such himself. I don't think he thought too much of Darby for a name, but then he never needed anything but Shea so far as I could tell.

"I might know him," I finally replied. "What's he look like?"

"Skinny boy with nut brown hair, as I recall. Had a scar across his chest left by an overfriendly grizzly."

"Like this?" I asked, rising enough that the faint claw scratches were visible. "And who'd you be anyway? I never saw such a mound of dust talk in all my life."

"Dust?" he roared. "Why, any good trail scout carries a bit of his trail with him. That way he doesn't get lost."

I couldn't help laughing, and Shea replied in kind. Then he tossed his hat aside, pulled off his shirt, and jumped from his horse into the pond. In moments he shed the rest of his clothes and was rushing after me like a hungry wolf.

"Hold on there," I pleaded as he reached out and snatched my arms. "I've grown some since you used to sling me over one shoulder."

"Grown a lot, have you?" he asked, bending low, then heaving me onto his back as effortlessly as I might have lifted Bessy.

"Put me down!" I pleaded. "I'm stark naked, and there are women hereabouts."

"Apt to get an eyeful, are they?" Shea asked as he let me splash back into the pond.

"Wouldn't want them complaining to the reverend, you know."

"I know," he said, growing solemn. "Passed by the Hogans a bit back. They directed me here. You had some sad news, I hear."

"Some," I admitted.

"I spent the last hundred miles wonderin' if you'd still want to head out with me. Had a notion you would've come two years back. Now you've got a farm and all."

"My gear's packed," I said. "You wouldn't take me two years ago."

"Your pa needed you."

"Maybe so. He doesn't now. I'll be seventeen soon."

"Won't be leavin' anybody behind, eh?"

"My sister," I told him. "Little niece. A place that's been a home of sorts, and some good friends. But I've got an itch to see the high country."

"Powerful itch, that one."

"I remember you told me once it was a good place to ease your grief."

"Fair," he said as I took his hand and gazed at the stubs of the two severed fingers. "You know, Illinois, it's hard country up there anytime, and worse when it snows."

"It'll make a better test then," I answered.

He nodded, then led the way to the bank. We shook off the water and got dressed. Then he gripped my shoulders and gazed deeply into my eyes.

"I can't be no second pa to you, boy," he said, trembling.

"I can't be a second son, either," I replied. "I was a fair companion once, though. And you were a good teacher. I wouldn't mind more of the same."

"Life does its own teachin' most times."

"I'd say so," I agreed. "So, what do you think? Will I make a mountain man?"

"Make anything of yourself you choose," he said, nodding somberly. "Care to pass the night here at your place or head on along?"

"Well, Mary's got Mama's way with biscuits. She'll have my hide if I leave straight away."

"Then it's best we head out first thing tomorrow. Lingerin' don't help the sayin' good-bye, you know."

"Sure."

I climbed up behind him on the horse, and we rode back the house. Three pack horses were tied to the fence, and

26

Mary stood on the porch waiting.

"I asked Shea to supper," I explained as I hopped down. "That all right?"

"He's more than welcome," she responded. "And your plans?"

"We leave tomorrow," I explained. Shea nodded his agreement, and Mary turned abruptly and marched inside.

"You realize there's a bit of work to get done first, don't you?" Shea asked as he dismounted.

"What?" I asked. "I've got my gear together, and you can tell Snow's ready to ride."

"Well, just look at you, Illinois. I can't take to the mountains with a farm boy. You need proper boots, some buckskins, and a fit hat!"

"The buckskins can come once I drop a deer," I said. "I've got some good boots. As for a hat, I've got a bit of cash."

"Best keep it," Shea argued. "Apt to need it for whiskey to get me drunk enough to take you along."

"I'll pull my weight."

"Well, I guess you might," he admitted, walking over to the pack animals. He then drew out a tan, broad-brimmed leather hat and tossed it to me.

"Mine?" I asked.

"Got it for you at The Dalles. We'll get some hides and such to outfit the rest of you on our way east."

"Thanks, Shea," I said, clasping his hand with my own.

"There's a bit more iron in your fingers," he observed, grinning as he probed my arms. "You've swung an ax some, I'll wager."

"And worked the fields."

"Haven't worked a razor much, though," he said, laughing.

"Nor have you," I added, pointing to his beard.

We went on exchanging barbs until Mary announced dinner. Then, sitting across the table from Mitch and Mary, we spoke of old times and future adventures.

"Darby, no," Mary finally said, setting her spoon down hard on the table.

"Got to, Sis," I told her.

"It's a crazed thing to do, Darby," she argued. "I won't

27

let you!"

"Couldn't stop me short of cutting off my feet," I assured her. "Mary, I'll never be happy anywhere else. Look at me. I'm near smiling for the first time in two long years. Papa's gone now, and . . ."

"I'm still here," she said with reddening eyes. "You're all the family I've got left."

"You'll soon have all the family you can fit under this roof," I said, grinning at Bessy. "Don't make it harder, Mary. Please. Leave me to head out on good terms. Let me make my farewells quick. It's to a better life I'm headed."

"I wish I could believe that," she grumbled.

"I do," I told her.

"Shea, you'll see he comes to no harm?" Mary asked.

"I got no promises to make on that, Miz Mary," Shea answered. "It's not for me or anybody else to say. But you can't hold onto a bit of the wind, can you? Me and Illinois here, we're cut of the same cloth. Bound to roam, and there's no remedy save open skies and high mountains."

"You'll write, Darby?"

"When there's a chance," I told her. "And if we get back this way, I'll visit."

"I'm going to miss you, little brother," she said, rising and hurrying around the table. She drew me to my feet, then wrapped her arms around my waist and hugged till I could scarcely breathe.

We stood together for close to ten minutes. Then Mary released her grip, and I began helping clear the table.

Shea and I passed the night in my room, he enjoying the rare comfort of the bed while I lay in a pair of blankets near the window.

That night a fierce wind whipped up, and thunder crashed across the mountains. Lightning flashed, and the very earth seemed to tremble while rain and hail lashed the farm. I tossed and turned, awakening four different times when the window rattled alarmingly. Shea slept through it all without flinching.

After breakfast I splashed outside through the farmyard to the barn and saddled Snow. Shea appeared shortly and helped with the pack horses. When all was made ready, I

28

led the way inside.

Mary fixed a hearty breakfast, and she handed me a large bag of provisions as well. She also insisted I take twenty dollars cash to ward off need, and I took the money more to ease her fears than out of necessity.

"Watch out for yourself, Darby," Mitch said as we shook hands.

"Look after Mary and Bessy," I answered as I bent down and kissed the little one. I shared a longer, silent farewell with Mary. Then Shea led the way to the horses, and we rode off together.

It's hard leaving people and places behind, and my heart was heavy as we set out. Papa knew that, and he wouldn't have been surprised to read the frown on my face. He never would have understood the eagerness with which I gazed at the far slopes, though.

"Be a hard trail ahead, most likely," Shea warned.

"Most likely," I agreed. It mattered little, of course, for I was in good company. I rode with that other bit of the restless wind known as Tom Shea.

Chapter 3

I suppose we must have managed twenty miles or more that first day.

"Halfway to Mt. Hood anyway," Shea judged.

I trusted him to be right, for I'd only been down the Barlow Road twice—once with the wagon train and later on a visit to the Hogans. The first time I was on foot, and the second I bounced about in the bed of a wagon. Riding Snow, I barely felt the miles at all. He took to the trail with an eagerness that rivaled my own. If not for the slower pack animals, I figured we might have ridden halfway to the Rockies.

Shea rode a bit ahead of me, as if to ward off danger. He always said it was to avoid my constant jabbering, but I knew better.

"Never did see a human boy jabber such as you!" he often complained. "Goin' to have to stop callin' you Illinois and rename you Jabberhead."

"Can I help it?" I asked. "I've been saving up questions for two years. How am I to learn if I don't ask things?"

"Jabberheaded fool!" he exclaimed. "Got myself a jabberheaded fool for a partner."

I noticed, though, that the wrinkles had departed his forehead, and he smiled more often each mile.

We made camp on a mountainside beside a small spring.

"Halfway spring," he explained. "Named it for bein' midpoint between the mountain and trail's end."

"Just now or before?" I asked.

"Oh, years back. End of the trail's slow goin' west-

30

bound, but I always make fine time headin' back to open country. I been too much with people lately, you know. They even had me shavin' my chin and wearin' a shirt with lace cuffs back in Independence. That Cap'n Ripley had more than his share of sensibilities, I tell you. Wasn't till I chased some Cheyennes from his horses that he settled down and let me be me."

"How come you signed on with him?" I asked. "Lots of folks coming west now. Seems to me you could pick your outfit."

"Usually do, too. Found myself in a spot of trouble back in Missouri, though. Had a nip or two from the jug and got crosswise of a fellow. Notched his ear, you see. Turns out his brother's the judge thereabouts. Locked me away a month, he did, and nary a thank you for not carvin' up his brother the way anybody else in town'd done."

"So you set out late again."

"And cursed with fools," he muttered. "I was half of a mind to ride back and summer with the Crows."

"But you didn't."

"Well, I felt the need to hear my own tongue spoke at me, and I like the taste of biscuits cooked by a white woman. A man can turn mountain mad if he stays too long in the high country, Illinois. Besides, I made a promise to a certain boy I figured to've grown tall."

"Disappointed he hasn't?"

"Oh, there's different kinds of tall," he said, grinning. "You stand high enough to travel with me. May not be a lot of you yet, but what's there'd be prime by any man's judgin'."

It wasn't any man's judging that mattered. One approving nod from Tom Shea was enough for me.

Once we unsaddled the horses and led them to a fresh pool, Shea handed me a rifle, took one himself, and led the way along the mountainside.

"Saw a turkey up here," he whispered. "Fine eatin', turkeys."

I was of the same opinion, and I kept my eyes alert for movement on the hillside. Shea led the way to an outcropping, and we hid in the rocks as he began making strange warble sounds.

"I heard a fellow call ducks once, but never a turkey," I told him.

"Hush and watch," he answered brusquely.

He continued making his guttural sounds, and I fought back the urge to laugh. Shea made a mighty poor turkey. The only bird to appear was a cackling crow.

"He wouldn't make much of a supper," I grumbled as Shea reached for his rifle.

"Wasn't so sure I'd eat him," Shea explained. "Sure would like to shut him up. Likely he's been drawn by a certain jabberhead."

"Thought that was supposed to be a turkey."

He reached over and yanked my hair so that my hat flew off. The crow, alarmed, set off for less dangerous ground.

"Boy, a Sioux'd likely be done with you for such words," he warned. "Only Cheyennes put up with such as you, Illinois. They favor brown hair, too. On their scalp belts mainly."

I thought to answer, only at that moment a turkey emerged from the underbrush. I pointed at the bird, and Shea glanced at my rifle. I swallowed hard, checked my powder, made sure the percussion cap fit, and shouldered the gun. It didn't feel awkward as it once had. I held it steady, aimed, and fired. The hammer slammed down, striking the cap and setting off the powder charge. The rifle seemed to explode against the hollow of my shoulder, and a cloud of smoke stung my eyes as it enveloped the mountainside.

A fowling piece might have done a better job on the bird, for the rifle ball put a considerable hole in the turkey. Shea walked to the bundle of flesh and feathers, picked it up by its lifeless feet, and announced, "You killed it. You pluck it."

"Seems to me if I did the shooting, you ought to pluck it," I argued. "That's how it always was back home."

"You're in the mountains now, Illinois," he reminded me. "Code of the high country says a man shoots a critter, he skins or scales or plucks it."

"Code of the high country?" I asked somewhat suspiciously. "That's one I never heard of."

"You will," he assured me.

Shea wasn't entirely idle while I plucked the feathers, though. He gathered wood and built a fair-sized cooking fire. Then he cut a green limb and trimmed away the bark.

"Best way to get her cooked is to turn that bird on a spit," he told me. Next thing I knew he took the skinned bird, cut out the innards, and pierced it with his arrowlike limb. He managed to mix up some awful-smelling brown paste and smear it over the turkey. Then, once the fire burned down a bit, he shoveled some coals between a pair of forked sticks, set the spit in place, and began turning the bird over the coals.

I hauled out a dutch oven, rubbed its sides with a slab of lard, then began mixing dough for biscuits.

"What you doin' there, Illinois?" Shea called.

"Thought you favored biscuits," I answered. "I'm not half the cook Mama was, but I figure to keep us from starving."

"You cook?" he asked, his eyebrows rising halfway to his hairline.

"I can do lots of things besides ride a horse and shoot turkeys. And jabber. When Mary was heavy with child, somebody had to stir a kettle. If I'd left it to Mitch, we'd died sure. Only one I ever saw serve charcoal eggs. And Papa, well, there's just so many meals you can make of apples and peaches."

"So you took on the cookin', did you? Like I said, Illinois, there's lots of ways a man shows his height."

While he turned the spit and I rolled out biscuits on a breadboard, we recalled other times and places. It wasn't until later, after chomping on a turkey leg and chewing biscuits, that he spoke of those past two years.

"Was with the Crows mostly," he explained. "Passed that first winter with the Taylors just west of The Dalles, renewin' friendships and such. Since the Whitman mission was wiped out in '47, the Taylors've started ministerin' to pilgrims, takin' in trail orphans, and helpin' others get a leg up on life."

"I've heard of them," I told him.

"They come out with me in '45, part of my first train of pilgrims. Tom Fitzpatrick, ole Broken Hand himself, set me to scoutin'. I was with him in '43, you know, shootin' game and watchin' out for trouble."

"The Taylors must have been glad to see you. The Kershaws settled right next to us, you know. Other folks nearby, too. It always seems special, visiting with the folks who were with us making the crossing. I used to see Mr. Hogan every time he brought his family into Oregon City. The McNamaras sat beside us at Sunday services, that is except for the times I was playing the piano."

"Not many pianos in the Rockies."

"Oh, the mountains make their own music," I said, sighing. "The wind and the birds and the rivers."

"Takes a special heart to hear 'em. You'll like the Crows, Illinois. They'll take to you straight off."

"Won't mind me jabbering?"

"Oh, they tolerate their children doin' most anything. Near as bad as the Cheyenne. Good men, Crows. Women are handsome, too. I wintered with one a few years back."

"She gave you a son."

"That's been a long time now," he said, gazing into the distance. "Didn't winter with a woman this time. Little chance. Crows have it hard since the pox took so many of the young men. They got the Blackfeet fightin' 'em up north, the Sioux east and south, and the Shoshonis west. Lot of enemies and scant rest."

"They must have welcomed you."

"Well, they weren't too unhappy to see me. Glad of the powder and shot I carried."

"Did you hunt buffalo with them?"

"I tell you, Illinois, we come across a herd that stretched from now to tomorrow. Swallowed the whole Yellowstone Valley, it seemed. Plenty of full bellies last winter in the Crow camps."

"And then you headed for Independence."

"Hooked up with the Ripley party. Poor bunch to ride with, as I said. Near as many fools as with you, and nary a soul as good company as that scrawny squirrel of a youngster you used to be."

"None of Mama's biscuits, either."

"That's a fact!"

"I can still taste them, you know. Sometimes, too, when

the shadows fall or the moon's real bright, I think I see her, hear her whispering."

"Likely so. She worries for you, I'd guess."

"It's just shadows. And loneliness."

"Oh, I've seen some powerful spirits up high," Shea told me. "If you were a Crow boy, you'd starve yourself crazy, then sit up on a hill and wait for a vision."

"A dream?"

"Well, a strange kind of one, I suppose. You might not be asleep, you see. Maybe an eagle'd come and visit you, or a fox or elk. Animal does the choosin', you see. From then after, he's your brother, and you seek his help when times are bad."

"But you can't really see a dead person."

"Can't you?" he asked. "I see my boy every night when I close my eyes, Illinois. He gets older and taller each year. I don't know I'd write off spirits as shadows. There's a comfort knowin' somethin' else's here besides us and the land."

"You mean God."

"I mean whatever it is to you or me or the Crows, somethin' sure walks the high places."

I nodded my agreement, then began putting the uneaten biscuits in a provision bag. Shea cut slices of turkey and salted them, then added them to the bag. He set it high in a tree.

"No point to feedin' varmints," he declared as he carried the leavings well away from camp and left them to the scavengers. "Time to stomp out the fire now and make a bed."

I poured the rest of the mud-colored coffee over the coals, then began extinguishing the last of the fire by turning earth over the faintly-flickering embers. When the fire was cool enough to touch, I collected my blankets and walked uphill to a flat area Shea had located.

The mountain was covered with pine needles, and I observed how Shea built up a bed of them before unrolling his blankets. I followed his example, and when I shed my pants and climbed into bed, I felt as if I'd fallen into a cloud.

"Soft, eh?" Shea asked.

"Better than a feather mattress."

I rolled my shirt and rested it beneath my head, then closed my eyes and listened to the spring gurgle nearby.

"You miss the farm some, Illinois?" Shea whispered.

"Some," I confessed. "Little Bessy didn't bounce on my knee tonight. I got no kiss from Mary."

"Won't be much tenderness up high. It's a hard life. No Mama's cookin' and tendin'."

"No," I said, feeling a solitary tear weave its way across my cheek. The wind whined through the trees overhead, and an invisible finger seemed to brush the tear away.

"Darby, I'll look in on you," Mama's voice echoed through my memory the same as if she'd been reassuring me after a nightmare. I blinked open my eyes and gazed overhead at the million stars shining down from the ebony sky.

I'll be all right, I silently told her. I'm in good company, remember?

I half hoped Papa's spirit voice would have words for me as well, but perhaps he was still getting acquainted up there. Or maybe it was because my memory held few comforting words spoken by him.

The wind seemed to acquire an icy bite, and it gnawed at my face so that I drew the blanket up over my head. It shut out the fiery glow of the stars, too, and I shuddered. An overpowering sense of loss hammered at my soul, and I realized Mama and Papa were both lost to me now. There would be no gentle shoulder offered generously by Mary, no Mitch to provide understanding or humor.

I was alone.

I shivered as the wind tore at me. Then a heavy curtain seemed to fall over me, draping itself over my feet and nestling gently against my chin.

"Mama?" I cried.

"Just me," Shea spoke. "You seemed a bit chilled. This ole hide wasn't doin' much good thrown over my saddle."

I ran my hand along the soft surface of the hide. It was elk, worked patiently no doubt that long winter among the Crows. I'd thought Shea asleep, but he had always proven a watchful sort, and my sadness had not gone unnoticed.

"I was feeling lonely," I told him.

36

"This is a lonely place," he replied. "Wind seems heartless tonight, cryin' like an orphaned wolf pup or a widowed Indian."

Or a wayfaring boy, setting off alone into the Rockies, I thought. No, not alone. There were two of us.

Chapter 4

We set out early that next morning, toward a hazy horizon painted golden by the rising sun. Behind us the faint echo of civilization grew silent. Ahead the hostile emptiness beckoned.

Those next five days Shea spoke of many things, each one a nugget of wisdom interspaced by seas of silence. He named trees, pointed out landmarks, even taught me to make rabbit snares and set traps. And always, toward nightfall, he mentioned the wayward wind.

"It speaks to a wayfarer's soul," Shea explained. "Calls him on to the next ridge, the valley beyond. Hear it, Illinois?"

"It sounds lonely to me," I declared. "Awful lonely."

"Is, I suppose. That comes of the mountain quiet. Nothin's so quiet as a mountaintop smothered with snow. But up high a man gets acquainted with himself. Can't lie to the wind or cheat a blizzard. And if you've got good company, the loneliness passes. Truth is, I been lonelier in the flatlands, even with people all about."

"How?"

"Well, up high you run across a fellow, he's apt to treat you same as himself. Even Shoshonis'll take you to their camp most times. Low country folks, well, they put on airs, think themselves better'n most. They spend all their time diggin' in the ground, frettin' over rain or sun or somethin'. Up high men take the world as it comes, and they don't save their prayers for Sunday. Crows say every day well lived is a kind of prayer in itself, and they thank the spirits every time the sun comes up."

38

"Mama was religious." I recalled. "She used to say life was a test of our faith. If it's so, I've had a bitter hard road to walk."

" 'Cause you've known death?" Shea asked, laughing to himself. "You'll know more of it 'fore you're full grown, I expect. You've lost a mama and papa, but Illinois, you had good folks to start with. Most don't. You've been in good company most all your life, and lots of people never know a fair day. Your road's not been so hard."

"I guess not, if you look at it like that."

"No other way to see it. Now let's get along."

From Mt. Hood onward, we rarely camped alone. All along the Barlow Road we found orchards or lumber camps. In exchange for a bit of kindling chopped or perhaps trout plucked from the Sandy River, some fruit-grower would share his supper and give us leave to sleep in a barn. In the lumber camps Shea's tall tales of the Rockies earned us a welcome.

Whenever it came my turn to speak, I told of the grizzly that might have taken my life. When the doubting loggers grumbled about a pint-size dropping a bear, I opened my shirt and showed off the claw marks. The lumbermen hooted and howled thereafter, and any lingering suspicions faded like a mountain mist.

My favorite moments were spent fishing the river or hunting the mountains. The oneness Papa felt for the land when working the fields I came to know walking the tall forests or sitting beside the rushing waters. Shea could, I suppose, have sat beside a stream for hours without twitching the line tied to his fingers or speaking a word. If the trout didn't entertain me, I usually grew restless.

"Well, there's the Crow way," Shea explained when I grew particularly anxious. "Kick off your boots, roll up your trousers, and wade into the water."

He showed me, and I followed suit. He then rolled up his sleeves and eased his arms into the river. His hands moved like snakes, and for all the world it seemed like they became trout. In time they eased up to a fish and then, pop! Shea grabbed the poor thing and flung it onto the bank.

"Your turn," he said as he marched back to dry land

and drew out his skinning knife.

I began cautiously. The water was cold, and my toes were growing numb when I finally spotted a trout approaching. The river there was clear as glass, and I had no trouble working my way close to the trout. But when I made a grab for the thing, my foot slipped on a rock, and I plunged face first into the Sandy.

"Lord, help me!" I cried, shivering from head to toe.

The trout, as a final insult, swam right past my nose. It was a mistake. Angry and humiliated, I grabbed the fool fish and wrestled it to the bank.

"Well, you got a big one there, Illinois," Shea declared when the fish and I flopped onto shore together.

"Fair-sized," I admitted.

"Got an interestin' way of doin' it, I'll admit. Most use a bit of patience."

"Patience!" I complained. "Couldn't wait all day, could I?"

"Oh, you in a hurry? Truth is, patience brings you most everything you want . . . in time. It's all that's required for the important things. Even growing tall."

I expected to hear his usual croak of a laugh, but instead there was a stern, quick nod that told me it was a truth to be noted and remembered. I did so.

While I dried my clothes and cleaned the trout, Shea wandered downstream a bit. Later, he led me to a narrow point on the river caused by fallen trees and a mound of earth and leaves.

"Beaver dam," I told him. "We had three of them on the creek. Before that, back in Pike County. Papa was glad of them, said the dams slowed the water's rush and stemmed floods."

"They do that, all right," Shea readily agreed. "There for a time the beaver was mighty popular for hats, too. We 'bout trapped him out of bein' in the Platte country, along the Missouri, and up where the Medicine Bow twists and turns. He's a strange fellow, that beaver."

"Oh?"

"Would you look at the work he's done, Illinois! Little animal takes on a whole river, tries to bridle it with a few logs, bend it to his will. He's just about done it, too."

40

"They pound the ground down with their flat tails," I explained. "Amazing what they can do."

"Do it out of pure stubbornness, I'd say," Shea declared. "See a bit of wild water, and they set to work on it. Like your papa, these beavers. Tame the land, shake all the wildness out of it so crops spring up, and people settle in."

"He's not a wayfarer, I guess."

"No, there's the wayfarin' fellow up there," he said, pointing to a hawk turning circles overhead. It fell like a shot into a trio of sparrows, dropping one to the ground.

"Yeah, we're hunters," I agreed.

There were other hunters about as well, I soon learned.

We passed Barlow's toll gate that night. Shea wasn't one for putting coins in another's pocket when it could be avoided, and we wound our way along the riverbed a mile south of the trail.

"I bring him enough business," Shea told me.

We also skirted some large lumber camps and the beginning of a town before starting the long climb to Barlow Pass. We were just short of the summit when I spotted two riders up ahead.

We'd been leading our horses the past quarter mile so as not to overtax their strength, and Snow and I'd gotten maybe five yards ahead of Shea. I turned to announce the riders, and found Shea motioning a halt.

"We're almost at the top of the pass," I argued.

"Get back here, Illinois," he said sternly but quietly. "Stay behind me awhile."

His face flashed concern, and I did as instructed. The riders proved to be a pair of amiable-looking fellows, the Mallorys, out scouting the country for timber.

"You cut trees, do you?" Shea asked.

"Well, the crew mainly does that," Ben, the taller of the two, admitted.

"We find 'em and mark the ones to cut," the younger one, Wake, added. "You look to've been through this country often. Know any good spots?"

"Seems to me most cut well west of here," Shea muttered, pausing long enough to secure the pack animals to a nearby pine. "Let's take a rest, Illinois. I think that third pack horse has gone a bit lame on us."

41

"You sure?" I asked, tying Snow's reins to a small spruce before trotting back to check on the horse.

"Must be a heavy load you're totin', friend," Ben Mallory said, following me to the pack animals. "Mind I ask what you'd be carryin'?"

"I mind, and I'm not your friend," Shea barked. "What's more, I'd as soon you two stay clear of the boy there and our gear, the both of 'em."

"Didn't mean to alarm you," Ben said, holding his hands out to his side. "Just longed for a bit of conversation, the two of us seein' no white face for better'n a week now. Didn't mean to offer offense."

"No, indeed," Wake agreed. "You say there's a good deal of cuttin' west of here. Well, that's reason enough to look hard out this way. We can't compete with the big operations, bein' just a small outfit ourselves."

"Ever heard of the Hogan crew?" I asked.

"Who hasn't?" Ben replied. "He's made a killin' cuttin' trees in these mountains, I can tell you."

"We worked for him once a couple of years back," Wake added.

"That'd been what, summer of '48?" Shea asked.

"That's right," Ben said, nodding. "Cut some tall trees that year, yes, sir."

"I met Mr. Hogan headin' . . ." I started to say.

"Headin' up the Barlow Road," Shea finished. "We camped with his people. They said Hogan broke his leg July of that year. You recall that?"

"Might've been July," Ben said, shifting his weight nervously. "Summer sure."

Shea flashed an alarmed look at me, but I failed to take the cue. Instead the Mallorys began examining Snow.

"Looks to be Nez Perce raised," Wake observed. "You buy it off 'em?"

"Was a gift," I answered. "Return of a favor, I guess you'd say."

"Nez Perce sure know horses, don't they, Ben?" Wake asked. "He's a dandy. I'd give you fifty dollars and my old black there."

"Generous offer," Ben pointed out.

"We don't need your money," Shea announced.

"He's special, you see," I explained. "I came part of the trail on his back, and toward the end my papa rode him. He's close to family."

"I see," Wake said, turning to his brother. "Still, for sixty, you might part with him."

"No," I said, grinning as I ran my hand along the white stallion's flank. "I've got a lot of miles to ride, and I need a horse I can rely on."

"Seventy-five?" Wake asked.

"Wouldn't matter if you offered five hundred!" Shea growled. "He told you the horse isn't for sale. Now why don't you fellows back away and leave us the road?"

"You'd turn down that much?" Wake asked in surprise.

"Told you we didn't need your money," Shea said, any hint of a smile fading.

"Well, you got that much money, maybe we should sell you somethin'," Ben declared. "Like maybe your hides."

"What?" I asked as Wake Mallory threw open his coat and grabbed for a pistol. Ben did likewise, and I froze in my tracks. Shea's hands had rested in his pockets for a good five minutes. Now I knew why. His right held a new Colt, and it exploded three times before I even knew what was happening. Shea's coat ignited a moment, but it was but a powder flash and was easily extinguished.

Wake Mallory fell backward, a neat round hole in his right cheek. Shea's second and third shots ripped through Ben Mallory's chest seconds after the taller gunman discharged a single shot. Ben's bullet would surely have killed me if not for Shea's prompt action. As it was, the bullet nicked my right earlobe.

"Lord, Wake, I'm kilt," Ben said then, dropping first to his knees, then wheezing as a rush of air left his punctured lungs.

"Illinois, boy, you're shot!" Shea cried, pulling me over and prying my fingers from the side of my face. Blood covered my cheek and flowed down my neck, and part of my ear dangled loose. Shea lifted me onto one shoulder and carried me to cover.

It couldn't have been easy, sewing that ear back together. I was howling with pain and shock, and my arms and legs flayed like a singed rooster.

"Settle down, boy!" Shea barked, then sat on my chest so that the air was squeezed from my lungs. I instantly gasped, and my arms and legs ceased to move. The needle worked quickly then, and afterward he wrapped the side of my head with white linen.

It wasn't until later that I got my senses back. Shea had already dragged the Mallorys off and buried them past the trail.

"How'd you know?" I asked as he led their horses along.

"If you'd use that head of yours, boy, you'd figure it out. How'd they work with your friend Hogan that summer when he was comin' west with your papa's company?"

"Couldn't have,' I admitted.

"There's more. Any man talks business to you on his feet's not to be trusted. He takes an interest in your goods, you watch out. Those two weren't half clever about it, either. Likely they took us for fools. By the size of their poke, they've found a good livin' workin' this pass."

"You took their money?"

"Wouldn't do them much good," Shea pointed out. "Not likely theirs, either."

"We can't keep it."

"Could, but I figured to send it along to Miz Taylor. She helps those that suffer trail's misfortunes, and it seems less than likely we'd find those who come across those Mallorys ahead of us. Road agents in the Cascades! Next thing you know we'll be robbed by tree frogs! World sure can be a crazy place, Illinois."

"Seems so sometimes."

"It troubles you some, the killin'?"

"Yes," I confessed. "Happened so sudden."

"That's how it comes out here, Illinois. Worse in the open country. Remember that boy got hit by a rattler walkin' the Platte?"

"Yes," I said, shuddering.

"This is hard country, and it's full of graves. You know that well enough. Won't be the last death you'll see, son."

"No," I said, gazing up into his somber eyes. He'd never called me son before. More and more it fit.

"It's not too late to turn back, you know."

"Yes, it is," I told him. "Don't worry. I learn fast."

"You do, don't you? Shame to that, too. Life sours a man as he grows."

"Or kills him," I pointed out. "I'll be in better spirits tomorrow, though. I promise. Unless my ear falls off in the night."

He grinned a bit, and I managed to laugh. But my dreams were full of dying faces that night, and I awoke haunted by a nightmare that had come to be reality.

Chapter 5

The killing of the Mallory brothers didn't fade into memory as I would have liked. As we continued along the trail those final days of September, the faces of the dead plagued my dreams. Every shadow seemed to contain lurking road agents, and the snap of a twig at night roused me from my bed.

"Can't let it weigh so heavy on you," Shea advised. "Death's just part of life, you know. You learned that comin' out here, Illinois. Couldn't've forgotten that much, not even spendin' ten years on a farm."

"Farmers know about death," I told him. "You plant new life and reap come autumn. But cutting wheat or picking corn isn't the same. To kill men . . ."

"You didn't kill anybody."

"What about next time?" I asked. "Isn't that why I've got that pistol stuffed in my belt? Isn't it why you handed me a rifle?"

"It's good the thought's a hard one, you know. Killin' shouldn't be easy."

"Shouldn't it? You did it easy enough."

"That what you think, boy? Isn't that way at all. Some things tear at a man like grizzly claws. Just 'cause I did it doesn't mean it came easy. Shoot, Illinois, out here livin's hard, and a man does what's needed."

"And afterwards?"

"He lives with it, knowin' there was no choice. They pulled their guns, don't you see? They chose the tune. I'd been no happier buryin' you back there. So I swallow hard and try to wash it out of my system."

"Ever do it?"

"Not altogether," he confessed.

I frowned, took note of the revelation, and followed him in a kind of reverent silence. Later that afternoon, as we fished a small stream two days short of the Columbia, I made my own confession.

"It's not just thinking about the killing, you know," I said, sighing.

"Oh?" he asked.

"I'm afraid."

"You?" he asked, laughing heartily. "Illinois, you haven't got the sense to stay clear of grizzlies or Cheyennes, and you call yourself fearful? That's the highest manner of foolishness I ever heard."

"No, it's not," I said, shuddering as I pointed to the shadows cast by the pines on the far side of the stream. "I look over there and see men hiding, ready to jump down on us, shoot us for our gear and horses. I hear sounds at night and think somebody's set up an ambush."

"That's caution, not fear."

"Caution doesn't turn your insides to mush, doesn't have you shaking half to death."

"Does sometimes," he argued. "It's fine to be wary, you know, especially of dark places and unknown country. I'm along, remember? I know this stretch better'n most, and I can smell trouble for thirty miles. Thing you have to do's tell the danger shapes and sounds from the ordinary."

"How do I do that?"

"Pay attention, listen, and let me teach it to you. Shoot, a Crow boy half your age'd know the difference between a prowlin' skunk and a creepin' thief."

He bid me put aside my fishing line, then led me into the woods. Soon I was sitting on a rock, my eyes closed. With Shea beside me, I listened for the near silent sounds of the forest. It wasn't long before I could detect the difference between the sounds of leaves rattling in the wind, the flittering of birds, and the more distinct noise caused by Shea's footsteps.

"Smell can tell you things, too," he explained.

That next day I continued my education in life on the trail. At first it was difficult to distinguish between the scent of a deer or a horse, but with Shea's help, I began to note differences. Men were an easier task, for they often carry with them the aroma of a cook fire, a whiff of wet leather mixed with sweat, or the acrid smell of powder.

Men were loud, too. Five miles short of the Dalles I heard voices on the wind and pulled up short. Shea nodded, then waved me off the trail and into the trees. As we watched from cover, a second pair of riders trotted by, their boastful voices betraying them to anybody who cared to listen.

"How would you figure 'em?" Shea asked after the riders had passed.

"Not emigrants," I said. "Locals maybe. They're not packin' supplies."

"Anything else?"

"Their clothes," I said, shutting my eyes and imagining the riders. "They were clean, and their horses weren't lathered."

"So what were they doin' headin' west?" Shea asked.

"Visitin' somebody?"

"We pass any settlements? Not even a lumber camp lately. Well, boy, spit it out!"

"You figure them to be thieves?" I asked, feeling my thighs tremble. "Like the Mallorys?"

"Could even be part of the same bunch. Illinois, what would you do about it?"

"Ride hard into the Dalles, maybe pass word to the sheriff."

"He's got little interest in watchin' the Barlow Road," Shea explained, shaking his head. "Could be he already knows about 'em. They'd likely be lodgin' in his own town, after all. How far would a pair like that ride?"

"All the way to Oregon City, I guess."

"Think, boy!" he urged.

"I am!" I growled.

"No gear, no supplies, eh? How far would they ride?"

"I guess no farther than they'd get before it was time to come back to town tonight."

"Why would that worry us?"

48

"Well, I guess we wouldn't want 'em falling on us from behind."

"Now, you've learned something after all," he said, smiling with approval. "We'll ride along till there's a good place to camp. Could be a farm or an orchard. There's more'n a few of 'em up the way. Not far from the big river now."

"The Columbia?"

"That's right. Lead away, Illinois. Watch the trail ahead. My eyes'll be on our backs."

There was something reassuring about having Tom Shea guarding our rear, and it caused me to set a brisk pace toward the river. We were heading almost due north now, and when the wind hit just right, I could smell the river. The Dalles had been a pleasant enough place when Papa camped our company nearby back in '48, and I thought rather kindly of the town. The horses began to tire toward the middle of the afternoon, though, and Shea called for me to head toward the first farmhouse we reached.

The creeks that fed the Columbia along our route were named like milestones. First there was Fifteenmile Creek, then Eightmile Creek, and so on. The farm we visited straddled the banks of Threemile Creek.

As we rode toward the house, we passed a pair of boys slightly younger than myself carrying egg baskets from a coop. A tall spindle-legged girl of perhaps fourteen churned butter on the porch. Two tiny ones rolled a ball back and forth beside the door.

"Better you go greet 'em." Shea suggested when we came to a halt. "You got a better way with civilized folk."

"I do? I thought you were the scout."

"Leave the wild Indians and road agents to me," Shea countered. "Go, Illinois."

I dismounted and walked slowly toward the open door. The girl abandoned her churn and raced along the porch ahead of me. She vanished, and before I could rap my knuckles on the door to announce my arrival, a tall woman of generous proportions arrived carrying a double-barreled shotgun.

"Well?" she called. "What you want?"

"Please, ma'am," I said as the barrels swung in my

direction. "I mean you no harm. My friend and I, Tom Shea there, are headed up the trail toward the Dalles, then into the Rockies. We sometimes pass the night in a barn, chopping firewood or doing odd chores to return the favor."

"And eatin' poor folk out of a month's feed," she suggested, tapping my ribs with the shotgun barrel. "Got seven boys to chop wood, and the barn needs no vagabond strangers lightin' a pipe and burnin' it down. Besides, we've had trouble from thieves along here lately."

"Any of them named Mallory?" I asked.

"Two," she said, narrowing her eyes. "You see 'em?"

"Buried them," I said, nodding to Shea. "They came on us a week back in the Barlow Pass."

"Get the whole lot?" a slender man dressed in brown overalls asked, joining the woman.

"Two," Shea called from his horse.

"There's two more I know of," the man said, stepping out to have a look at Shea.

"Might be we passed 'em a way back," Shea explained. "I figure they'll ride back 'fore nightfall. That was one reason I thought to pass the night under cover."

"They huntin' you?" the woman asked.

"They never saw us," I explained. "But we've got horses and goods belonging to those brothers."

"See, Ginny," the man said, sighing. "Told you there'd be a reason they'd have those two horses. Thieves don't pack so heavy, and they don't take on boys with calloused hands. Eat better, too. I'm Rod Mevert," he added, extending a hand. "This is my Virginia, and the herd of youngsters here and there are ours."

"Darby Prescott," I said, shaking the man's rough hand. "My friend, Tom Shea."

"Heard of a fellow name of Shea," Mevert declared. "Hard man who brings folks west. Likes to ride horses and men into the dust."

"That's him," I said, grinning as Shea took the farmer's hand. "So, have you got work we can put our hands to?"

"Looks like you've already earned a mark of gratitude from the folks hereabouts," Mevert said, pointing to the horses. "And it wouldn't be very hospitable to leave you out in the open tonight."

"I always earn my way," I declared, stiffening my shoulders so that I appeared a bit taller.

"Well, ever mended harness?" Mevert asked.

"Since the day I was born," I answered. "Lead me to it."

"And you?" Mrs. Mevert asked, turning to Shea.

"Well, now the boy's seen to, I thought to take these two horses and the goods into town, see they get sent along to the Taylors downriver. There's a fair sum of money there, and . . ."

"You know anybody to tend to such business?" Mrs. Mevert asked.

"Not a soul," Shea confessed.

"Well, you put the horses in the barn, then bring me the money and the goods. I've got a brother plans to haul supplies to the Taylors' mission middle of the month. He can be trusted to see things get where they're intended. You know the Taylors?"

"Suprised?" I asked.

"Well, he doesn't look to've been in many churches," Mrs. Mevert told me. "Most'd keep money taken off road agents."

"I brought 'em west in '45," Shea explained as he climbed down from his horse. "I've left stranded pilgrims at the mission over time, and I figure Miz Taylor would know what purpose to put money to."

"She would," Mrs. Mevert readily agreed. "Now, you see to your horses, and I'll slice some apples for a pie. When you finish, you might join the boys down at the creek. The both of you look to need a wash."

"Yes, ma'am," I said, shyly hiding my face with my hat.

"Trail dust'll do that to you."

We then led the animals inside the barn and removed packs and saddles. While Shea carried the Mallory goods to the house, a boy about my size and shape appeared with buckets of water for the animals.

"I'm Job," he told me as he showed me the bad harness. "I'd gotten to that myself tomorrow or the day after. Still will, if you'd like."

"No, it just needs a bit of lace," I explained. "I'm glad of the work."

51

"When you finish, Ma says you're welcome at the creek. Might stuff your ears some, as it's noisy thereabouts. There's seven of us boys, you see, and just the two girls. Washin' gets pretty interestin'."

"Yeah," I said, laughing. "I have brothers, three of 'em older."

"Me, too," Job said, muttering to himself. "Like as not, that's why they gave me my name. Job in the Bible had his share of trials, and I've had mine."

"Six brothers," I said, whistling. "Trials indeed!"

By the time I had the harness repaired, Shea had started washing the dust off the horses. I took a brush and started to help, but he waved me along.

"Be along time till you've got other boys to chase around a creek," he told me.

"Together we'll finish quick. Then you can join us."

"Better I stay out of view," he warned. "Those riders came along. They're up on the hill, watchin' the house. Another boy won't be noticed among Miz Mevert's brood, but I'd surely be spotted."

"How?"

"I know one of 'em, Illinois. Pierce Lloyd. Used to work the Columbia ferry."

"You've ridden through here often enough. It wouldn't surprise him, would it?"

"Might. Anyway, I'd as soon those two not know there's an extra man handy with a rifle nearby."

"You think they'll raid this farm?"

"Could be they'll try."

"And if they do, there'll be more killing."

"Possible. Shootin' starts up, Illinois, you get to cover. Mevert and I'll tackle that pair."

"Can't be that way, Shea," I argued. "I took to the trail with you. I'm bound to share the dangers."

He frowned heavily, and I half expected him to take out after Lloyd and the other rider then and there. Instead Shea went on with his work. I set the brush aside and headed for the creek.

Job and his brothers were as loud as predicted, especially a pair of eleven-year-old twins Hardy and Howie. You couldn't tell them apart in the water, and they tormented their elder brothers without mercy.

Ross and Rudy, the two oldest, must have been near twenty by my reckoning, and they busied themselves looking after the very young ones. That meant Job and his slightly younger brother Noah received the lion's share of attention. Except today I was along, so I was tormented as well.

I barely got shed of my clothes when one of the twins climbed on my back and began picking at my bandaged ear. The other one took offense at his brother getting to the newcomer first and set to splashing both of us. Then both twins climbed atop, and I took a sudden plunge. If not for Job's timely rescue, my trail days might have ended at the bottom of Threemile Creek. I bobbed to the surface gasping for air. Suddenly all grew quiet as Noah pointed to the scars on my chest.

"You do that, twins?" Job asked angrily.

"Ain't human claws, Job," Noah announced. "Some kind of animal done that."

The twins ceased their antics long enough to examine the marks, and I knew I had the whole bunch. Boys were as prone to hear a good tale as lumbermen, and once again my wild adventure with the grizzly earned me peace.

A bit later, while seated at the supper table, Hardy shared his own version of the story. I ended up revealing the scars. Shea grinned, and the elder girl, Tasha, batted her eyes in wonder.

"That's the problem with this wild country of ours," Mrs. Mevert declared. "It's got boys ridin' the mountain trails, facin' wild animals and naked Indians."

"Indians aren't the worst, nor grizzlies, either," Shea grumbled. "It's white men prey on their own. An Indian, given half a chance, will give you a fair fight. These fellows watchin' your house'd come by night, shoot from the shadows, and it wouldn't matter who caught their bullets so long as there was gold for 'em after."

The younger Mevert children weren't aware of the pair of riders, and they stirred restlessly in their chairs. Quiet, it seemed there were a hundred of them. Now I believed Mrs. Mevert must have sat the whole state down at her table.

"Time to cut the pies," Mrs. Mevert announced, and the uneasiness seemed to pass, for the moment at least. Afterward, Shea set off with Mevert, Ross, and Rudy. I knew they were organizing a night watch.

It proved necessary. A bit after midnight I was awakened by Snow's restless stomping. I glanced at Shea's blankets, saw him gone, and quickly pulled on my trousers and set off to discover what was astir.

Shea huddled beside the barn door, holding a rifle in readiness as he stared out the narrow gap left by the slightly ajar door.

"Visitors?" I whispered.

"Back of the house," he whispered. "One of 'em anyway. Don't worry. I can see a shotgun barrel standin' ready."

"And the second man?"

"Second and third," he explained. "Comin' at the front."

"Can't we help?" I asked.

"Sure, Illinois. We can watch and cut off the retreat. If we try anything else, we're like to get a load of buckshot for the effort. Shotguns aren't particular who they ventilate."

I nodded, then began loading my rifle.

"Put that aside and grab your handgun," Shea advised. "If it comes to a fight, you'll need the shots, and you'll be close enough."

"I never really shot at a man with the notion of killing him," I pointed out.

"Well, I'd say it was time to learn quick, Illinois. They might try to pepper more'n that ear this time."

I swallowed my fear and recalled the fiery flash of pain. I quickly rested the rifle against the wall and fetched my pistol. Then, as I readied to follow Shea into the melee, the world seemed to explode before my eyes.

Pierce Lloyd was the first to fire, I think. He aimed his rifle at the front of the house, and yellow flame sent a bullet ripping through the front door. The outlaws raced forward as one, only to vanish as doors opened, and shotguns blasted a storm of shot and powder smoke.

"Let's go, Illinois," Shea said, darting out of the barn as a single shadowy figure stumbled away from the house. Shea drew a pistol from his belt, but before he could fire,

Rudy Mevert unloaded his shotgun into the fleeing bandit.

"Got 'em, Pa!" Rudy called, inspecting the slain.

"Another one dead back here!" Mevert yelled. "Anybody hurt?"

"Just my window," Mrs. Mevert complained. "Looks like Job got cut some from the glass."

"I'm all right," Job said, stepping beside his mother as she lit a candle. The younger children raced out to inspect the dead, then shrank back from the horrible sight.

I stumbled back toward the barn, glad the pistol resting in my hands had remained cold and unused.

"We brought this down on them," I mumbled when Shea joined me.

"No such thing," he argued. "Might be we helped 'em some, warnin' about the men watchin' their farm."

"Three more men dead," I said, staring into his clear, calm eyes. "Five of 'em now, and we've been gone only half a month!"

"Was them took to the outlaw trail, Darby Prescott. Wasn't your doin'—nor mine."

I was surprised to hear him speak my first name, and he noticed.

"What happened to Illinois?" I asked.

"Not a thing," he answered. "A good name for the trail, but just now, well, wasn't a wayfarer I was speakin' to."

"Who then?"

"A boy growin' into a man," he explained. "Tryin' to understand things that, well, go past understandin'. World down here doesn't make sense all the time. Up high, well, nature calls the tune, and there's a rhythm to the seasons."

"It's good to know there are better days ahead."

"May get us through hard times," he agreed. "Best take to our blankets now. Tomorrow we'd best be headin' on."

I slipped off my trousers and returned to my bed, but I slept rather poorly. Death's shadow had again fallen across my path, and knowing those three earned their deaths didn't lighten the burden I felt one ounce.

After sharing breakfast with the Meverts under a shroud of silence, I helped Shea ready our horses. Packs were secured, and cinches were tightened. We tied our rifles back of our saddles in anticipation of troubles yet to come.

"Where will you be goin' now?" Mrs. Mevert asked Shea when she handed him a flour sack full of provisions.

"The high lonely!" he bellowed. "And peace!"

Chapter 6

The first half of October proved uneventful. Shea and I rode fifteen to twenty miles each day, pulling off the trail only when the horses appeared to tire or a suitable opportunity to wash the caked traildust from us appeared. We went from the rainy west of Oregon into the arid east, alternately fording swollen rivers and creeks or riding through choking dust swirls. South of the Umatilla River we spotted bands of Indians.

"Ahead's the Blue Mountains," Shea declared, pointing at the distant peaks.

"I remember," I told him. "Nez Perce country."

"So you haven't forgotten it all," he said, smiling. "Grizzly country as well."

"I remember that, too," I said, touching my chest as if the scars burned through my shirt. "Snow knows, eh, boy?"

The white horse seemed to snort a reply, and I laughed.

"Your spirits are better," Shea observed. "Must be the high country."

Yes, I thought, or the peace.

We reached the Grand Ronde River crossing on an unseasonably warm day, and I abandoned Snow as soon as I reached the southern bank and jumped, fully clothed, into the cool waters.

"Ought to shed your clothes first," Shea complained as I splashed water at him.

"Why?" I cried. "They're more in need of a wash then I am!"

Shea shrugged his shoulders, secured the pack animals,

57

and rummaged around until he located a cake of soap. He tossed it to me, and I began peeling off pieces of clothing, scrubbing them with the soap, and then hanging them in the branches of a nearby willow. The tree seemed to sprout a second Darby Prescott. Then Shea began hurling his dusty, sweat-stained garments into the river, and I repeated the process.

As the willow began sporting a third shirt, and then a fourth, a pair of youthful riders appeared on the far shore. By their sleek ponies and long, straight noses, I recognized them as Nez Perce. For a minute I thought they might join us in our madness, but they only pointed at the crazed whites and laughed heartily. A third rider, likely a father or uncle, came along shortly, and then the three of them rode off.

"I kind of wish they'd come down and visited awhile," I told Shea. "We haven't had much company since The Dalles."

"None we'd care to have to supper," he added.

We had, in truth, evaded small bands of horsemen more than once. After crossing paths with the Mallorys, we'd turned cautious.

"Lot of wagons have come through since I was here," I noted, gazing at the deep ruts cut in the sandy bank of the river.

"More each year," Shea agreed. "Kind of sad, those ruts. Makes the trail seem tame. I was always partial to the Blue Mountains, and now folks pass through almost without lookin'."

"I look," I told him. "Was near here the Nez Perce gave me Snow. I never had a horse of my own before. I felt about ten feet tall, riding alongside Tom Shea, wagon train scout."

"Not many call me Tom anymore. Three Fingers, that's a better name for a scout."

He raised his maimed hand, and I touched my scarred chest, then gazed at my reflection in the clear water of the Grand Ronde.

"Does it show much?" I asked, turning my head in an effort to detect the damage done my ear.

"Got to look hard to even see the scar," Shea assured

me. "Let your hair grow a bit, and nobody'd ever know."

It was just what I wanted to hear. I nodded silently, then stretched out in the water and swam to the willow. The sun and the wind had combined to dry my trousers, and I hurried out of the waters and began getting dressed. My shirt, having merited a hard scrubbing, seemed reluctant to dry, so I left it awhile.

"You tired of the river?" Shea called.

"Beginning to wrinkle up like a prune," I told him.

"Grab your rifle and see what you can find us for supper then. Don't wander far, and leave the grizzlies be this time."

"Sure," I agreed, laughing at his jest.

I walked maybe a quarter mile upstream before spotting a plump goose swimming near the shore. I took aim, cocked the hammer, and fired. The ball hit the goose in its chest, sending feathers flying. Birds nearby honked their displeasure and took flight.

I retrieved the dead goose and set off for the crossing. I devoted the next hour to plucking the bird, cleaning out its innards, and washing the meat. By then Shea had finished his wash and had a fire blazing near the river. He then set off to remove the dry clothing from the willow branches.

I'd only helped Mary roast a goose once, and I was less than an expert on the operation, but the turkey Shea had turned on his spit was tough and nothing like I remembered Mama made. So I took out the dutch oven and went to work.

If that goose had been an inch longer, I would've been finished to begin with, as it never would have fit in the oven. I went through our supplies and found we had little to compliment the bird. I cut up a couple of potatoes and mixed in some onions I'd dug from the trail. Mary'd added cream and spices, but having none, I sprinkled salt and pepper into the mixture and melted a bit of lard. It made a rather jumbled stuffing, and I began to have my doubts as to the result. Not prepared to admit defeat, however, I rammed the concocted mixture inside, then rested the goose atop an inverted pie pan and began pricking the skin to let the fat drain.

By the time Shea returned with our clean clothes, the lid

was on, and the reddening coals glowed both below and atop the oven.

"You put a goose in there?" he asked.

"Sure did," I told him. "Smell it?"

"I'll admit it's fair pleasant to my nose, Illinois. You ever do this before?"

My eyes betrayed the answer, and he laughed to himself.

"We can always dig out some worms to eat, I suppose," he grumbled.

Actually, we were close to doing just that by the time the goose got cooked. It took close to three hours, and we were near starved by then. The horses grazed on the soft grasses growing beside the river, and Snow in particular seemed amused that we should be so hungry when there was such good pasture at hand.

By now a chill crept through the air, for the sun had gone down, and mountains weren't known for providing mild autumns. I hurriedly put on my shirt, then added a woolen coat.

"That as warm as you can get?" Shea asked, grabbing a buffalo hide and carrying it over. "We'd best hunt us some elk and get you proper outfitted. Boots'll never make spring, either."

"Papa was going to buy me a new pair with some of the harvest money."

"Guess he never had a chance," Shea said, frowning. "Well, once we get into the Rockies, we'll tend to all that."

"Sure," I agreed as I draped the hide around my shoulders and huddled closer to the fire.

"Roast goose, eh?" he asked as I lifted the lid with a hooked stick and spooned grease over the browning bird. "Does smell fine. You figure we'll live to eat it."

"Probably," I said, grinning.

Actually, the goose wasn't half bad. The stuffing was a trifle bland, and I wished I'd some cream or butter as Mary had. As for the goose, it was pretty good once salted and peppered some.

" 'Course, I was ready to eat an old shoe," Shea commented. "Your goose's considerable better'n that. Next time we turn her on a spit, Illinois, and you use your time to bake some biscuits."

I nodded my agreement.

I was nearly exhausted when we finished eating and got the plates and dutch oven cleaned up. Shea took the leavings well clear of camp, and I noted with satisfaction that we'd salted away the rest of the goose for the days ahead. I spread out the coals of the fire so that they couldn't ignite the nearby grasses, then rolled out my blankets a few feet away. Shea did likewise, and the both of us were asleep moments after we hit the ground.

I'm not altogether sure when the Indians came. My first hint they'd arrived came when a rough hand reached out and dragged me bodily from my blankets. Three young warriors helped me to my feet, then nudged me along to where Snow waited, nervously pawing the ground a few feet away.

"Hold up there!" I protested, gazing around for Shea. He'd vanished. "I've got to get my pants," I explained, pointing to where they rested at the foot of my blankets.

A young Indian laughed, then pointed to my bare legs. They were thin and ivory white, a strange contrast to the muscular bronze thighs of my captors. The warriors paused long enough for the boy to bring my trousers, and I managed to get at least halfway dressed before they threw me atop Snow and escorted me at a gallop from the camp.

I'd never even been half as confused about anything as I was about my abduction by the Nez Perce. They, after all, had given me Snow, had celebrated my killing of the grizzly. Were they angry about all the wagons? Had they simply gone mad? Had I violated some tribal law, perhaps by killing the goose? And above all, where was Shea?

I soon had one answer. The Indians led me to an encampment some five miles north of the river near the base of a rounded mountain. Shea was already there. His appearance offered little comfort, though. He was tied hand and foot, gagged, and sat beside a plump old woman who reached for a pine log if he even flinched.

When I appeared, the Indians howled their pleasure, and the camp became a beehive of activity. Men raced here and there, and a gang of children collected around Snow's feet. They spoke to me, often, but I understood nary a word. A tall man finally reached up and pulled me from

61

Snow's back, then conducted me to Shea's side.

"You all right?" I asked him.

Shea tried to speak, but his words were muffled by the gag.

"We've done nothing to you," I said, glancing around at the encircling Indians. "I've got no guns with me, and neither has he. You needn't tie him."

The large woman cackled, and Shea flinched. I expected her to lay the log on me next. Instead small hands reached out and touched my hips, legs, even my belly. I fended them off with my arms as best I could, but that only made them try harder.

"Stop it!" I cried.

Then a great silence fell over the camp. A white-haired old man emerged from his lodge, accompanied by a teenage boy close to my own height. The old man's tired eyes fixed on my confused face, and he seemed equally confused. He then made a motion and muttered several words. A warrior held my arms while his companion opened up my shirt to the waist and bared my chest and shoulders. I couldn't help recalling stories of mutilation and human sacrifice shared by some of Papa's friends. I shuddered.

The old man grinned and shouted. He then approached me slowly and outlined the scars on my chest.

"He says," the boy at his side explained, "that you are Bearkiller, the remembered one. You have grown, but still you ride the white horse at the side of the three-fingered one."

It took me a moment to catch my breath. For an instant I thought I'd heard my last English words—ever.

"I don't understand why you brought me here," I said. "Why you've tied up Shea!"

The boy spoke to the white-haired old man, who then called to his people. The crowd laughed heartily, and the boy trotted over to free Shea.

"He didn't wish to come," the boy explained as he removed the gag. "We didn't wish to hurt him."

"Well, I wish somebody'd told that old woman there," Shea complained as he regained his freedom.

"We bring you here to share a buffalo feasting," the boy

told me. "Grandfather says you are too thin to face the snows. We will smoke the pipe and eat and dance. Come."

"Shea?" I asked.

"I'd go ahead with 'em, Illinois. Never heard of Nez Perce harmin' white men, and their food's got to beat your goose."

"We have horses and goods back at our camp," I told the boy.

He waved to my left, and I saw other Indians had brought along the pack horses. I guess there's no turning down some invites.

In truth, it turned out to be a fine time. I was invited to sit around the fire with the men and touch the pipe to my lips. There were great mounds of buffalo meat and every manner of tuber grown in eastern Oregon. Three horses were given away in my honor, and all night the boy, who said his name was Fly Over The Mountains, translated Nez Perce stories of courage and adventure told for my entertainment. Small children touched the scars on my chest for luck, and a tribal dance topped it all off.

"You will share our lodge this night," Fly Over explained when I yawned.

"How is it you speak English so well, and no one else seemed to understand?" I asked him. "When I was here before . . ."

"My father worked among the whites for a time," he explained. "Others, too, speak, but not so good. Grandfather would talk to you in your own tongue if there were not so many here."

I nodded. The old man might recognize the need for learning the white man's language, especially for his grandson, but among the warriors it was important they know he was Nez Perce first.

"Come," Fly Over said, leading the way to the lodge. I turned to look for Shea, but he was off throwing dice with a pair or warriors, and I left him to his game. My blankets were waiting, and I all too eagerly began undressing. I didn't much envy the Nez Perce their style of garments, especially the bare thighs come winter, but I'll admit they have a practical side where taking to your bed's concerned. Fly Over The Mountains simply untied his belt, wriggled

63

out of a vest, then climbed naked between two buffalo hides. I'd barely gotten out of my shoes by that time!

Shea came in a bit later, grumbling that his luck had deserted him.

"Bad enough to get bound and gagged like a tenderfoot," he explained. "To get took at dice by Nez Perce!"

He climbed into his blankets then, and the white-haired old man followed shortly, together with a pair of old women and two smaller boys. I was half asleep when, for the second time that day, a hand touched my leg. I sat up immediately this time, only to find that instead of a band of warriors the cause of my awakening was a slender girl perhaps a year or so older than myself.

"I share," she said, tugging at my blanket.

"You what?" I asked. "This is my place. My blankets."

A gaggle of laughter flooded the tipi, and I glanced around, surprised to see everyone watching.

"You don't understand, Illinois," Shea said. "She's here to make you comfortable. You're an honored guest."

"I'm comfortable already." I declared, holding the blankets tight against my bare chest. "And I don't need her help."

"Wasn't exactly what she had in mind," Shea said, laughing.

"She will keep you warm," Fly Over said, rubbing his hands together and snickering.

"No, she won't," I said, wide-eyed. "Can't they see I'm young for such doings?"

"You old enough," the girl insisted.

I must have been three shades whiter than before by now, and I was half prepared to wrap a blanket around my waist and make a break for open country.

"Isn't there any way out of this?" I pleaded. "Papa held it awful sinful, what she's got in mind. Besides, I don't exactly, well, Shea, help me."

"Tell 'em you're religious," he suggested.

"That's right," I said, making a cross sign with my fingers.

"Yes, cross," the girl said, making a motion across her chest in the shape of a cross. "Christian father."

The other women similarly crossed themselves, and

Shea laughed at the girl's disappointed face. She turned and departed.

"Now I understand," Fly Over said, smiling as he nodded. "You are a Christian father. You would lose your spirit power. We know of other fathers, but they come to us in black robes."

"They think you're a priest," Shea whispered.

At that moment I didn't care if they thought me the devil. I was so full of relief that I near fainted. Seconds later I was fast asleep.

Early the next morning Shea led me aside.

"Thought of a way to even things with those dice players," he confided. "You figure you can ride that white horse of yours fast?"

"Like wildfire," I told him. "Snow's as fast as anything on four legs."

"Fast as that gray?" he asked, pointing to a gray speckled stallion twenty feet away.

"I never saw him run," I confessed. "Don't know."

"Is it worth the pack horses to find out?" he asked.

"The horses?" I gasped. "What'd you lose last night?"

"Close to everything else, includin' most of our gear. Well?"

"I guess Snow better run fast. Elsewise, I got a feeling I better get used to sleeping with company and eating buffalo meat. You're sure to wager me next."

I said it with a smile, and he answered it in like manner. So it was that I practiced the second great sin Papa preached about—gambling. And if I lost . . .

I imagine near every man and boy had some sort of wager on that race. A friend of Fly Over bet me a pair of beaded moccasins the gray would triumph, and Fly Over himself wagered so that he confessed he'd likely pass the winter naked if I lost. Me, I'd only be shy my woolen coat, which was close to too tight anyway.

I couldn't claim to being as fine a horseman as the young Nez Perce who sat atop that gray, but I had a lot more at risk. I couldn't think of setting off into the Rockies without supplies, and Fly Over wasn't much to look at without a breechclout and vest. He'd be frozen purple by November.

To make matters worse, the Indians set a roundabout kind of course, and they placed blue and red strips of cloth on nearby trees to insure both riders kept to it. Speed wasn't enough. You had to collect the cloth flags as you went.

"Do your best, Illinois," Shea bid me.

"Remember your naked friend," Fly Over added.

Other warriors shouted their encouragement as well, the bigger part directed at my opponent. Then a boy led the way to our starting point, lifted his arms, and shouted the race was on. The gray set off like an arrow, and I urged Snow after him. We were a good ten yards behind when the Nez Perce rider plucked the red strip from the first tree. He paused to do it, though, and I simply edged Snow over, reached out, and collected the blue strip at full gallop. Warriors howled as I cut inside the gray and raced for the second tree.

Snow had found his pace now, and the scent of the gray seemed to breathe fire into both of us. I galloped full speed toward the second tree, never bothering to glance back. The blue strip awaited, and again I reached out and grabbed it.

By now the gray and rider were nearly even with us, and as I stuffed the cloth strips inside my shirt, I felt something sting my thighs. When it happened again, I glanced over in time to see the other rider flay my leg a third time, this time opening up a gash in my thigh.

"Come on, Snow," I cried, hugging close to the sleek horse's neck as the lash slashed my back, then barely missed my ear. Snow ran with every ounce of strength and heart, but still we couldn't pull away. Just ahead the strips waited on the third tree. I took a deep breath, dodged the other rider's lash, and forced the gray wide. Then, reaching out at the last second, I snatched the blue strip. The gray screamed as its rider drew in the rein and frantically fought to reach the red cloth.

"Only one more," I whispered as Snow struggled onward. The final tree lay fifty yards ahead. Then all I had to do was make the turn and race back to the camp.

The gray's rider hurled insults after me as he resumed his run. I paid him little mind. The lash was safely behind

66

me now, and the last blue strip loomed ever closer. I reached out, grabbed it, then stuffed the last two strips in my shirt with their brothers. Snow whined in triumph as I turned him toward the last stretch. Then, over my shoulder, I spied the gray coming like a thunderbolt.

I judged the lash had found another victim, and I read a fierce scowl on the Nez Perce's face. That race meant more than a few pack horses. Pride was also riding those horses. Well, I wasn't short of that myself. There were no more trees to round now, no cloth strips to snatch, just a line to reach, and I howled like a madman as Snow picked up speed. The gray was closing now, though, and I guess it was a matter of which horse gave out first. The pair of them would have been a match for any team under God's blue sky.

The line seemed close enough to touch now. Twenty yards, then ten, I felt my face catch fire as the gray pulled even, and when the other rider's lash hand rose again, I threw my left hand out to my side. The sudden movement unsettled him, and he lost perhaps a step. It was all Snow needed to surge ahead across the line and win the race.

I'd never heard anything to match the clamor that greeted the close of the race. I slowed Snow, then nudged him toward a nearby pond.

"Thank you, boy," I said, running my fingers along his flanks and burying my face in his mane. "I knew we could do it, Snow, lash or no lash."

I close to fell off my horse then, and for a minute I leaned against him for support. Then eager hands reached out, plucked me from my feet, and carried me victoriously to the finish line, where the downhearted losers were paying their wagers.

"Look!" Fly Over cried as he wrapped a fine elk robe around his shoulders. I saw everything from brass buttons to a chamber pot exchange hands. For myself, I welcomed the moccasins.

"Should've warned you about the lash," Shea grumbled as an old woman dabbed putrid-smelling white paste onto my torn thigh, leg, back, and cheek. "But I guess you handled yourself fair. That little shove took the wind out of him, didn't it? I thought he'd mess his britches when

67

you cut inside him at the tree."

"You ride like a Nez Perce," Fly Over The Mountains added. "You are white outside, but I think red underneath."

They carried me around for close to ten minutes, passing me from one band to another like a war trophy. When I finally touched ground again, Fly Over's grandfather grasped me by both shoulders, pulled me close to his chest, and whispered, "You are the one with us now, Bearkiller."

The old man called all the people together and spoke to them. Then Fly Over led ponies out and presented them to members of the tribe.

"What's happening?" I asked Fly Over The Mountains. "Did he lose a wager?"

"No," Fly Over said, frowning. "Grandfather won much. Now he gives away horses in honor of your naming."

"Naming?"

"He's given you a name, Bearkiller. You are Nez Perce now."

"What?"

"He's adopted you," Shea explained, patting my shoulder with a large hand. "You got yourself a new papa."

"It's good," I said, smiling. "I feel almost at home here."

"Want to stay?" Shea asked.

"It wouldn't be so bad. They seem like good people."

"It's different some, livin' with Indians," Shea said, gazing at his missing fingers. I knew he was remembering his Crow wife and son.

"You rode on, though, and you would this time, too," I said.

"Got my heart set on the Rockies."

"Then I guess we'll leave in the morning, now we've got our supplies back."

He grinned and slapped my back. I returned the favor.

We passed one final night in the camp of the Nez Perce. As I lay in my warm blankets, remembering the race and feeling the contentment that comes with a full belly and a day well lived, I spotted the girl in the oval entrance to the lodge.

Her face was pleasant, and her manner almost shy. Someone had braided her hair, and a fine elk robe covered her thin frame. Her eyes filled with a plea of sorts, and she smiled at me.

You don't understand, I spoke silently. I'll leave tomorrow.

She opened the robe, letting the faint glow from the embers of the fire behind me dance across her. I swallowed hard, then slowly shook my head. She pulled the robe tight, then smiled as she made the sign of the cross.

Yes, I thought. Think it that. You'd never understand how I can kill a grizzly bear, win a horse race, and still be too young.

I closed my eyes and listened as her soft feet trod quietly away from the lodge. I figured in the cold of winter, I'd likely dream of her and wonder if I might not have been happier as a Nez Perce horseracer and bearkiller. Things being what they were, I dozed off, knowing tomorrow I'd ride at Tom Shea's side eastward toward the Snake River.

Chapter 7

Ft. Boise clung to the Oregon Trail where the Boise River merges with the Snake. Shea and I approached the old trading post the first week of November amid flutters of snowflakes that threatened to paint the world winter white.

"Winter's come," Shea announced soberly.

I knew what was on his mind. We were yet a month from the Rockies, and the snows had found us. Ahead the Snake River rolled on. I turned and gazed behind me at the trail ruts, now smothered by snowdrifts. Already the tracks of our horses were swallowed by ivory winter. I feared the same fate might await us.

"We're crossing into Jordan, the promised land," Papa had announced when our train had surged across the Snake into Oregon. I couldn't help sensing we were leaving that promised land now for a kind of snowbound Purgatory, a haze-clouded region where death forever lingered close at hand.

"Illinois, let's get on with it," Shea called, shivering from the cold. "Fort's just the other side of the river. We're sure to find cover for the night there."

I nodded, then followed toward the river. Patches of ice formed on the bank, and the water appeared bitter cold. A fine mist rose smoke-like from the surface, and Shea scowled.

"Throw a rope over the trailin' pack horse," he suggested. "That way we can keep 'em 'tween us."

I did so, then allowed Shea to splash into the river. The pack horses followed, whining reluctantly as Shea pulled

70

them into the frigid stream while I nudged them from behind. The river proved deep in places, and when Snow's hooves sank into the muddy bottom, my feet caught fire. I urged the poor horse on, fearing a moment's hesitation would surely turn us both to ice.

"Come on, boy," I cried. "No blue flags to snatch this time. Just half a river and a bit of a hill waiting."

And so we kept going, shivering from the cold and the damp, shutting out the shrieks of the horses and the haunting whine of a shrill north wind. The bank seemed to hover just out of reach. I blinked away a numbing pain and saw it vanish in the haze. Then Shea bellowed in triumph, for he'd reached the far bank. The pack horses hurried along now, and Snow, sensing the end of his torment, splashed through the shallows with renewed vigor, and we were across the Snake at last.

Our ordeal was far from over, though. The wind tore at my drenched trousers, sending icy slivers of pain racing up my legs. I coughed and shivered, and Shea waved toward the huddle of buildings that composed Ft. Boise. I thanked God we need not cross the Boise River as well, for Shea had kept us north of that river so as to reach the fort unhindered by a second stream.

For several minutes I rode along in a stupor, sensing more than knowing where Shea rode. The rope meant to keep the pack animals in file served to steer Snow toward the fort now. Flakes fell in white waves, stinging my eyes and numbing my lips. If I hadn't thought to wrap my ears in a woolen scarf, they surely would have suffered the ravages of frostbite.

I scarcely recall reaching the fort itself. I have faint memory of hands pulling me from my horse, of loud voices and heavy feet thudding along wooden walkways. Somewhere along the way cold and exhaustion swept me away, though. When I awoke, I found myself lying in a wooden tub of warm water, tended by a sour bespectacled demon of an old woman.

"What's happened to me?" I gasped, blinking my eyes as if that would rid me of the apparition before me.

"Near snowblinded and partly froze, but it's done nothing to curb your tongue, has it?" she grumbled. "That

Shea's brought you to Ft. Boise, at least that part of you's not melted away in my tub."

"Who are you?" I cried, covering up as best I could.

"Molly Bostwick," she said, grinning as she handed over a scrubbrush. "Little late for modesty, I fear. I had to cut those britches off you, for they were froze to your bottom. What's a boy with farmer's hands doin' with the likes of Three Fingers Shea anyway? You ought to have better sense."

"He's a good man," I argued. "And better company than you."

"You'd hardly know that," she grumbled. "It's me thawed you and washed you, and now you've got cross words instead of gratitude. Men!"

"Could you bring me some clothes?" I asked.

"Now you want more favors! I'll be hanged if I didn't half expect such from Shea, but you've got the look of a decent sort. I expected better."

"I'm sorry," I said. "It's just, well, I'm not used to being tended by anybody. My mama's been gone going on three years now, and I'm a little ill at ease . . ."

"Orphan, eh?" she said, nodding. "Ought to've known. You soak awhile, sonny, and I'll have some clothes brought you."

"My name's Darby," I told her. "Darby Prescott."

"I'm Molly," she said with a friendly grin. "You soak some, Darby. We'll find you something to put on yourself more fitting for winter."

I saw no more of Molly Bostwick for a time. Shea appeared with a pair of buckskin trousers borrowed off one of the trader's boys, together with a woolen shirt and a buffalo hide.

" 'Fore we get much higher, we'd best get you better outfitted," Shea declared. "Little dip in the Snake, and you near freeze yourself."

"The horses?" I called.

"Bedded down in a shed. I gave ole Snow a sound brushin' with my own hands."

"Thanks, Shea. I can't understand what hit me. I've known cold before."

"Likely the river chilled you more'n you knew. Does it

sometimes. Miz Bostwick did a fair job with you."

"Who is she?"

"Laundry lady hereabouts known for takin' in strays. Got a houseful, by what I hear. Trail orphans or trader kids, they all of 'em gettin' by one way or another."

No wonder her face is wrinkled and her hair gray, I thought.

Once I was out of the tub and all the moisture was rubbed out of my skin, I got dressed and followed Shea across the fort compound to a large building. There the post's principal trader, Duncan Macilvain, awaited us.

"He's a Scot, too, you see," Shea whispered.

But Macilvain was a far cry from Tom Shea. The trader stood bare-kneed in Highland kilt, and when we introduced ourselves, Macilvain responded by placing a set of bagpipes on his shoulder and treating us to a series of wild Scottish tunes.

The piping painted Shea's face white as the snow outside the windows, and I was surprised to hear the weathered, hard-as-granite scout strike up a tune in a muddle of Gaelic the likes of which I had never heard. Macilvain piped even louder, and the two of them took to throwing out their arms, then kicking high and dancing around like a pair of loons.

They went on for close to an hour. Then they set off for a corner of the store, drew out a smoky bottle, and began sharing old tales of a land neither one had seen for a score of years.

"Scotsmen!" Molly Bostwick declared later when she called them to dinner. "Lot of crazed fools. And you, Darby Prescott, not a lot better."

"What'd I say?" I cried. "I've been sitting here minding my own business most of the day now."

"And never a thought that there might be work waiting to get done? And I thought you raised on a farm of good folks!"

"I was," I insisted. "So, what can I do to earn some supper?"

"Thought you'd ne'er ask," she said, ushering me along to a side room where a pair of tables stood. Plates and bowls lay on a sideboard. She merely pointed to the table, and I set about preparing the table for a dozen diners. Shortly thereafter a pair of girls aged ten or so added pewter spoons, forks, and knives, and a boy somewhat younger topped each plate with a gingham napkin. Four older children followed, carrying steaming kettles of stew or platters of biscuits.

"Now where've those Scots gone to?" Molly complained. The smallest boy darted off instantly. He returned with Macilvain and Shea almost immediately, and Molly waved toward the tables. I waited for the others to grab seats, then sat at the remaining place just opposite Molly Bostwick. She then gave thanks for the food, urged all to keep the Lord's commandments, and we set to work emptying the plates.

It was quite a meal, for I'd almost forgotten the delightful taste of carrots and peas. A bit of celery or parsley spoke of a home left behind, and I was grateful beyond measure.

"Well, there'll be dishes to get washed," Molly told me when I expressed my thanks. The other children grinned, and I accepted my fate without comment.

Shea and Macilvain passed the evening swapping more tales of Scotland. When I'd finished my kitchen duties, I joined them for a bit. They spoke thick Gaelic words, though, and even when mingled with English, the conversation was beyond me. I finally made my way to a corner of the store and stretched out atop a stack of trade blankets.

"That's no place to sleep," a dark-haired boy of fourteen told me. "You're to share our quarters tonight, Miz Molly says. Come along. I'll show you."

I followed without questioning. It seemed my life had taken a course of its own, and I was powerless to direct it anymore. The boy bundled himself in a heavy elkhide coat, and I hurried over, grabbed my buffalo hide, and likewise braced myself for the chill wind. Molly Bostwick's house was adjacent to the trading post, and I had but a few feet of open ground to cross. Nevertheless, trudging through snowdrifts with the wind slashing at my face, it was far enough.

"This way," the boy said when we entered the house. It

74

wasn't but a single room kept warm by an aging Franklin stove in its center. A blanket hung over a rope set Molly and the girls' quarters off from six slat bunkbeds inhabited by the boys. The four lower bunks were already occupied. My blankets had carefully been set atop the highest bed on the right side.

After we removed our soggy boots and set our coats to dry beside the stove, my guide climbed the precarious ladder and hopped into the empty top bunk opposite my bedding.

"Welcome to Ft. Boise," he said, waving me along.

"Thanks," I answered. "I'm Darby Prescott."

"Jubal Boyd," he answered. "I'm a quarter Paiute, you know."

"No," I said, studying his features. It didn't show.

"You ride 'long with Three Fingers?"

"Crossed the mountains with him in '48. Then came down from the Willamette Valley with him this year."

"Late to cross the Snake," Jubal commented. "Lucky you didn't freeze, Miz Molly says. Should've seen her muttering about it, how she had to cut off your clothes and soak the ice off your feet. She was proper mad, I'll tell you."

"Why?" I asked. "She doesn't know me."

"Don't know the whole truth of the tale," Jubal confessed, "but I heard Macilvain say once that she lost four of her own kids comin' west. She buried the last one here and swore she'd go no farther. She cooked and did washin' for a time. Then Henry and Clark Paget lost their ma and pa. Sheila Brooke came next. 'Fore long, Molly had a new family. I saw her wrestle a big Iowa pig farmer to the ground for lashin' his boy back in July. She's got a soft spot for young ones, I suppose. Took me in, and Lord knows nobody else would."

"That's a truth," one of the boys below agreed. "Go to sleep, Jube!"

Jubal shrugged his shoulders and began peeling off his clothes. I followed suit, then climbed snugly beneath the blankets and enjoyed a kind of warm snugness I could barely recall knowing.

The snow which had welcomed us to the Snake was but

the prelude of the first winter blizzard to hit the Snake River country. All night the wind howled furiously, and the skies emptied a foot and a half of white powder on Ft. Boise those next two days. Even had we wished to leave, there was no way to open the huge swinging gates of the stables and get our horses out, for the hinges were frozen in place, and snowdrifts three feet deep piled against the outside.

The horses themselves weren't in peril. The stable had been designed with such problems in mind, and a wooden catwalk led from the second floor of a storehouse to the stable loft. Jubal and the Paget boys negotiated the walkway twice daily, seeing that fresh water and oats were provided the stock.

I think Shea was glad of the delay. He and Macilvain were much alike, and though I had a feeling their wild tales little resembled any truth, it didn't seem to matter. I devoted my own time to stitching a new pair of buckskin trousers for myself, helping Molly Bostwick as needed, and entertaining my fellow inhabitants with stories and songs.

For besides collecting children from the trail, Molly Bostwick also gathered discarded odds and ends left behind by emigrants rolling westward. Her prized possession was a maple pianoforte, but up to now no one had brought the strings to life. I set that to rights straight away, and my fingers filled the fort with music. After dinner our second night, Duncan Macilvain blended his pipes with my notes, and we played until the icicles on the eaves began to dance.

The music plagued Shea with a strange wave of melancholy, and he took to strong spirits for the first time I could recall.

"It's the pipes, son," Macilvain told me. "It passes."

I hoped so, but the music brought a new glow to Molly Bostwick, and her assorted charges were forever pleading with me to try a fresh tune.

I found time for more than music, though. As the weather finally abated, and the sun reappeared, the younger inhabitants of Ft. Boise spilled outdoors and engaged in fierce volleys of snowballs. Jubal and I squared off with the Pagets for close to an hour. Then the younger kids ambushed the four of us, and it was a contest of whether we could plant small bodies in the snowdrifts faster than they could escape and rejoin their fellows.

Afterward, while thawing out beside the stove, I hummed a tune and sewed up the hems of my new trousers.

"What's a boy with such a gentle spirit doing in the company of that rascal Shea." Molly asked as she took a pair of clippers to Jubal's hair.

"Looking for some peace," I told her.

"In the high country? There's none to be found once the snows come, Darby. Better you to stay here till spring."

"That's well enough for the Paget boys," I admitted. "Jubal even. But me, I'm a restless sort, and I long to see new sights. It's me begged to come, you see. Molly, he's not so different from you. He's got a heart that feels for those in need, too. You must've been awful lonely before you took in Henry and Clark. Shea's no different, though he'd never admit it."

"We'll miss the music," she said, taking my hand.

"As I will," I told her. "The food, too. But I'm bound for the Rockies."

"My folks died just this side of the American Falls," Jubal said somberly.

"My mother's buried above the Bear River, just short of Ft. Hall," I told him.

"It's hard country, full of graves," Molly noted with a sigh. "You see to it one doesn't have your name carved on it, Darby, or I swear I'll come after your ghost with a big stick and thrash you proper!"

"She's the one to do it, too," Jubal said, laughing.

I nodded, then tied off my knot and stepped into the new trousers. They fit fair enough, though I relied on a pair of suspenders for the present. I had a notion to do some growing, after all.

Shea and I spoke few farewells when we rode out eastward. A wave sufficed for Jubal, and Molly would have cried in any case. Macilvain played the pipes, and the shrill notes followed us as we rode along the Snake.

Once we passed from sight of Ft. Boise, I was overpowered by the loneliness of the land. The whole world had been painted white, and for as far as I could see in any direction, not a single footprint marred the smooth ivory surface. We were men apart—alone.

Shea noted my frown and set to work seeing there was little time to reflect on the cold and eerie silence. We were in the mountains now, and there was work to do.

"To begin with, it's time you had a proper coat," he declared. "Buffalo hide's fine to cover you at night, but you've got need of an elk's hide to fend off the cold. A proper hat would help, too."

"So lead away," I told him.

He did just that. I'd learned to recognize tracks and scents, but I was a newborn babe compared to Three Fingers Shea. He had a nose for game like no man I ever knew, and he soon took us north of the river into the tall trees. Near a small pond we waited half the day for elk. When they appeared, we sought only the larger ones, those who'd had their best winters.

"That one with the broken antler," Shea whispered at last. I took aim, steadied my rifle, and fired. The ball whined across the hillside and struck the elk's heart. It turned, stumbled, and fell. Shea dropped a second beast before the others scrambled off to safety. We then set about the hard work of skinning the animals and butchering the meat.

For a week we ate well from the meat of the elk. Each night I worked on the hides, first drying and later tanning them. Finally it was time to shape and cut the robe and fashion two hats.

Shea showed me how to cut a slit in the center for my head. He then measured the arms, shoulders, waist, each in turn. Finally I trimmed the robe and drew out my needle. Thereafter I sewed as I rode, as I sat beside the campfire, even while fishing the river. At last I had a winter coat fit for a mountain man. Shea then fashioned himself a hat and showed me how to do likewise. The final touch proved a pair of tough boots of buffalo hide he'd bartered from Macilvain. At last, clad in elkhide, buckskins, and buffalo boots, I sat atop my snow-white pony as a Rocky Mountain wayfarer should.

"Now we can set to some real adventurin'!" Shea declared.

So we did. The balance of the month we continued up the Snake, hunting and fishing, Shea teaching and I learning. The snowbound character of the country came to bother me less and less, and when the skies disgorged upon us, we found shelter in caves or constructed thatches of pine and spruce branches that leaned against rocky outcroppings and provided us respite from the wind and weather.

"Feel at home yet?" Shea asked me as we headed at last toward the American Falls of the Snake.

"No," I told him. "I don't know it's possible here. It's such a windblown, silent world, after all."

"Maybe," he admitted. "Me, I like the quiet, though."

Overhead a majestic eagle made a long, wide circle. I watched it in awe, and Shea grinned. A second eagle then appeared, and the pair rode the clouds until they disappeared beyond the treeline.

"It's their country really," Shea said, nodding. "Theirs and the tribes. White men just pass through."

"For now," I said. "Later on, when the Willamette fills with farmers, others'll see the magic in these mountains, notice the good water, and they'll build towns and cut the earth with their plows."

"Seems likely," Shea confessed, shaking his head. "Seems it's always the same. Sad, too, 'cause then there'll be no place for wayfarers. We'll sit drunk in saloon corners and talk of times nobody remembers."

"Oh, they'll be folks around to remember," I assured him. "As for you sitting around a saloon, I don't figure the grizzlies and the Sioux and the rattlesnakes have finished with you yet. And right now we're supposed to be adventuring, aren't we?"

"Sure are!" he bellowed, urging his horse on through the snow. "And we will, too!"

79

Chapter 8

Those final days of November, I couldn't help thinking that we had become true wayfarers. Wind and snow erased our trail almost as soon as we made it. Any shelter we constructed was dismantled before our departure. Perhaps a bit of ash might be spotted in some cave or another, but for the most part, only the eagles overhead noted our passing.

I felt a sense of pride in our ability to cope with the raw weather, to hunt for our sustenance. Shea said little as we rode, but I caught him grinning or nodding at me by and by, and I knew he wasn't displeased with the man I was growing to be.

We made our second crossing of the frigid Snake River just above American Falls. Ft. Hall was now but a day or two away, depending on the weather, and Shea was on good terms with the traders there.

"I remember Ft. Hall well," I told him. "Mary and Mitch said their vows there. Mama's buried just south of here, you know."

"I recall it. Was a sad time for the both of us," he said somberly. "She was a woman to know, Illinois. Made the finest biscuits I ever ate."

"Better'n mine?"

"Well, you're improvin' some, I'll admit, but you don't have a woman's way with flour. You do better with biscuits than goose, though. We'll have to get a fresh sack of flour at the fort."

I nodded my agreement. The ground was far too frozen to dig tubers now, and I was eager to taste something

80

besides meat turned on a spit. I believe I would have welcomed a wild turnip or some Indian squash.

The flour would have to wait, it turned out. That night the wind ushered in December with a violent snowstorm. White powder choked the land, and I was grateful Shea had insisted we construct a shelter. Even so, the pine branches of our small lean-to strained under a heavy burden as snow collected. Our fire struggled to fend off the cold, and I fretted for the horses. We'd built a shelter of sorts for them as well, but they often set off to forage for themselves, and if in the open, they would have a fearful time of it.

I grew up in Illinois with hard winters and heavy snows, and I was well acquainted with both. The blizzard that hit us was as bad as any described around grandfathers' fireplaces or recounted at community gatherings. Next morning the snows continued to rage, and when I tried to make my way to the horses to assure myself they were all right, the blinding white fury sent me sinking into deep drifts instead. I barely managed to pull myself out and stumble back to the shelter.

I tried again around noon. The wind had begun to die down, and the snow lightened enough to allow me some vision. The horses proved well enough, though they'd exhausted the forage we'd left. I opened a precious bag of oats for them, patted Snow's nose, then turned back toward our own shelter. I got only a few feet when a shapeless white monster uttered a horrifying call and stomped toward me.

"Shea!" I shouted, retreating through the drifts. "Shea!"

"What you got yourself into, Illinois?" he asked impatiently.

"There's something out here!" I yelled.

"What?"

"I don't know," I said, staring with wide eyes as the white phantom suddenly ceased its charge. For a moment it paused. Then it collapsed into the snow.

No longer threatened, I began to calm myself. It was clearly too small and much too slow for a bear. Or a buffalo. Or a horse. In fact, its shape matched nothing in my memory. Curiosity got the better of caution, and I approached it. If not for a fringe of brown cowhide, I might have never found the intruder. Every other inch was coated with snow and ice.

"What you got there, Illinois?" Shea called as he finally emerged from the shelter.

"Don't know," I said, nudging it with my toe.

It moved slightly and uttered a low moan. I bent over and pulled on the cowhide. It proved to be a scabbard containing a knife. My monster was no doubt human. The realization filled my chest with a sense of urgency. I pulled at the rest of it, clawing away ice and snow with my fingers until at last I located a neck, then a head, and eventually a face half covered by a woolen mask. I pried off the mask and discovered a pair of eyebrows painted white, a nose barely drawing air, and a mouth reddened and blistered with frost.

"Who are you?" I asked.

"Help," a voice managed to mutter.

I reached low, grabbed legs now thinned by ice shaken loose, and slung the snow creature over my shoulder. Helped along by Shea, I carried it to the shelter. We placed our mysterious burden beside the fire, then began unwrapping it. What began as an almost rounded hulk of a figure soon grew thin and gaunt as we pried one coat after another from a frail youngster that might have been Darby Prescott two winters before.

"He's near dead," Shea declared. "Get some water heated. Then get the rest of these things off him and rub the skin. We best have the blood stirrin' again, or he's apt to lose fingers, toes, maybe arms and legs."

I nodded, then dragged a kettle outside, filled it with snow, and set it on the fire. Shea had laid a pair of buffalo hides beneath our frozen visitor, and I began peeling icy fragments of a shirt from flesh as pale and lifeless as a skinned rabbit.

"Wish we had a tub," Shea grumbled. "It's what we used on you at Ft. Boise. It'd help to have a woman like Molly Bostwick along, too, one accustomed to such work."

I understood what he meant. Neither of us had much gentleness. All I knew to do was tear away the frozen garments and rub the ice-boy's fingers and hands, arms and shoulders. Shea likewise started with the toes. As the water warmed, I bathed the boy's face and hair, then dried the abused skin with a cotton shirt.

Color did return, but for the most part the flesh seemed burned from the summer sun. His breathing was heavy, labored, and I feared any moment he might simply give up. Then his teeth began to chatter, and his eyelids cracked open.

"Who?" he mumbled. "Where?"

"Friends," I told him, rubbing his chest with new vigor. "On the Snake near American Falls."

"Need help," he added.

"You've found it," I assured him. "You're in good hands."

"Not . . . me," he said, coughing violently. "Others."

"He's part of a group sent for help, Illinois," Shea declared. "Where are the rest?"

"With . . . with me," he whispered, closing his eyes.

"You stay and keep at it," Shea told me. "I'll see if I can spot the others."

I looked up as if to plead for his help, but I said nothing. He was right. If others remained out in that storm, they were surely as desperate. I let him go and continued rubbing life back into my patient.

"Lord, you brought me through the chills," I whispered as I dipped a cloth in warm water and massaged the boy's chest. "Bring him through, too. This place holds enough graves already."

Perhaps the Lord was listening, or maybe the boy was stronger than I first judged. Whatever the reason, my efforts began to bring him to life.

"Wiggle your toes," I said. "Fingers, too."

"I'm sooo tired," he moaned.

"Do it!" I barked. "You're half frozen. I can't do it all. You have to help."

I turned him on his side and wiped off what seemed to be a small lake of moisture from his back. As his fingers began to regain some movement, I gave him a cloth and let him work on himself.

Soon he was bending his knees. His breathing eased, and he managed, with my help, to sit up.

"You'd better sip some water," I suggested. "Then I'll heat some food. First, though, you'd better put some clothes on or all that work'll be for naught."

"I'll admit they'd be welcome."

"Yeah," I said, grinning as I remembered awakening in Miss Molly's tub. "Bet you thought to have happened upon lunatics. I took the cold myself a month back and came to with a strange woman rubbing me half to death."

"Wouldn't mind if'n she was pretty," the boy remarked, a trace of a smile happening across his face.

"She was old and wrinkled like a prune," I grumbled as I began tossing the few extra odds and ends of clothing I owned at him. "May not fit any too great, but I'm closer to your size than old Shea."

"I'm used to passed down things," he declared, easing himself closer to the fire. "Got four brothers."

The smile then faded, and he stared toward the narrow slit of a door leading outside.

"They out there, too?" I asked as I filled a cup with warm water and passed it into his trembling hands.

"Two. Other two's back at the train."

"Wagon train?" I asked. "You mean there's a company nearby?"

"If they're not all froze. We left 'em three days back near starvin', with two axles busted, and the horses run off or down from cold. We took the six mounts best fit for ridin' and headed for Ft. Hall."

"Where's the train?" I asked, only now sensing the true tragedy we'd blundered upon.

"Down the valley. Scouts said we were just short of Ft. Hall."

"You got turned around some," I told him, "We're maybe fifteen miles from the fort ourselves."

"Nothin's ridin' fifteen miles through that," he said, dropping his face in his hands. "They're all dead."

"You don't know that," I argued, helping him slip his arm into a shirt. "When Shea gets back, we can make a map, ride to Ft. Hall, and get help there after all."

"I got a map," he said, pointing to the pile of frozen clothing. "In the pocket of Judd's army coat. My brother served in Mexico, you know."

I nodded, then pried the coats apart until I located the blue campaign jacket. In a pocket was a small, hastily-sketched map showing the train maybe eight miles south and east of the fort on the main branch of the Oregon Trail.

"You figure we can get help there?" the boy asked, passing the empty cup back to me.

"Don't see why not," I responded. "Weather's improved some, and I've got a horse that can pure ride like thunder."

He brightened some, and as he got into my oversized clothes and wrapped himself in the buffalo hides, I could see he'd be all right. His face was splotched some, and his lips were cut and bleeding, but his ears seemed all right, and as he warmed his fingers over the coals of our fire, they began to lose their white-blue tint.

Shea returned two hours or so later. He motioned me outside, then shared sour tidings.

"Mountain spirits must smile on the young," he declared. "The other five were caught in a rockslide. They're all dead, Illinois, buried by rock and snow so you can't reach em' 'fore first thaw.

"There's a train," I said, passing him the map.

"Lord, they weren't even headed the right way. Can't say I'm surprised. Must've started miserably late to hit Ft. Hall in December.

"What do I tell him?" I asked.

"Not a thing, Illinois. You figure he's up to a hard ride?"

"He's near dead!" I exclaimed. "I've only just thawed him out."

"Can't leave him here alone, and one of us needs to find that train while the other gets help at Ft. Hall."

"You head for Ft. Hall," I suggested. "They know you, and you're sure to get help. I'll copy the map and find the train."

"Illinois, you don't know this country," Shea argued. "You're apt to get lost just like those pilgrims."

"No, you'll get me halfway. Then all I have to do is cut across the trail and find the train."

"In all this?" he asked, waving at the snowbound countryside.

"He found us, Shea. I'd guess he smelled our fire. I'll do the same.

"And if they don't have a fire burnin'?"

"Then they're dead, and it doesn't matter," I said, sighing. "You're always saying to trust things'll turn out. I can't believe that boy got to us so we can save him alone. We've got enough meat put by I can carry some with me for the folks on that train, and you know Snow's up to the ride. I am, too."

He pulled me over beside him a moment and nodded grimly.

"We'll let the horses rest some, get some good feed. Tomorrow, first light, we head out."

"Sounds best," I agreed.

That was just how we did it, too. Next dawn we secured our belongings on two of the pack horses, then put our weary companion atop the third and tied him in place. The sun appeared shortly, and I considered it a fine omen for success. The ground along the river offered a bit of a trail, and we made fair time the first six miles or so. Then Shea declared it was time for me to cut east, and I turned Snow into the drifts.

"Good luck!" the boy called. "Lord, I don't even know your name."

"Darby Prescott," I answered.

"Tell 'em Tim Frey got through!" he added. "You'll tell Ma?"

"I will," I promised. "Mind you keep pace with Shea, hear? He's a fair man to follow."

Shea gave me a concerned look again, but I waved it off and urged Snow along. Soon we vanished in a sea of white.

The map Tim had provided showed the wagon train stranded along the main trail. Though the snow hopelessly erased all signs of ruts, I recalled that stretch of trail as treacherously narrow. The rest of the countryside was heavily wooded, and it would take a hundred feet of snow to conceal the gap in the trees that marked the trail.

A bigger problem was keeping Snow clear of drifts and away from dangerous embankments. Shea's tale of the rockslide kept me alert for signs of boulders and fissures on the surrounding landscape. Otherwise, I scanned the slopes for some hint of danger, or for anything that might mark the recent passage of riders or wagons.

For the longest of times I saw nothing. The sun reflected off the snow with a brightness that burned my eyes, and the deep snows soon penetrated my boots and froze my toes. Snow suffered even more, and I prayed as we climbed hills that the drifts would prove more shallow. They did, as it happened, but the thick underbrush barred more rapid progress.

I paused near midday to give Snow some oats and chew a bit of meat. Then, abandoning the idea of starting a fire to warm my toes, I set off eastward again. I rode less than a hundred yards before locating the trail. I spotted a half-buried wagon a bit later, and two prowling horses a half mile later.

As for the train itself, I might well have ridden past except for Snow. The horse sniffed out the woodsmoke and dipped his head anxiously. He surely hoped for a warm barn and was probably disappointed when instead I located a mound of snow topped by a thread of white-gray smoke. From within came the faint refrain of a half-forgotten hymn.

"Anybody there?" I called.

A child's cry followed. Soon another whined, and the mound stirred. Great sheets of ice and snow broke away as a bundled figure emerged from what proved to be a square formed by four wagon boxes. A canvas roof kept off the snow. When I crawled inside, I discovered twenty starving travelers—men, women, and children—crammed together in a foul-smelling, smoke-clouded hell.

"Is there somebody here named Frey?" I asked.

"They got through," a man declared. "The Frey boys and Marcus Tolbert, my Jeff and Madison."

"Mrs. Frey?" I asked.

"Next square," an exhausted woman said, pointing to another mound of snow.

"No, wait," the man called. "Tell us when the rest'll be here."

"Soon," I said as I headed for the next square.

Mrs. Frey was, indeed, there, huddled with two small

boys.

"Tim said to tell you he got through," I explained. The small faces at her side brightened, and Mrs. Frey cheered considerably. Their fire was near out, so I took an ax and set off to cut some firewood. A dead pine lay near buried in the snow, and I began trimming limbs. A pair of men managed to stir from the shelter, and I had them break the limbs apart and carry the wood inside.

"I'm Charles Cavett," one of them announced. "This is my company. Did you bring any food?"

"I've got some smoked elk in my pack there," I said, pointing to Snow. "You divide it up as best you can, seeing the children get theirs first."

"I know what's to be done," he growled.

"That why I've got the ax?" I barked. "That why a boy shorter'n me rode down to fetch help?"

"I sent my brother and four good men as well. Tim went because his brothers wished to lighten their mother's load here. She lost her man in Mexico, you know."

"I didn't," I explained. "Still, it seems you might have kept the fire burning."

"Easily said by a man's who's eaten."

I frowned. It was true enough. Of course Tom Shea would have found game to shoot. And Papa never would have sent anyone out in a blizzard and stayed back!

I didn't know it, but I hadn't scratched half the truth. As word spread there was food, people began emerging from the wagon boxes. I heard a shout from up the hill, and a man emerged from a third square.

"You mean there're others?" I cried, driving the ax's bit into the pine log and struggling toward a white-faced skeleton of a man.

"Don't," he said, collapsing against my shoulder. "Don't!"

I didn't understand, and when others took him away, I peered inside the shelter. No flame flickered. Snow and ice had penetrated the smoke hole, turning the occupants into ghastly human ice sculptures. One or two were moving, and I began dragging them out of their frozen tomb. As others arrived, they joined in the rescue. In all five people remained alive. A dozen were frozen as they sat.

"Get a fire built!" I pleaded with the men still milling around. "We can get a fresh shelter built."

"Food!" someone screamed.

"There's some in my pack. More's on the way. We've got to get these folks unfrozen."

"Where's the food?" a grizzled man cried, grabbing my coat and wrestling me to the ground. "Food!"

"Oh my . . . horse," I mumbled.

"Shoot the horse," someone urged. "Eat it!"

I believed they might have done just that had I not kicked myself free and pulled my pistol.

"Fools!" I said, firing a second shot. "There's a rescue party on the way from Ft. Hall. I brought some meat. Where's your captain? He took it."

"There he is!" a young girl shouted. A hundred eyes turned like angry wolves on Cavett. He sat beneath a pine stuffing bits of meat into his mouth. Angry travelers rushed at him, and I turned away. Like as not it was a kind of justice. Still, I had no stomach for the savagery of it.

"Come along, son," Mrs. Frey said, gripping my shoulder and leading me along. "There's another group."

"No," I said, shaking my head. "I can't look at anybody else frozen to death."

"They're alive," she said. "We've got a fire goin'. We need hands, and yours've got more strength than this old woman's."

I followed her toward the fourth square. Inside twenty children wailed and wept. Their starving eyes pleaded for help, and the younger ones shivered from cold and privation.

"Let's get 'em out of this stinkhole," I suggested. "Drag a couple of the boxes around, and we'll close the other side with a wall of snow. We can dig out the middle and get a fire going. Are there some dry clothes to be found?"

"Plenty," a tall woman remarked. "Lots of us don't need 'em now."

. I nodded grimly, then set to work. It was strange, but as the trembling youngsters emerged from the shelter, those same starving men and women who had moments before been at the throat of their captain over a bit of meat now put their shoulders to digging out a shelter, labored to move wagon boxes, and in no time created a new shelter as large as the old four. Canvas covers were stretched across the top, and a long bed of fire was dug which soon melted away the lingering snow. Pine needles were spread like hay across the floor, and small bodies were undressed and warmed by sympathetic hands.

I busied myself tending to the fire. The sight of all that suffering troubled me. I was equally uneasy around the sobbing children rocking on parents' knees or huddling together around the coals. I was too near Mama's grave not to recall the warmth of her touch, now missing for two and a half long years.

I was still splitting pine logs when Mrs. Frey reappeared. She introduced me to Tim's little brothers, Miller and Ron.

"Should we prepare for bad news?" she asked.

"Tim's fine," I said nervously. "He's with my partner, Tom Shea, no doubt resting easy in some Ft. Hall parlor this very minute."

"You've said nothing of the others," she reminded me.

"I didn't see them," I said, running my hands along the ax handle.

"But you know they won't be coming back," she said, sighing. "Judd was with his pa at Buena Vista, you know. Came back from a war to die in this Godforsaken country."

"Not Godforsaken," I argued. "God got Tim to me and Shea, you know. Nigh frozen and barely alive, that boy, but he held on so help'd come. You know how I found you? Heard hymns. I'm not religious as my mama was, and I never was much on miracles, but if ever there was one to happen, I'd say it was here and now."

No sooner had I spoken than a voice boomed out, "Illinois! That you?"

"Here, you old mountain goat!" I yelled in answer, and Tom Shea emerged through the snowdrifts at the head of six wagons and a small column of traders and trappers. A great outcry followed as those pilgrims able enough raced forward to welcome their rescuers. I greeted Shea with a salute, and he jumped down into the snow and gripped me by the shoulders.

"Been worried some," he told me. "Once you left, that boy warmed up his tongue and told me there's been a good deal of trouble among this outfit. Seems their cap'n . . ."

"There," I said, pointing to the lump stretched out in the snow fifteen yards away. "Took the food I brought for himself, and the folks kind of went wild."

"Not the first death on this trail," Shea noted. "Guess somebody best cover him up."

Shea did so himself. The rescue party paused only long enough to feed the hungry travelers, then see them all packed in the wagon beds with such of their belongings as could be carried. All heavy gear was left behind, and many a cherished treasure had already been swallowed by the white nightmare.

"Darby, will you ride with us?" little Ron Frey asked as I led Snow along beside Shea.

"Go ahead, Illinois," Shea urged. "You pony's clearly spent, and you look to need a nod or two yourself. You did fine this day, son."

"Thanks . . . Tom," I added, waiting to see if he reacted to my use of his Christian name.

"You get to callin' me that, I'm liable to take a likin' to you, Illinois Prescott," he said, giving me a good-natured slap on the back.

"Guess I'll run the risk," I answered, tying Snow behind the wagon, then climbing in.

Chapter 9

I settled in between the Frey boys and a tall, plain-faced sixteen-year-old Mrs. Frey introduced as Celia Flowers. Her sour frown troubled me, and after a bit I struck up a conversation.

"I'm sixteen, too," I explained, "though I have a birthday coming along in the spring."

"You look to be younger," she grumbled. "Boys must run small in your family."

"Or girls tall in yours," I answered. "Why so angry?"

"You expect different? I've left a brother and sister back in that snow, not even proper buried. Pa just threw a bit of rock and dirt over 'em."

"I lost a little brother myself," I said, frowning. "Was just three. I was a lot smaller myself, though."

"Judd and Tom're dead, too," Miller Frey said.

"Lots of death on this trail," I said for what seemed the hundredth time. "My mama's buried above the Bear River. But look around you, Celia. There're plenty still alive who might be frozen."

She scowled, then crawled to the back of the wagon. A boy of seven or so nestled in under my arm, and I felt nervous. Matt had been dead a long time, and I wasn't accustomed to little brothers. My eyes turned in panic to Mrs. Frey.

"Why not tell 'em a story," she suggested.

I managed to free myself from the seven-year-old without bruising his feelings. Then I struck up a story Fly Over The Mountains had shared in the Nez Perce camp, a strange tale of a brave young warrior forced to fight a devil dog.

"Every time that warrior about had the dog killed, that devil'd turn himself into stone," I explained. "Break the spearpoint or bounce the arrows off quick as you please. Finally you know what that warrior did?"

"No," the huddle of children cried.

"Well, he went and changed himself into a rock, too, only he was a bigger one. He pounded that devil right into the mountain and stayed there even to this day. I saw the rock myself, and you'll pass close by it on your way through the Blue Mountains."

"That far?" Miller asked.

And so I described the trail ahead, the long sandy trail along the Snake, the hard river crossings and steep grades leading to the Columbia, all topped off by Barlow's toll road.

It soon grew dark, and the children began to whimper and shiver. Mrs. Frey and the other women held them close, rubbing their small chests with their hands as if to share what warmth remained. The wind began its phantom howling, and again a small head buried itself in my side.

"Here, sit on my lap," Celia said, returning to my side and taking the boy in her arms. "He wouldn't bite, you know."

"I'm not used to people anymore," I told her. "Shea and I ride alone. I buried my brother, my mother, my father. I've got nobody to feel for."

"You had a brother, though," she said, her voice betraying her feelings. "It's dark now. One little body feels pretty much the same as another."

I nodded, and she passed the boy over and drew another to her lap. I enclosed the child's small hands in my own, and he sank his head onto my chest. Celia was right. It wasn't too different from having little Bessy sit with me in Papa's rocker.

Mrs. Frey then struck up a hymn, and the other women joined in. Celia sang as well, and though the words were unfamiliar to me, I quickly picked up the tune and hummed along.

"We close, Darby?" Ron asked.

"Pretty close," I answered. "See those little pinpricks of light way up ahead? That's Ft. Hall."

"At last, thank God," a woman in the back proclaimed.

"Yes, thank God," Mrs. Frey said, bowing her head. The others did likewise, and even the children seemed to be whispering their private thank yous.

"I guess you'll stay around the fort awhile now, won't you?" Celia asked me.

"More likely we'll ride on once the horses rest up," I answered. "We're bound east of here. The high country."

"Some would consider this high enough," she said. "And cold enough."

"Some would," I agreed. But not Tom Shea.

An amazing thing happened when we arrived at Ft. Hall. A small army of traders' wives ushered the poor pilgrims into their homes and stuffed them with food, offered clothing and solace and every manner of comfort available at the isolated trading post.

I felt a hair deserted. The Freys and Celia vanished before my eyes. An eerie silence seemed to descend on the now empty wagons.

"Guess you were expectin' pipers, eh?" Shea called. "Get your horse and follow me."

I rolled out of the wagon, untied Snow's reins, and did as instructed. The pack horses were quartered in a small shed, and once we unsaddled our mounts and saw to their needs, we left them there as well.

"I asked Macleod, the trader, to put us up a day or two, and he gave us leave to have the loft."

I eyed the place warily. The shed smelled of horses, and the loft was little more than a narrow shelf cluttered with hay. To make matters worse, Mrs. Macleod soon arrived with a dozen boys and saddled us with seeing they were bedded in that same loft.

"We'll be alone quick enough, Illinois," Shea reminded me as I set to grumbling. "Wouldn't hurt to have a bit of company tonight."

Twelve youngsters free of their mothers and fathers was not the kind of company I relished, and I rolled out my own blankets beside Snow's stall. The rustling about of the

94

horses was fairly tolerable. I even found the smell an improvement over the loft. Halfway through the night Shea also had enough. He tossed a pair of youngsters into the hay stacked below and warned the next one to draw his ire might get a firsthand demonstration of how Crows scalp their enemies.

The second night was little better, and I longed for the chill nights bedded in a Rocky Mountain snowbank. Then the sky darkened, and nature lashed at us with a worse blizzard then ever. Shea and I stared at the white slopes in the distance, at the drifts building up against the wooden walls of the fort buildings, and we sighed in disappointment.

"It's only going to get worse, isn't it?" I asked.

"I'd judge it so," he confessed. "Be late to get a cabin built, and there's no chance of layin' in meat."

"So what do we do?"

"Winter here, if I can work a trade with Macleod."

"I know a dozen boys we could swap for something."

"Don't know he'd give much for 'em," Shea said, laughing. "He's a sharp Scot, that Macleod. I hear he swaps stable dung to the minister's wife for vegetables from her garden."

With a small army now quartered at Ft. Hall, though, the post had countless needs. In return for partial use of a small storeroom, Shea and I agreed to keep Macleod supplied with wood and fresh meat for the duration of our stay.

"It'll be some work, I'll admit," Shea said as we moved our gear from the shed to the storeroom. "But I won't mind the huntin', and this winter seems bitter hard to spend in the open. We'll find the mountains patient. They'll wait for us."

And so we became woodcutters and hunters. In truth, I was glad of the work. The Snake River Valley abounded with elk and deer, and we rarely returned empty-handed. We worked the hides and sold them to some of the emigrants, rarely for the price they would have fetched elsewhere perhaps, but for a bit of coin that would stand us in good stead come spring.

Woodcutting soon grew tiresome, though. Fires had to be kept burning, and pine consumed itself painfully fast.

Cutting the hardwoods meant driving wagons farther and farther along the trail. Toward Christmas we decided it was best to load up every able-bodied man and fill four full wagons with wood before returning.

Our stay at Ft. Hall wasn't all work, though. In the evenings, Shea and I would share yarns with the youngsters. The ladies from the wagon train had bake-offs, and I delighted in tasting a bit of Norwegian pastry or Austrian gingerbread. There was plenty of singing and a bit of dancing. Macleod was near as fine a piper as Duncan Macilvain, and Shea taught me some of his wild Highland steps. I even convinced Celia Flowers to join in a sword dance, and we hopped between the crossed blades quite expertly after a time.

My joy during those days was gathering with the young ones for a bit of singing. Tim proved quite adept at playing a flute, and the melody helped whittle away our despair.

"Was Judd's," Tim explained. "I'll never make it sound sweet like he could, but a tune in the winter warms you some."

"Better than a fire," I told them.

It did, too, and although Tim never matched the sounds I made on Molly's piano, I got to where I enjoyed the singing even more for its greater need among the survivors of the Cavett train. Even Shea admitted that flute fought off the melancholy some.

"Nothin' like the pipes, grant you, but it's fair music just the same."

Shea's heart was truly elsewhere, and after Christmas, I saw his eyes following hawks or eagles often as they sailed overhead.

"Weather's easin'," he'd declare. "Won't be long 'fore we'll ride on out of here. Thought about which path we should take?"

"Doesn't matter," I declared.

"You been some taken with that Flowers gal. Thinkin' 'bout the Willamette?"

"If I'd wanted a family, I never would've sent that Nez Perce girl off," I told him. "Anywhere you head us, I'll follow."

"Mighty nice country up in the Tetons. Pierre's Hole isn't so far. They held a rendezvous there what, twenty years back. Not so long ago, twenty years. Oldtimers still talk of it. Back then the beaver was thick."

"There'll be elk enough to keep our bellies full."

"I'd say so," he said, grinning.

As December gave way to January, I, too, began to grow restless. Celia noticed and drew me aside one afternoon.

"You haven't been around too often in the evenings lately," she observed. "Anything wrong?"

"I've been working hard, cutting wood and such. I take to my bed earlier."

"What'll you do when the weather warms?"

"Head for the Tetons, I think. Shea says the peaks there are close to as grand as any on earth. I've only caught a glimpse of them, back on our way up South Pass. From there we might head out into the Big Horns, maybe shoot buffalo up near the Missouri."

"There are other choices."

"There are?" I asked.

"You've tasted my cooking, Darby. You know I'm no beauty, but I'm strong of heart, and Pa's still got enough money to buy a nice section of land out in Oregon."

"I've got no spare ponies to trade for a wife, Celia," I told her.

"I'm not a Nez Perce. Pa wouldn't want ponies. He'd only ask you to be a good husband, and I know you would be."

"I'm no farmer, Celia. I've worked fields half my life. They never bloom for me as they did for Papa. I passed two years counting the days till this winter would come, and I could ride out with Tom Shea. I've yet to turn seventeen. I barely have a beard. I feel warm sharing your company, Celia, but you have to give me leave to go. There are lots of farm boys in Oregon to make you happy. Me, I'll always be a wayward soul."

"It doesn't have to be that way," she argued.

"You don't understand," I said, gripping her hands. "It's how I want it to be."

She sadly shook her head, and I regretted those first words spoken to her in the back of a rolling wagon. It was better to be like Shea, keep at a distance.

As February arrived, I noticed Shea, too, had taken some of the wagon folk to heart. He spent long hours with the men, sketching out the route and helping them buy new stock from a band of Shoshonis camped upriver. The littler Frey boys took to riding his shoulders around the fort, and I know it bothered him some when they offered to pay him to guide them along to Oregon come spring.

"I've done that," he explained. "I have no heart for trailin' wagons every year. Season after maybe. Illinois and I've got our eyes on the Tetons."

The snows continued to fall, but as mid-February came and went, he roused me from my bed and declared it time to leave, snow or no snow.

"It'll be hard, I agree, but it's time we slept under an open sky," he explained.

"Then I'll saddle my horse," I told him.

I was in the middle of saddling Snow when a small delegation of new friends arrived at the shed. The Frey boys offered me a hand with the bridle, and a pair of little ones saw to it the pack animals had fresh water to drink.

"I thought perhaps you'd convince Mr. Shea to scout for our company," Mrs. Frey said.

"Darby, you know the trail, too," Celia said. "You could take the job."

"I could," I told them, wiping my forehead with my sleeve. "Won't. I'm headed in another direction. You'll make it all right, though. Wait for the grass to turn green. You little ones keep a lookout for snakes, and if a grizzly takes after you, run real fast."

They laughed as I made a claw of my hand and took a swipe at one or two of them.

"Then I guess this is good-bye," Celia said, gazing at me with hard eyes.

"Au revoir, the French trappers up here say," I explained. "Means until we see each other again. I'll be back through Oregon one of these days. Maybe then you'll have youngsters of your own to put on my knee."

"Maybe," she said, rubbing her eyes.

"Au revoir," I told the others as Shea finally appeared.

"Au revoir," they echoed.

I then tightened Snow's cinch and helped Shea get the packs secured. Shortly thereafter we rode out of Ft. Hall, headed for the Tetons or whatever high place Three Fingers Shea determined as our destination. It didn't much matter to me. I was, again, a wayfarer.

Chapter 10

Snow clung stubbornly to the land, and as we rode northward along the Snake, the rocky terrain grew more and more difficult. The river had cut a deep gash in the land, and we had to head into the mountains. No twenty miles flew by beneath our horses anymore. Sometimes, winding up treacherous, ice-covered trails, we were lucky to manage four or five. The sun set early and rose late, too, and much time was required for erecting shelters and shooting fresh meat.

I confess I missed the clamor of Ft. Hall, especially the singing and the tale spinning. Briefly the Freys had been a family of sorts, to Shea as well as to me. I'd been able to share some of my feelings with Celia, and her smiles and laughter had brought a refreshing softness to what had again become a hard world.

I was grateful to the trader Macleod for the sacks of beans and flour we carried along. Best of all, we had enough coffee to last us a couple of months. With winter's icy breath greeting us each morning, a touch of steaming liquid was most welcome. And when my moods turned to melancholy, I hummed a few tunes and imagined adventures yet to come.

Sometimes, if given encouragement, I would sing as we rode. From time to time Shea would hum along, and once in a great while we would sing to the clouds some trail song, often as not giving it a few fresh lyrics that would hardly have been welcome in Mama's parlor.

A week on the trail honed my wits to their old sharpness. I noticed my voice had deepened some. I could no longer hit the high notes. Furthermore, my chin had begun to collect a fair amount of growth, and new iron gave my arms and shoulders a broader look.

Shea didn't often speak of it, but I could tell he approved of the changes. Often now he let me take the lead, and he trusted me to lash the shelter poles or tend the horses. Always before he'd found an excuse to look over my work. Now I was respected as an equal.

"That's as it should be," he told me. "You're near a man in every way that matters up high."

"I'll grow some more," I told him.

"Won't make you more of a man," he declared. "As for growin', a man stops doin' that, he starts dyin'."

I knew he meant there were still things for both of us to discover, to learn, and to understand. That was what he called "adventurin'," and I loved it as much as he did.

It was early March when we happened upon a small band of Shoshonis camped in the Teton foothills. I grew instantly cautious, but Shea only laughed and waved me along.

"It's Two Knives," he declared, freeing his horse from the pack animals, howling across the hillside, and then racing toward the Indians like a crazed loon.

I held back, figuring anyone named Two Knives was probably capable of using at least one of them on a shaggy-haired white boy. And sure enough, the Shoshonis responded to Shea's charge by knocking him from his horse with the shaft of a lance. Three Indians then pounced, and I began my own charge, drawing my pistol as I rode.

Shea must have sensed my lack of understanding, for no sooner had Snow started his gallop than Shea stood up, grinning, and waved me off.

"It's all right, Illinois," he called. "We're old friends, Two Knives and me."

The Indian grinned as well, and I drew in my reins, turned about and returned to the pack animals. Only later, when women and children appeared, did I feel safe to enter the encampment.

Two Knives proved to be both genial and generous. We were given our own lodge for the night, and a young girl prepared a fine supper of elk steaks and assorted plants ground into a pasty mush. It wasn't much to look at, I suppose, but it was pleasing enough to the taste.

That night, seated around a council fire, I listened to another round of warrior tales, most of them about the fierce Shoshoni chief, Washakie, and his exploits against the Crows and Sioux. Two Knives had some fine stories of his own, and through Shea I again explained how I'd gotten the scars on my chest.

"I guess I've told that story a hundred times by now," I told Shea afterward. "It's stretched itself well beyond the truth, I fear."

"As a tale should," he explained. "The deed hasn't changed, you know. And the better it sounds, the larger your standing among the young men."

"What will that matter when we leave tomorrow?" I asked.

"Wasn't plannin' to leave straight off," he explained. "Two Knives says there might be Sioux ridin' the hills ahead. If so, there's safety in numbers."

"But he's fighting your friends, the Crows."

"Once. Now the Sioux are the real enemy."

I nodded without truly understanding.

The Sioux were hundreds of miles to the east of us by all accounts, though, and I soon swept them from my mind. I was readily welcomed by the younger Shoshonis, especially Two Knives's three nephews—Long Nose, Beaver, and Snake Boy. In no time they introduced me to various games of chance, skill, and daring. I proved occasionally lucky at the first, hopelessly clumsy at the second, and somewhat foolhardy where the third was concerned. Still, my three tutors took each false step in good-humored fashion and did their best to help me mend my ways.

Years of trading with westbound emigrants had taught many Shoshonis a working vocabulary of English words, and together with hand signs, frowns, and nods, we got along well enough. I learned the hard way to run when Long Nose yelped. A stray porcupine rewarded my slow retreat with a barrage of quills.

"Give you somethin' to remember your time here," Shea told me when he dug the last one out of my tender right hip.

"I'm just glad it wasn't a grizzly," I remarked.

Perhaps to make up for the porcupine attack, Three Knives invited us on a hunt the next morning. I lay on my side most of the night, cleaning my rifle and making paper cartridges. My new friends were envious of the percussion cap piece, for they still used flintlock rifles.

"Now if you want to see a real rifle," Shea said, drawing a bundle from one of the packs, "you'll have to look at this one here."

The gun was far from new, but it considerably outweighed my aging weapon. I balanced it in my hands and judged it a good dozen pounds.

"Traded Macleod out of it," Shea explained. "She's a Hawken .52 caliber."

I'd often heard of the Hawken brothers from St. Louis. Their arms were favorites among the old trappers, it was said. I wasn't all that sure the Hawken rifle, heavy as it was, would prove superior over the newer gun I rested on my knee.

Shea read my thoughts and grinned.

"We'll see soon enough," he whispered.

And so we did. After sipping coffee and chewing a bit of jerked venison, we set out on foot across the wintry landscape, trudging through deep snows glistening with morning frost. The tall pines were wrapped in ivory shawls, and icicles occasionally fell like winter daggers into the snow. Some of those icicles were a foot and a half long, and I took care to stay out of their way. Their sharp points might make a big hole in me, elk coat or not.

It wasn't long before Beaver spotted deer tracks. He said nothing, just made an antler sign with his fingers and led us off into a thick forest. Two Knives hurried to the van, followed by Long Nose and Snake Boy. Shea and I remained to the rear.

Soon the deer trail crossed other, heavier tracks. The snow had deepened, and it was impossible to recognize hooves. What was clear was that here was an enormous animal, big as two or three men. And it was close.

"Look," I said, stepping to a nearby pine and prying loose a tuft of long white hair.

"Buffalo," Long Nose said, his eyes brightening as he

showed the white hair to his brothers.

"There have been few buffalo in these mountains for many snows," Three Knives declared as he returned the hair to me. "This is strange."

"White hair," Shea mumbled. "Ever see a white buff, Three Knives?"

"Only Buffalo Calf, who knows the medicine ways, has seen the white buffalo," Three Knives answered. "We must stop and smoke over this thing you have found, young one."

For myself, I was eager to see the white buffalo. At first I figured snow must have whitened the hair, but when it remained ivory after so much handling, I realized it truly was sign of a white. Two Knives sent Beaver to his camp to tell of the strange event, and the boy returned later with a wrinkle-faced oldtimer named Buffalo Calf. The old man walked about, sniffing the air, then touched the white hairs and spoke.

"He says there's powerful medicine here," Shea explained. "The white buffalo is sacred to the spirits. It must not be harmed."

Harmed? I thought. We waste any more time, we won't even see it!

Buffalo Calf walked around, touching the tracks and smelling the air. He touched my hand, then my forehead. He spoke quietly, and Shea bid me accompany the old-timer.

"It's all right, Illinois," Shea said, waving me along.

I followed the medicine man into the pines a way. He sat on a large black boulder, and I rested on a second boulder nearby.

"Many years ago I, too, saw the white," Buffalo Calf explained. I was surprised to hear him speak English, and he nodded to acknowledge the ruse. "I was very young, and very unwise. I set after the buffalo with my bow, and it never returned to guide me on my path."

"I don't understand," I told him. "I didn't see it. I only got a bit of hair."

"Did you see that?" he asked. "He will come again to you. Listen to his voice. It is a gift, the power he will bring. Use it wisely, and your path will be a bright one. Now I must go."

"And me?"

"You must wait for the buffalo spirit."

"How long?"

Buffalo Calf shrugged his shoulders and headed back to the others. If anyone else had bid me sit on a frozen rock amidst a snow-covered hillside so a white buffalo could come and speak to me, I would have had cross words for the loon and set off back to Two Knives's camp. Something etched in Buffalo Calf's face—a kind of immense sorrow—caused me to stay.

After a bit I took off walking. I couldn't, after all, depend on a white buffalo to do all the work. Once in motion, my feet seemed to carry me across one hill and then another. I wasn't altogether sure where I was going or why, but it felt right. Then, as I neared a steep embankment, I saw the buffalos.

There were eight of them, all monsters. Their woolly brown backs stood out in stark contrast to the white of the snow. I'd seen buffalo the first time at Chimney Rock, and even now I recalled the tender taste of the hump meat. I thought to fire, then recalled I wasn't out to shoot our dinner anymore. I slipped behind a pine and watched the creatures dipping their hairy chins lower to dig through the snow to where the grass lay buried.

Suddenly the ground shook, and I gazed up in surprise. Perhaps five feet behind me rumbled an enormous bull buffalo. He was entirely white, all but his pinkish eyes. I shuddered as I waited for him to lower his head and tear at me with his horns, but instead he halted. The great bulk of his head seemed to dip to one side as if wondering why I didn't flee, why I hadn't shot.

My flesh tingled as the wind whined eerily through the branches overhead. The white buffalo stared at me a moment, then romped past me and rejoined the herd. Seconds later the nine of them thundered on.

"Is that what I was supposed to wait for?" I cried. "I heard no words, did I?"

There was a terrifying barrage of icicles just then, and I ducked for safety. When I returned to my feet I saw a great sea of dark shapes emerge from the distant trees. There were no white creatures—just an enormous herd of buffalo. The white and its companions had disappeared.

So, was that the message? I wondered. By not killing the white, had I brought the Shoshonis a herd to follow? Who could know? I turned and set off to find Shea.

The others sat where I left them. Snake Boy was the first to rise.

"Where are the buffalo?" he asked.

"Buffalo Hump said there would be a large herd," Shea explained.

"There is," I said, waving them along.

A fresh wave of eagerness filled the faces of the young Shoshonis as I led the way toward the herd. Two Knives was no less excited, and I do believe Shea even betrayed a trace of a smile.

We closed on the grazing animals, each taking care to line up his own shot without imperiling a companion. Shea nodded for me to fire first, so I took aim and pulled the trigger. The big rifle boomed. A large bull fell, writhing, to the ground. As I fought to reload, Shea shot a second animal cleanly through the lungs. Two Knives fired his own rifle while his nephews opened up a shower of arrows on the buffalo. By the time I finished my kill, two other creatures lay lifeless in the snow.

"Now comes the hard work," Shea grumbled.

"I remember," I said, grinning as the recollection of that first hunt returned. "Hard work, yes, but worth it."

Shea nodded, then helped me start the skinning.

A great celebration was held that night among the Shoshonis. The white hairs were passed around so often I thought they might have concealed a golden nugget. Buffalo Calf told of his own encounter with the ivory buffalo, and every belly filled with buffalo steak.

"This was your hunt, Darby," Shea told me as we cut the last fragments of meat from the hides. "For as long as you live Two Knives will welcome you to his side. They've given you a new name, you know."

"Oh?"

"Buffalo Dreamer."

"I didn't dream any of this. It happened."

"There are lots of dreams a man can have," Shea explained. "Often they come to him in broad daylight, with drums bangin' and voices cryin' to high heaven. Inside, though, you know a spirit's talkin' to you. It's a kind of prayer, I guess you'd say."

"That was kind of how it was," I admitted. "But I was close enough to that buffalo to stare into its red eyes. It was real, Tom."

"So what'd you hear?"

"Nothing," I said, dropping my chin onto my chest. "Not that I wasn't listening. Later I saw the buffalo herd, but there was no voice."

"It wouldn't've come from out there," Shea explained, gesturing at the world all around us. "Spirits speak to your heart. What did you think?"

"I'm not altogether sure," I confessed. "I felt really alone. Cold, too. And . . ."

"Go on. Tell me."

"At home."

"Yeah, it spoke to you, sure as I'm sittin' here. That buffalo spirit read your heart. It knew you still had a bit of an urge to take to the low country, plow up a field and plant corn. It told you here's home, that you belong in the Rockies."

"How can you be so sure?"

"I don't have to be. You are."

"I am?"

"I read it in your eyes. Thing is, son, I brought you up here to teach you mountain ways, and you seem to be pickin' 'em up faster'n I can remember what to say. Here you are, growin' taller by each sunrise now, gettin' to look more like your mother save for you've got your papa's build, of course."

"Really?" I asked, running my fingers along my chin. There was a considerable growth there now, and Shea passed me a looking glass so I could see clearer.

"Crows'd pluck those whiskers," he explained. "I got the tools."

"You don't pluck yours," I noted. "Still, it doesn't look like much as is. I've got Papa's razor in my gear. Think maybe I should shave it off?"

"You ask a man with a beard as long as mine 'bout

shavin'?" Shea asked, laughing heartily.

"Once I'll bet you cut it regular."

"Long time past," he said, nodding. "Was a bright-eyed girl to chase. You cut yours, some Shoshoni gal's apt to send you lookin' for horses."

"It'll be awhile before that," I said, blushing.

"Well, I best show you how to make a lather. Wouldn't want you cuttin' your chin off."

"Then they'd have to name me somethin' else," I said, laughing. He grabbed my neck and gave me a shake, then pulled away in surprise. I grinned, slapped his back, and began searching out Papa's razor.

It wasn't half as easy as I expected. Shea had me hone the blade on a whetstone, then wash my face with steaming water. Last of all, I dabbed on a soapy paste and took the razor in my fingers while Shea held the looking glass steady.

"Take short, easy strokes," he advised. "Tighten the skin, but relax your hand. Then just leave the razor to do its job."

I took a deep breath and began. The razor slid along my cheeks easy enough. Twice, though, I cut my upper lip, and I nicked my chin as well. Shea dabbed the red droplets with tiny bits of cloth, and soon the bleeding ceased. I touched my chin and cheeks and found them hairless, but strangely hard.

Shea frowned, and I turned to him in surprise.

"Bit hard seein' the boy fade to memory," he explained. "But I got to admit to feelin' prideful as well. You're comin' to be a man worth knowin', Darby Prescott."

"Like somebody else 'round here?"

"And who'd that be?"

"Tom Shea," I told him as I returned to the buffalo hide. "About the best man I ever come across. My partner."

I saw his face light up as never before, and for once he allowed himself the compliment without turning it to another direction.

You brought the Shoshonis meat, I told the buffalo spirit that night in my dreams. You brought me a second father and a better, warmer path.

Chapter 11

We passed the remainder of that hard winter with Two Knives and the Shoshonis. As the March sun began to pry winter's grasp from the land, I awoke to find myself turned seventeen. The whiskers had begun to come regularly now, and I employed Papa's razor often, much to the amusement of my Shoshoni friends.

"We will call you Spotted Face," Snake Boy jested, pointing to the latest slices torn from my chin.

I laughed along with them. Though I now spoke a smattering of their language, I had no way of explaining the fondness I had for putting Papa's blade to work. For that razor made me one with a family a thousand miles away, with brothers I would not likely see again and a sister with her own family to build. I enjoyed my wayfaring days, but I'd learned to appreciate the invisible roots that kept a man erect in the fierce wind that loneliness could raise.

When the snows finally left the valleys, the Shoshonis began breaking their camps. They would head east, toward the rivers and hills where they passed the summers. Shea declared it was time for us to go as well, into the Tetons, those towering peaks that rose to the misty north.

As I saddled Snow, I felt sad to be leaving my many friends. The same reluctance flashed across Long Nose's face. Beaver and Snake Boy made a jest of it, saying my scalp would be easily spotted on a Sioux's belt. No great show was made of our parting, though, for it was understood the world was a circle, and paths would cross again.

Shea muttered to himself a lot the first day on the trail, but soon he brightened. This was, for me, new country, and he took to pointing out the streams and mountains as he once had shown me the landmarks on the trail to Oregon. I'd long neglected my journals, and I now began mapping our wanderings. I'd lost track of the days or even months, but I guessed it would soon be April, and I knew the year was 1851.

"Still makin' your white man's scratches, eh?" Shea would ask, laughing to himself.

"Can't very well disguise myself," I said, pulling my hat off so that my long sandy brown hair fell down to my shoulders.

"Seems a bother, that hair," Shea grumbled.

"Is," I agreed. "Maybe you'd clip it some. If you've got shears."

"Do," he told me. "Might take a bit of my beard, too. Beginnin' to look like an old grizzly wakin' from his winter's sleep."

"Smellin' like one, too," I pointed out.

And so we paused at the next stream to bathe, wash our clothes, and clip our hair. I was amazed to find the long winter had paled my skin near white as the lingering snow.

"It's just this water," Shea observed. "Like to freeze a man's hide off his bones."

I had to admit as much myself, only it felt so good to be shed of three months' accumulated smoke and odor I'd gladly done so again. I noticed my trousers were an inch and a half short of my boots now, too, and I thought it a fine thing that I wasn't, after all, destined to be a dwarf forever.

We reached the meandering stream known as Teton Creek later that week, and Shea again told me of the great rendezvous held at Pierre's Hole. We then rode up the creek into the very lap of the massive Teton Mountains.

"Wasn't so long ago this was fine country for trappin' beaver," Shea told me. "Mostly it was before my time, mind you, but they still trapped this country heavy a dozen years back. Till '40 or '41. Then the fur trade lost its glow."

"Lost its glow?"

"Was never a gold mine, Illinois. Too much hard work, and none too safe with the different tribes and all apt to turn temperamental by and by. But you could work your

110

pelts, get 'em down to a trader, and make a fair livin'. Then, well, the price fell. Too many of us, some said. Indians started noticin' the beaver dyin' off, and they saw the white men cuttin' roads through their huntin' grounds. Tribes like the Cheyenne and the Sioux took it unkindly."

"So you started earning your way scouting the trails?"

"Oh, it put some money in my pocket, I'll admit," Shea said, pointing to a flock of geese overhead. "I guess wayfarer that I am, I felt a need to be around people some. And it's a good feelin' a man has helpin' pilgrims along to a better life."

"Even with all the death and sadness on the trail?"

"There's bein' born, too. Take those folks we dragged into Ft. Hall. Mighty hard time they had. But how many little ones got born while we were there?"

"Two, no three," I said, smiling at the thought.

"So there's forever new life breakin' out even among a burned wood. Got to bear that in mind."

"Where you headin' us?"

"To a fork just ahead. This is hermit country mostly, but I wintered here once with a partner name of Thompson. Good enough man. Had the bad luck to get crosswise with Eustace Blackburn, big bear of a fellow. Eust, well, he cut Thompson up some, and we buried him in the hills above the Green River ferry. I figured our cabin might have lasted, though. I build things fair, and that wasn't but five winters back."

"Don't need a cabin so much now it's spring," I observed.

"Darby, if I had a silver dollar for every time I been snowed on in June up here, I'd be a wealthy man."

"Darby?" I asked, shaking my head. "One minute I'm Illinois and the next Darby. You plan to make up your mind?"

"Well," he said, nervously fidgeting with his hands, "I figured if you had to call me Tom, I might as well use your civilized name. Can't call you boy these days, and, well, there's times when Illinois seems like somebody else."

"You mean when we talk serious. And I have grown some since scratchin' my name on Independence Rock, haven't I?"

111

"In all the right ways a man ever does," he said, nodding. "Now let's quit jabberin' and find that cabin."

We left the creek and started up a nearby hill. The snowdrifts remained deep beneath the pines, and we made poor time. Finally, though, Shea spotted the place. It was half buried in white powder, but that didn't keep Shea from charging ahead. I took the pack animals and found an easier path.

The snow wasn't packed hard, and Shea's horse managed to traverse the drift easily enough. Shea then leaped into the snow, and when he rose, I saw it was close to waist deep. Nevertheless he dug out the door, swung it open, and stepped inside.

I approached slowly, allowing him time to recall those earlier times he'd passed there. When he hadn't reappeared some ten minutes later, though, I decided to see why. I left the pack horses fifty feet away, then urged Snow along the narrow path Shea had cleared. When I rolled off into the snow, I slipped, and the white sea swallowed me whole. I scrambled to my feet, spitting snow and laughing like the fool I was. I then stepped inside the cabin.

Shea stood near the fireplace. Snow had fluttered down the open chimney and spilled into the cabin, and eerie panes of ice formed on the windows, casting the place in a strange yellow light. A tall man with raven-colored hair sat beside the table, holding a Hawken rifle and gazing with lifeless eyes toward the window. Wooden splints braced a fractured leg, and sunken cheeks explained hunger had likely taken his life.

"It's young Palmer, Sime Palmer," Shea explained. "Come up here to see Thompson maybe. Sime was his nephew or cousin or some such. Starved or froze most likely. Looks to've broke his leg, likely from fallin' in the ice. Had your habit of writin' things," Shea explained, tossing me a small leather-bound notebook. "You might like to read what he thought sometime."

"Maybe," I said, setting the journal aside. "Come on out into the sunlight. You look pale."

"I'm all right," Shea insisted. "Give me a hand with the fellow. Best we get him under some rocks 'fore he starts to thaw. I seen illness come of such."

I stumbled over and gripped Palmer's rigid shoulders. Shea pried the young man's feet from the floor, and we carried him outside. Shea then led the way up the hillside where a rockslide had formed a mound of boulders. We left Palmer there and covered the corpse with rock.

"Ought to say something," I said, "maybe cut him a marker."

"Didn't have anybody to remember him," Shea muttered. "Had no notion of religion. No, whatever's left of him's made its peace months back. We got other work to tend."

And Shea was eager to get after it. First of all, he passed me a shovel, and I cleared snow away from the cabin. I next climbed the roof and hollowed out a smoke hole of sorts in the snow-clogged chimney. Shea then placed some rocks on the hearth and built up a fire. In no time, the smoke and heat began melting the rest of the snow, and a small river ran down the chimney, over the hearth, and spilled into the cabin itself.

We dragged the sparse furnishings outside and gave the windows a sound scrubbing. Next we cleaned the smoky walls. The bright April sun tended the rest, and toward nightfall, the cabin was inhabitable once more.

There had once been a pair of slat beds along the wall near the fireplace, but Palmer had likely burned the wood when he could no longer travel to his woodpile. That night we built beds of pine needles and spread our blankets atop them on the floor. The fire gave the place a cozy warmth, and I expected a restful sleep.

It didn't come. Instead my mind cast me out on a lonely, windswept plain. Snows covered the world, smothered the sky, and sent shivers down my spine. And through it all there appeared the phantom shape of the white buffalo.

"I'm the ghost of death, friend," an eerie voice whispered. "I came for Palmer. You now walk his path. Prepare yourself, Darby Prescott, for I come for you next."

I awoke shivering, panting for breath. It seemed I could feel the buffalo's hot breath on my face, could feel icy hands reaching out for me. I tried to scream, but my voice was muted by fear. I shook wildly and stared at a ghastly face peering at me from the window.

"Illinois, boy, you all right?" Shea asked, shaking me to my senses. Still the face glared at me with haunted eyes. "Son, wake up! You're all right!" Shea said, gripping me hard and restraining my wild movements.

I blinked my eyes as if to chase away the ghost. Only then did I realize the apparition was, in fact, myself.

"I, uh . . . had a dream," I mumbled.

" 'Bout the white buff?"

"You saw it, too?" I asked.

"No," he said, steadying me. "Heard you moanin'. Strange places, these mountains. Always been a home for strong spirits."

"I saw Palmer," I told him.

"Oh," he said, frowning. "Yeah, I should've thought of that. Death has a way of troublin' a man sometimes."

"Not you, though."

"I've made his acquaintance too often for that. Now talk it out, Darby. What'd you see?"

"The buffalo," I explained, "only it said it was the ghost of death. It came for Palmer, and it said it was coming for me."

"Bunch of nonsense, that," Shea said, shaking his head. "Pure nonsense. White buff's your spirit friend."

"What?"

"Boys turn your age, they starve themselves half crazy to have a dream. A wolf or a bear . . . or a buffalo comes to 'em, tells 'em somethin' to set 'em on their path. White buffalo come to you. He's not about to bring you harm. Truth is he was likely there to chase off the evils lingerin' in this place."

"You think so?"

"Can't figure it any other way. Smell the smoke. There's pine scent, and it carries a good spirit with it. Can't let a fool dream bother you anymore."

"Guess not," I agreed.

"Ever read Palmer's scratchin'?"

"No," I confessed.

"Turn to the last page and see what it says."

I crawled over to the table and snatched the journal, then carried it to the fire. By the flickering flame, I made out his final feeble scribbling.

"'I pray the man finds me will cover me up so the wolves don't get me,' he wrote," I read to Shea. "'If he's a man knows guns, I'd have him put my Hawken to good use. I paid fair money for it down in Green River and can't abide the . . .'"

"Read the rest," Shea instructed.

"I can't make it out."

He took the journal and stared at the faint lines. Shaking his head, Shea managed a smile.

"Fool youngster likely meant he hated to think his good money went for naught. He was always closer to his pennies, that one, than with his friends."

"So you swapped for the Hawken back at Ft. Hall for nothing," I said, amused somewhat, for Shea watched his pennies, too.

"For nothin'?" Shea asked. "I'd say Palmer left that rifle for you, son. So you see, that white buff brought you favors after all. Got yourself a proper huntin' gun now."

I hoped he was right, for I'd seen all I cared to see of Teton ghosts.

In fact, they didn't return. After cleaning the Hawken, I tested the rifle's aim and found it pulled some to the right. Shea adjusted the sights, and I worked at holding the heavy rifle steady. In a week's time it brought down a fine elk, and as April yielded to May, we grew strong on Teton game and trout from the creek.

Once the snow finally melted away from the grassland, our horses began to regain their strength as well. Shea taught me the country, devoting special care to showing me which tubers and plants gave sustenance and which brought on illness.

"Land can be a jokester sometimes," he told me. "Some of these plants'll both give and cure a sickness. Trick's to know how much to use or which season to pick 'em."

I knew I'd never remember it all, so I started sketching the plants and making notes about them in my journal.

"Fine thing to do, Darby, but don't forget to study 'em. It's in your head they'll do good, not sittin' in some book collectin' dust."

"Sure," I agreed. I couldn't imagine ever recalling half the things he knew, though.

I was off studying my notes and digging roots when I first saw the wild boys. There were three of them, dressed in frayed buckskins, bare-legged and skeleton thin. At first I didn't know what to make of them. They walked with a lurch forward, and they gazed right and left, ahead and behind like prairie dogs fearing a diving hawk.

I started to call to them, but something held me back. Instead I hid in the brush and watched them approach the cabin. The tallest, who might have been twelve, made scratching noises on the cabin door, and the others whined like anxious hounds. Shea opened the door, froze in amazement, and the boys scattered like frightened mice.

"Hey, boys, I mean no harm!" Shea called.

The wild boys never glanced back, though. Afterward I asked him about them.

"Don't know," he told me. "Weren't here when I wintered with Thompson. Too pale for mixed blood. It'd be far from the wagon trails for 'em to've come that way. Could be Palmer's kids, though I didn't know he had any. Said nothin' about boys in his writin', did he?"

"I didn't read it all," I said. "I will. Tom, you figure they were here all winter, near naked like that and all? I'll bet they're starving."

"You figure to tame 'em, do you?"

"Somewhere, sometime, they were human."

"Doesn't much matter now, not with 'em that young," Shea declared. "They go mountain mad. Seen it before. A week or two in the rough, and they forget who they are, even what they are. They grow fearful of anybody. I once saw a girl, maybe nine years old, try to scratch her own ma's eyes out. That little one wasn't lost but a week. Those three've got a lifetime's muck on 'em. Not even Molly Bostwick could scrub it off."

"She'd try," I pointed out.

"Then I guess you will, too. Don't be too disappointed when it fails, though."

"Maybe it won't."

"Maybe," he muttered, clearly unconvinced.

I tracked the wild boys as I would have stalked any game. It wasn't easy, for they moved around from rocky ledge to small cave to treetop like nothing I ever saw. There was no pattern to their movements, and I judged them crafty beyond measure. I only got close enough to speak to them once, and that was early one morn when I stumbled across the three of them asleep close by the creek. I crept up on the oldest and nudged him awake. His fearful eyes greeted my appearance with unspeakable terror, and he shrank toward his fellow creatures, whimpering like a frightened child.

I had come down to the creek to do some fishing, and my pockets were full of fresh biscuits. I drew one out with my fingers, then set it on a rock. The wild boy sniffed at it, then took it in his teeth. Finally he tore off a corner and tasted it. Convinced it was not poison, he split the biscuit and set a portion beside his sleeping comrades. Then, with a tenderness I didn't expect, he roused the others from their sleep.

"You're not long wild," I told them. "Here."

I emptied my pockets, and they eagerly gobbled the food.

"Wait, and I'll bring you more," I promised.

Their eyes followed me toward the house, and I grabbed every bit of food I could carry.

"Mary always did say the way to tame a boy is to feed him," I mumbled as I raced down the slope. When I reached the creek, though, only crumbs remained of the wild boys.

"They been hurt sometime," Shea suggested when I told him the tale. "Thought I saw strap marks on the littlest one that day they come to the cabin. Could be Palmer gave 'em some food till he died. That'd explain 'em comin' here. Trail orphans, I'd guess, or maybe youngsters snatched by Sioux or Shoshoni and then set loose."

"They're not altogether wild," I assured Shea. "I close to had them eating from my hand."

"I seen men do that with raccoons. Even a bear'll take your food now and again. Doesn't mean you've tamed 'em, Darby."

But I wasn't about to give up. I continued setting out food, mostly at night, and it was always gone by morning. Twice more I spotted them, tanned and hard from rough life, but better fed and less fearful. Twice they left me bits of pine carved in animal shapes where I left the food.

"Maybe we should set snares for them," I suggested. "A bear trap maybe."

"No, they're too smart for that. They'd never lasted long here if they didn't use their nose to smell out trouble. First trap you set'd turn them from you for good. Maybe, in time, they'll come to you on their own. More likely they'll set off somewhere else."

Shea and I shot a pair of bighorn sheep on the far slope, and we worked the hides into the warmest kind of winter coats imaginable. I took my old elk coat down to the feeding place and left it near the food. I then crept up the slope and waited for the chance to speak again to the wild ones.

A bit after midnight I heard something thrashing around. It uttered low, strangely guttural noises, and I grew uneasy. I drew out my pistol and edged my way to the fringe of the trees. There, tearing into the mutton I'd brought for the wild boys, was a fiery-eyed gray wolf.

"No!" I shouted, stepping out and firing a shot in the air. The wolf raced away, and I sat beside my coat and sobbed.

"Wild things are best left alone," Shea told me when he found me there at dawn. "Wolves or bear cubs . . . or human cubs left too long in the rough."

"I know somebody befriended a lost boy once," I said, shuddering. "Remember? I set off on my own from the train, with nowhere really to go and nobody to trust. You brought me back."

"Was your papa sent me."

"You came. Then and last autumn. You're better at it than I am, it appears. I failed."

"You tried," he said, helping me to my feet. "I'm proud of you for it. Isn't everybody who'd take a chance knowin' the odds were set so hard against him."

"Only a fool," I muttered.

"Or a man knows about bein' orphaned."

"Yes," I said, nodding sadly.

Chapter 12

With summer's glow on the land, we departed the Tetons and headed north into the Yellowstone Valley. It was a strange, eerie land full of bubbling mud and foul-smelling pools of yellowish liquid. Oddest of all were the giant columns of water that suddenly shot skyward through cracks in the rocky surface. I was put in mind of a tale Grandpa Prescott spun about giant whales swimming the south Atlantic, blowing steam as high as a church steeple.

"Strange place," I told Shea as we made camp in a canyon cut by the Yellowstone.

"Crows believe strong spirits abide here," he explained. "These mountains always seem best suited to elk and grizzlies. I never knew a man to winter here two years in a row."

I could see why. Even the wind seemed bewitched, whispering unearthly tunes, and carrying a sulfurous scent. But when we continued northward, we found small parties of Blackfeet prowling the countryside. Their faces were painted for war. They brought along spare horses, but no women or children shared their camp.

"Blackfeet'd as soon scalp a white man as bid him good mornin'," Shea declared when he ushered me to the safety of a boulder-strewn hillside. "Nobody to tangle with, Darby. I've fought 'em before."

And so Tom Shea turned southward, and I followed, as always, in his wake. We crossed rugged country, leaving the Blackfeet far behind. Now we were in the land of the Absaroka—the Crow.

"We'll see 'em 'fore long," Shea assured me when we

119

made camp along the banks of a surging river.

"The Crows?"

"They'll mostly be out on the plain, shootin' buffalo now," he explained. "Or up north chasin' Blackfeet off their huntin' grounds. Crows haven't had an easy time last few years. Smallpox killed more'n a few, and the Blackfeet up north, Sioux and Cheyenne to the east, and the Shoshonis down south all creep in a bit here and there."

"The Shoshonis are our friends, aren't they?" I asked, recalling our pleasant times in the camps of Two Knives.

"This river here's called the Shoshoni," Shea explained. "North Fork anyhow. But today it's Crow country. Next week, well, who knows? Two Knives and his boys were fair company, and the Shoshonis don't hold the fondness for scalpin' white men that the Blackfeet have. Still, if we take to the Crow camps, we'd be no friend to the Shoshoni."

"You still have friends among the Crows, don't you? Relatives of your wife and son."

"Some," Shea mumbled, staring sadly off into the mountains. "If they've not all died of late."

"Then that's where we're headed?"

"Might be," Shea admitted. " 'Course, the wind might blow us elsewhere instead. Has before."

I nodded, then busied myself making preparations for supper. We had already snagged four plump trout from the river, and together with wild turnips and some water plants, it promised to be a fine meal. As I scraped scales from the fish, though, I detected a rustling among the cottonwoods upstream. Something thrashed about as if entangled in a snare, and I instantly grabbed my Hawken and set off to investigate.

I got no nearer to the trees than fifty feet when a low grunt sent shivers down my spine. I'd heard that sound before, up in the Blue Mountains in '48. My eyes caught sight of a silver-brown mass of fur, confirming my fears. For the second time in my young life, I was confronting a grizzly bear.

Often Shea had spoken of how bears are shy creatures. Given a chance, they will generally retreat from humans. But grizzlies can be ill-humored in the best of times, and the sight of an angry swarm of bees hovering over the beast's head explained the bear's foul temperament.

"Shea!" I cried.

My shout did nothing more than arouse the grizzly's anger. The beast bellowed so that the ground shook. Then it fixed its eyes on my thin frame and lunged forward.

"Lord, help me," I whispered as I raised the rifle to my shoulder, fixed a percussion cap in place, rammed back the hammer and prayed the charge remained dry. The bear loomed closer, and I pressed the trigger.

The rifle exploded, and powder smoke stung my eyes as I was thrown backward into a snowbank. My fingers grew numb, and I fought to regain my senses. The bear, meanwhile, emerged from the smoke dragging its left side. Blood stained the ground, and I knew my aim had been true. The grizzly wasn't dead, though, and what remained had vengeance in its eyes.

"Oh, Lord," I said, scrambling to my feet and retreating. As I moved, I drew out the rifle's ramrod and fumbled in my pocket for a fresh cartridge. How my fingers ever found anything is a great mystery, but in the end I managed to pause long enough to load the powder, ram down the ball, fix a second cap in place, and turn the rifle again on the grizzly.

The camp was a world of confusion by now. Horses whined and fought to escape their hobbles. The bear slung cook pots and blankets right and left as it chased me.

"Shea!" I called a final time.

There was no answer, so I leveled the rifle and fired. The Hawken again sent me flying, and this time I lost my grip on the rifle. I fell hard against the woodpile, catching a large length of pine in the small of my back so that a wave of pain exploded through me. I half rolled away and blinked to clear my eyes of the shroud cast over the camp by exploded powder.

The bear raised itself onto its hind legs and roared defiantly. I reached for the pistol normally carried on my hip, then recalled I'd left it elsewhere. I had but my skinning knife, and it would offer little protection from such a ferocious foe as that grizzly.

"No!" I yelled as the bear approached. "No!"

I closed my eyes and prepared for the wave of pain that

its massive paws would bring. I feared the sharp teeth, the deadly hug that would squeeze what life remained from my lungs. But the bear never touched me. Instead it cried defiantly, then fell with a dying shudder to the earth and expired.

"Lord, are you dead, bear?" I asked, shaking off my terror.

It was indeed, and I sank to my knees and offered thanks for my salvation. I was still praying when Shea appeared.

"Lord, you fool of a boy, don't you know better'n to square off with grizzlies?" he called. "Darby, you plan to get yourself covered from chin to toes with scars, do you? That bear could've killed you!"

"Close to did, too," I confessed. "Took two balls to down him. And I figured myself dead for certain."

"You're not hurt?" he asked, lifting me to my feet and having a good look. "No slices tore out of you?"

"Just a bruise here and there," I explained. "Guess I'd better get back to scaling those fish now."

"Leave that to me," he suggested. "You've got a bear to skin."

"Can't it wait? I've nearly been killed, you know."

"Bear meat's fair eatin', Darby, and there's a coat to be made."

"Sure," I grumbled, wishing the bear might have escaped. "Figure I can wear the claws around my neck?"

"Your bear," he told me. "I know a Crow wore a choker made of bone and grizzly claws. His name was Bearkiller. That's the one the Nez Perce gave you, isn't it?"

"Yes," I said, remembering. "Sounds better'n Buffalo Dreamer, too. Bearkiller Prescott. Fair enough."

"Well, you think on it while you get along with the skinnin'. We've got meat to smoke and pack now, and still dinner wants cookin'. Best get on with it."

"Guess so," I said, grinning at the approving glance he sent my way. It had been there before, but I don't think in quite the same way. Shea's eyes recognized me as an equal, as a man worthy to be his partner. I felt a hair taller, and as I skinned that bear, I began to feel like a true man of the mountains.

122

By the time we left the Absaroka Range and approached the broad shoulders of the snowcapped Big Horn Mountains, I'd completed my transformation. I rode Snow with a new self-assuredness, and with the choker of deer bone and grizzly claws adorning my neck and the bearskin rolled behind my saddle, I appeared as a man to be reckoned with, Three Fingers Shea or not at my side.

We were riding alongside the Big Horn River when we first met up with the Crows. There were but four of them, and the eldest was scarcely as tall as me. They gazed at us with suspicious eyes, but when Shea raised his three-fingered hand, they seemed to lose their uneasiness. He called out to them in their own language, and the leader rode closer. The young Crow spoke a few words slowly, then babbled away a mile a minute.

"This is Iron Heart," Shea explained. "His aunt was my wife. He remembers."

Shea paused to swallow a sudden surge of emotion, and I turned to greet Iron Heart.

"You are welcome to our camps," the Crow said when I raised my hand in friendship.

"You speak English very well," I said in surprise.

"Taught him myself," Shea boasted. "Your mother, Bluebird, is well? And Two Blows, your father?"

"Well," the boy said, smiling as he waved to his friends. The other Crows turned and disappeared into a stand of pines. Iron Heart then reached out, touched my choker, and smiled in approval.

"My name's Darby," I said, gripping his hand.

"Lately I call him Bearkiller," Shea added.

"Yes, Bearkiller," Iron Heart said, touching the claws again. "A good name."

"Not so good as Iron Heart, though," I said, grinning. He laughed and pounded his chest. Then he nudged his horse into a trot and waved us along. Shea nodded for me to go first, and I urged Snow along.

We rode three or four miles before reaching the Crow village. Their tipis were arranged in a broad circle alongside a small bubbling creek. Elk and deer hides stretched on a series of wooden frames, and kettles simmered with stewing venison. Women and girls tended the pots, scrubbed garments, or looked after the little ones. There were no men in sight. A few boys gathered with a pair of gray-haired grandfathers to craft arrows. The younger boys chased each other through the creek or wrestled in the mud.

"Here are my brothers, Little Heart and Far-seeing Hawk," Iron Heart called, waving two muddy youngsters from the creek. "You remember Three Fingers, our white uncle."

The boys gazed at Shea shyly, then stared at the bear claws around my neck.

"Here is Bearkiller," Iron Heart added, slapping my shoulder. "Maybe he will tell us of the brave hunt."

The younger boy howled and climbed up behind me onto Snow's back. The other one gripped my wrist, then raced back to join his companions at the creek.

"Come, my mother awaits," Iron Heart declared, motioning toward a smallish woman dressed in a yellow buckskin dress just ahead.

"Ride," Little Heart whispered, poking my ribs with a muddy finger.

I squeezed Snow with my knees, causing him to lift his forefeet in the air. Little Heart had to hold onto my back with all his strength to stay atop the big white horse, and I felt his hands claw desperately into my back. Afterward, as we followed Iron Heart to a nearby lodge, the younger boy remained still.

Shea introduced me to Bluebird, the pretty-faced sister of his dead wife. Shea must have seen the one sister in the other, for his face took on a fresh glow. She spoke little English, but she conversed to Shea at length in the tongue of the Crow.

"They are remembering," Iron Heart explained to me as we tended the horses. "Tonight we will feast his return, and stories will be shared. You will tell of the bear?"

"I speak no Crow words," I told him.

"I will speak them for you. In time you will learn. I will teach you."

"I, too," Little Heart added, joining us.

"You can only teach mud turtles," Iron Heart said, halting his younger brother. "Wash yourself."

Little Heart immediately dashed toward the river, and Iron Heart mirrored my grin.

"Have you brothers?" he asked.

"Three, all older."

"None younger?"

"Once," I said, sadly recalling little Matthew. "He died long ago. Sickness."

"Yes, we, too, know that sadness," Iron Heart told me. "Our people once were as the stars on a clear night. Now we are few, and our enemies force us from our hunting grounds. My father rides against the Sioux as we talk. Next time I will ride at his side."

"We saw Blackfeet up in the Yellowstone country," I said sourly. "Shea says they come farther south each year."

"Ah, Blackfeet are dangerous in the mountains, but on the plain it is the Sioux that test a man. They ride wild and unafraid into battle, and though we kill many, still they come. They fear Three Fingers. His rifle sings death for them."

"Yes, he's a good shot."

"You, too, carry a good rifle. Will you ride with us?"

"I've not got much heart for war," I confessed. "But I'll share your dangers if I share your camp."

"A good answer," Iron Heart said, nodding as he examined Snow. Other boys gathered as well, and Snow stomped nervously as unfamiliar hands probed muscle and flanks.

"He was a gift of the Nez Perce," I explained. "I killed a grizzly that had bothered their camp."

Iron Heart translated my words, and two of the young Crows touched my choker.

"No, not this bear," I told them. "It was another grizzly, three years or so ago. This one," I said, touching the claws, "was killed along the North Fork of the Shoshoni River."

The Crows whispered among themselves, and I could tell my standing in the tribe soared. Iron Heart clasped my shoulders with his hands, and the others gathered close as I narrated the tale of slaying the grizzly in the Blue Mountains. Later, when we went down to the creek for a mid-afternoon swim, I displayed my claw scars, too.

125

"Yes, Bearkiller is a good name," Iron Heart told me afterward. "You ride a brave horse, too. But if we ride to battle, you must ride another. A white horse marks you, my friend. It angers the Sioux. Even a man who has killed two bears should be careful with the Sioux."

"Yes," I agreed, hoping the day when I might have to ride to war would never come.

We passed two days and nights in the lodge of Iron Heart's father. Then the men returned from their raid, hauling with them fifteen Sioux ponies and a pair of captive girls. Two Blows was welcomed home by his three sons, and Iron Heart took the opportunity to introduce the tall warrior to me.

"He came with Three Fingers," Iron Heart explained. "We know him as Bearkiller."

"Darby Prescott," I said, gripping Two Blows's large hand.

Two Blows quickly turned to Shea, though.

"So, my brother returns," Two Blows said as he greeted Shea warmly. "We must feast. There has been victory over the Sioux, and now we grow strong with your return."

The boys howled in delight, and soon it seemed the whole tribe gathered. True to his word, Two Blows hosted a feast, and amid the dancing and eating, there was time for me to again tell of the grizzly fought and killed on the Shoshoni River. Two Blows gave away horses to honor his sons and his prodigal white brother, and a lodge was erected for Shea and me within the camp circle.

Our biggest surprise was yet to come, though. As we spread out buffalo hides to sleep on, a wrinkle-faced old woman appeared at the oval doorway.

"Tom?" I asked, turning toward Shea.

The old woman began babbling, and Shea's face bore first a frown, then a rather bemused expression.

"Says her name's Yellow Grass Woman," he told me. "Well, Darby, look's as if we've got a woman to look after us now."

"What?" I asked.

"Bluebird's aunt. Seems Two Blows got to worryin' a couple of men like us might take after somethin' younger to do our cookin' or tend our lodge, so he's sent this old nag over to keep after us. What do you think?"

"I think maybe I should've welcomed that Nez Perce girl," I told him. "This one's old enough to be my grandma."

"Well, see you're respectful, else she'll box you about some. These Crow women are accustomed to havin' their way so far as youngsters are concerned."

"I'm seventeen now," I argued.

"And I'm a good deal older, but I'd guess she's got years on the both of us combined. Be a while gettin' used to her, I'd guess, but there's somethin' to be said for havin' somebody around to wash and cook and mend. Such is a woman's lot, the Crows'd say."

I held back a grin. Mary would have bashed anyone who thought such to be a woman's lot. But I had, in truth, grown weary of doing those chores myself. Besides, the woman looked to have seen hard days. It was only charity to take her in.

Chapter 13

As I grew to know Yellow Grass Woman, I learned to look back on the days before her arrival as a time of freedom. She made a barely edible mush of corn and venison which we ate five meals out of six, and she was forever fussing at me to do this or that. I was never quite clean enough for her taste, and she took to poking my ribs with sticks and spouting off a string of Crow phrases a mile long. I understood none of it, and she seemed unwilling to learn English.

"Old sow," I grumbled more than once.

Shea took note of my poor disposition and drew me aside.

"Guess maybe you're like those wild boys back in the Tetons," he observed. "Been too long a wayfarer to take to camp life."

"I guess. It's just that she's forever picking at me," I complained. "Next thing you know, she'll be braiding my hair."

"Likely will," Shea said, grinning. "Got the cure for it, though. Two Blows says he plans to move his camp, set out after the buffalo. I'd guess when the boys set off to scout, you'll be asked along."

"You're the one used to scouting."

"Well, I've ridden out front a few times, I'll admit, but a buffalo scout ought to be young enough to ride all day. You'll find Iron heart and the other boys better company."

"Feeling old?"

"Older every day," he confessed. "Not so old I can't still turn you on your heels, though," he added, reaching out and lifting me off the ground, then flipping me head-over-heels so that I sprawled onto the sandy ground. I gazed at him with raised eyebrows, and he helped me up. Then I dusted myself off and joined Iron Heart at the creek.

"Shea says we're to hunt the buffalo soon," I told him.

"Yes, my father will send the scouts out soon," Iron Heart declared. "You will come with me?"

"White horse and all?"

"A man who has killed bears should hunt buffalo."

I didn't tell him of hunting with the Shoshonis or of seeing the white buffalo. Instead I sat beside him as he spun tales of the hunt, narratives of great peril and dangers beyond my imagination.

"Our hunt will long be remembered," he promised. "Iron Heart and Bearkiller will be the first to see the buffalo. We will be the ones to bring the winter food to the lodges of our people."

I nodded, though I didn't know how he could be so sure we would find the herd.

Half a week passed before we set out, though. Meanwhile everyone stirred with anticipation. Small boys played at hunting while some elder donned a buffalo robe and a horned bonnet. Older boys made arrows or molded lead into rifle balls. Women began packing up their family's belongings. The men held council and invoked the spirits through mysterious pipe ceremonies and deep prayers. The medicine chiefs erected a sweat lodge, and most of the men completed a purification ritual. Finally a great dance was held.

I understood little of it, but I'd learned enough to observe quietly and not badger Iron Heart or Shea with questions. For the first time since arriving in the camp I felt like a stranger, some sort of intruder who must be tolerated. My mood wasn't brightened by Yellow Grass Woman, who seemed particularly provoked when I wore my beaded Nez Perce moccasins. Between the old woman's nagging and Shea's snoring, I scarcely slept at all anymore.

Worse, my sole friend and great companion, Iron Heart, spent more and more time playing his flute near the lodges of young maidens. Fox Woman, in particular, drew his attentions. The tall, slender girl had dazzling brown eyes, and only a blind man could fail to notice her interest in Iron Heart.

"Crows take wives early, Darby," Shea explained. "Iron Heart's a warrior now. He's expected to support a woman, raise sons to hunt and daughters to continue the tribe."

"He's not much older'n me," I pointed out.

"You were offered a girl yourself, remember? I'd encourage you to give it time, for marryin' into an Indian tribe's not a temporary kind of thing."

"You did it."

"And was glad of it for a time. Brought me sorrow in the end. What's more, I never was altogether accepted by everybody, you know. It's a hard thing, tryin' to fit in a world you're not born to."

"I was born a farmer," I reminded him. "I never fit there."

"Different thing, bein' born to somethin', though. You take to the high country like I did myself. To the trail, too, in spite of its perils."

"That's what wayfarers do, isn't it?"

"Sure, but you've not got the restlessness I saw in you before. You've grown steady, Darby Prescott."

"Comes of getting taller, and surviving winter."

"Tall may help some, but it's mostly the way a man sets his jaw and sees his world. Wasn't so long ago you fretted most every day. Now you ride that white horse proud as a Nez Perce chief. Still, you watch yourself come the buffalo hunt. Crows aren't the only fellows settin' out after buffalo, you know. I didn't bring you this far to see you Sioux scalped. If that happened, I'd be mighty vexed with you."

"Wouldn't like it much myself."

He grinned, and I knew he understood the warning had been taken to heart. And yet when I rode out that next morning with Iron Heart, Tall Bear, Running Elk, and a younger Crow named Red-tailed Hawk, I could hardly conceal my excitement. Snow responded to the ride with boundless energy, and the others were hard-pressed to keep pace.

Ours was not the only scouting party sent out ahead of

130

the camp. In all six bands of boys scoured the creeks and hillsides for buffalo while the rest of the camp dragged itself eastward toward the broad plain which provided a natural path for buffalo heading south from the Missouri basin into the Big Horn Valley.

We found no buffalo that first week, but our days were not uneventful. Twice we shot deer, and we were forever snaring a few prairie hens or rabbits for the dinner pot. I welcomed the taste of fresh meat after so many suppers of Yellow Grass Woman's mush, and I amazed my companions by mixing up some dough and baking bread on a stick.

"You are a good companion," Iron Heart told me as we spread our blankets close to the embers of the fire. "Among our people a warrior may come to choose a brother-friend. Do you know of this?"

"No," I confessed. "What does it mean?"

"Brother-friends ride together into battle. One is sworn to come to the aid of the other. One takes the obligations of a brother born by the same mother. One takes the children of the other as his own, holds his brother's wife as a sister, seeing to their needs before his own."

"Yes?"

"I would take you as my brother-friend, Bearkiller," Iron Heart explained. "If you agree, I will speak to my father of it when we return to camp."

"I agree," I told him.

"Then it is good," he declared, smiling broadly. "And soon we will find the buffalo."

That night the white buffalo visited my dreams, thundering out of a cloud to lead me to a great herd of its brothers. I saw Iron Heart race between two great bulls and strike down each in turn. I rode at his side, striking with equal passion. Then a blood red sun appeared overhead, and I felt on fire. A dozen dark horses carrying riders with masked faces jumped from that sun and chased us. Iron Heart and I stood together, fending off the masked devils until they were no more. The other Crows then arrived, howling and celebrating our great feat.

When I awoke, I remembered the dream only slightly. I had no time to share it, for Iron Heart was anxious to set out, and we others, as always, let him lead us. We rode briskly up one hillside and down another. Then, near a bend in the Big Horn River itself, we spotted a mass of black specks stretching halfway to the horizon.

"The buffalo," Iron Heart said, pointing to the plodding beasts.

"Yes," I agreed.

Then, even as we were digesting our good fortune, we spotted something else approaching the fringe of the herd. Twenty horsemen rode from the cover of cottonwoods toward the buffalo, howling wildly as they turned the animals toward the south. Riders darted in to fire arrows at close range into the rumbling creatures' hearts.

"Another band's got there first," I said, sighing.

"Not Crows," Tall Bear pointed out.

"What?" I asked.

"Their horses are marked," Iron Heart explained.

I gazed in wonder. I could barely see horses at all in the swirling dust raised by hundreds of frenzied buffalo.

"Sioux," Tall Bear declared, drawing an arrow. "In our country."

"Killing our winter meat!" Iron Heart added angrily.

I looked nervously at my companions. They were readying themselves to charge twenty armed Sioux. It was folly, pure and simple, and I told Iron Heart as much.

"We cannot flee," he explained. "We must fight them."

"Five of us?" I asked. "What chance do we have of doing anything besides getting killed? Better we should send for help. With the rest of your people, we can have a great victory."

"The older ones will have all the glory," Tall Bear objected.

"Perhaps," Iron Heart said, looking over the valley with thoughtful eyes. "Perhaps not. The Sioux ponies will tire quickly, and the men will be hard at work cutting the meat. Tonight they will sleep well. We may perhaps be few to fight them and win, but we can surely take their ponies. Then our fathers will easily run them down and slay them all."

"Yes," Tall Bear agreed, and Running Elk grinned his approval.

Iron Heart then motioned Red-tailed Hawk closer. The two spoke briefly, and the Hawk prepared his horse for the long ride back to fetch the others.

"Perhaps, Bearkiller, you should go, too," Iron Heart said. "The Sioux are not your enemies, and there is danger."

"Am I not to be your brother-friend then?" I asked.

"It's good you will stay," Iron Heart declared, "but you cannot ride to war on a white horse. You will take Red-tailed Hawk's pony, and your white will carry him to my father."

"Agreed," I said, dismounting. I took my rifle and equipment, then turned Snow over to little Red-tailed Hawk. The boy was maybe twelve, and I was glad to have him headed toward the camp and safety. But once the Hawk left, Iron Heart led us to a stand of willows. As we tied off our horses and gathered together, he set about preparing his raid in earnest. And I began to fret anew.

Sioux and Crow bands had raided each other's horse herds since the world began, or so Iron Heart believed. To leave a plains tribe afoot was close to as great an indignity as to leave them hairless, and Iron Heart clearly enjoyed the notion. His plan was a simple one—namely club the pony guards senseless and race off with the horses. Darkness would provide its protective cover, and the weary Sioux would stagger, weary and confused, out of their lodges to find their ponies racing away in the night.

"It may be a good plan," I told Iron Heart, "but with only four of us, it will be difficult."

"Yes, it is a great thing," Iron Heart said. "Bearkiller, to be a man, one must do great things. To count coup on the enemy is greatest. Stealing his horses is almost as good."

I thought to argue, but my companions showed no trace of reluctance. Not a shred of caution troubled any of them. I sighed and studied Iron Heart's plan etched in the sandy ground. Later he spoke prayers and fed sweet grass to a small fire.

"I wish I had a pipe," Iron Heart complained. "It is better to smoke before entering battle. Perhaps the spirits understand."

I hoped so, for by twilight a dozen fires burned in the

Sioux camps below us. I feared a hundred warriors waited for us down there, each armed with arrows that would slice through flesh and penetrate the heart. I saw danger in every shadow. But when Iron Heart waved us forward, I climbed atop the brown Crow pony and rode at my friend's side.

As it happened, there wasn't but a sliver of moon out that night. Most of the Sioux had already taken to their beds. Two boys guarded the ponies, neither of them much older than Red-tailed Hawk. Iron Heart turned toward the nearer and pointed Running Elk toward the other. Quickly both young Crows dismounted and hurried forward. Iron Heart clubbed the first guard to the ground. Running Elk drove his knife through the back of the second, then cut away the young Sioux's scalp.

On another occasion Running Elk might have howled to the moon in triumph, but there were too many horses to collect—more than fifty by my own rough count. None of us had figured so many, and the four of us exchanged uneasy looks. Then Iron Heart remounted his horse, and we rode together to the rear of the herd. None of the animals wore hobbles, so when Running Elk and Tall Bear reached the flanks, Iron Heart shouted wildly, and the race was on.

Never in my life had I seen such a spectacle. Horses darted everywhere. Behind us men cried out in alarm as animals trampled lodges, upset stretching racks, and disturbed smoking pits. I couldn't help but laugh at two young men who raced after ponies reaching out with one hand while a second held a blanket to cover their nakedness.

I considered the confusion flooding the Sioux camp our best ally, for the four of us only drove a little better than two-thirds of the ponies off. The remaining horses escaped in one direction or another, and several were sure to be caught by the angry Sioux. Iron Heart realized that, too, and he kept us going as fast and as far as possible.

I suppose by daybreak we must have ridden ten miles or more. I recalled little of it. The fresh scalp dangling from Running Elk's belt combined with the dust and fatigue to fill my head with a dizziness I could not cast aside. I know

Iron Heart hoped to reach his father by first light, but Two Blows was nowhere to be found when the sun's golden rays found us.

"We're men of many horses," Iron Heart told me as we hurried our tired ponies along. "Now I can take Fox Woman to my lodge. You should meet her sister, Bright Owl. She will make a good wife, too."

"Just now I'd settle for old Yellow Grass Woman," I grumbled. "How much farther do you suppose your father is?"

The scowl on Iron Heart's face warned we were still far too distant for safety. Worse, I spied dust rising from the plain behind us.

"Sioux," Running Elk announced. We all knew he was right, but I wished he'd kept his thoughts to himself. There was little we could do save drive the horses onward and pray Two Blows was near.

Iron Heart suddenly rode past me and spoke to Running Elk. The two of them argued considerably. Then Iron Heart had a like conversation with Tall Bear. Again heated words flew. Finally Iron Heart joined me.

"The horses are most important," he told me. "You and the others will hurry them to my father while I stay behind to slow the Sioux."

"You won't slow them much by yourself," I argued. "I have a rifle, too. Together we can drop a couple of them, maybe put an end to the pursuit."

"I stay behind to die," he said, staring at me with hard eyes. "This is my raid. I must stay. You should go."

"A brother-friend would stay, wouldn't he?"

"We never spoke the words, Bearkiller."

"What have words to do with it?" I complained. "Come on. Let's find a good place to surprise them."

"No," he objected. "Go!"

"I've never been much good at running," I explained. "Bear near killed me once for being such a fool. I've got nobody to cry over me, Iron Heart, no brothers who'll know I'm dead, no parents to cut off fingers. There's just me."

"Three Fingers?"

"He's a good man, a father of sorts, I guess." I confessed. "But he'd stay, and we both know it. Now stop fussing about it and figure how we're to do it. If there's a chance of saving our hair, I'd as soon you take it."

"Yes," he agreed, brightening some as he led the way to a rocky hillside. We left our horses and made our way into the boulders. From there we had a good view of the five approaching Sioux warriors.

They were a good way back still, and our guns lacked the range to strike them. We loaded our rifles and made ready, though. Soon lead would strike bone and flesh once more. I shuddered to imagine the feel of burning pain. I found myself wondering about death, hoping it was but a long sleep and not the infernal damnation preached at me more than once on Sunday morns.

Iron Heart motioned to the approaching riders, and I fixed my aim on a slim figure on the right. Only as I prepared to fire did I see that figure belonged to a boy no more than thirteen. I should have sent my ball through his chest. Instead I fired low, toward his horse. Iron Heart felt no such compassion for the Sioux. His shot struck the Sioux leader in the chest and toppled him to the earth.

A cloud of smoke and confusion then took possession of the hillside. The young Sioux fought to extricate himself from his dying horse while Iron Heart and I battled to reload our rifles. As the smoke cleared, the three remaining riders suddenly charged the rocks. I fired and missed. Iron Heart managed to wound a man. Two others swept up the rocks and pounced on us.

I discarded my rifle and pulled my Colt, and the Sioux before me ducked behind the rocks. I shifted my pistol toward the Sioux locked in deadly combat with Iron Heart. They were too close for me to safely strike one without harming the other, so I concentrated instead on a band of riders hurrying to join the fray.

We stood little hope against the first batch, but the newcomers cast aside all doubt as to the eventual outcome. In no time two Sioux were hammering Iron Heart while three others circled me.

"Come closer," I urged them, waving my pistol. The Colt could put a large round hole in a man, and the Sioux seemed to know that. They kept a fair distance for a while as their companions broke through to Iron Heart and laid him low. I heard but a solitary cry. It was all that was needed. Swallowing hard, I aimed my pistol and shot the first Indian in the middle. As he buckled, I fired again, scattering the others as I hurried toward Iron Heart.

When I reached the bleeding figure of my friend, I felt a burning sensation tear at my left arm. The fingers went numb, and I gazed down in surprise to find an arrow embedded just below my elbow.

"So, they've killed you, too," Iron Heart said as he staggered to his feet. His chest and neck were bleeding from several wounds. At his feet lay one foe who had failed to accomplish his goal. Nevertheless Iron Heart's eyes grew large, and he muttered a brief Crow prayer.

I didn't see him fall. I was distracted by the whine of an arrow. Two Sioux taunted me from the far flank of the rocks, and another made a wild charge toward me. I fired, striking him in the foot. He fell, moaning, and I knelt beside Iron Heart.

"Brother?" I called.

He didn't answer. His eyes stared up from the ground, but there was no life in them. He'd died. I shrieked in anger, then prepared to empty my pistol at the next Sioux to rise from the rocks.

The Sioux hung back a moment. Then when one rushed forward, my pistol sent him hurrying to cover. There were three or four of them fanning out in a half circle, cautiously creeping closer. I huddled beside Iron Heart as arrows flew from the rocks. As my heart began to succumb to a wave of grief and hopelessness, a tremendous cry flooded the scene. From seemingly nowhere twenty armed Crows raced across the hillside, chasing Sioux from the scene with lances or blasting them with rifles. Shea was with them, and he rode to my side and motioned for me to leap up behind him and ride to safety.

"I'm watching Iron Heart," I explained, turning to my dead friend.

"He's got family to tend to that now," Shea argued. "You've got an arrow shot through your arm. Come along. Let's get it mended."

His persuasive voice silenced my objections, and I

pulled myself up behind him with my good right arm. We then rode off toward the river, and my eyes grew blurry. I recalled sinking into a soft green world of grass and reed. Then everything merged in a thick violet haze, and I lost consciousness altogether.

Chapter 14

I awoke on a bed of buffalo hides. My left arm was swollen and purple from wrist to elbow, and it ached as if stomped upon by a legion of cavalry. Yellow Grass Woman sat at my side, chanting and feeding a small fire with pinches of yellowish powder. When I lifted my head, she applied a wrinkled hand to my chest and prevented me from rising.

"You stay!" she commanded.

I did just that. Whether it was the sharp tone of her voice or the fact that those were the first English words she'd spoken that froze me in bed, I could never be certain. Whatever, the words worked their magic, and I thought I detected a trace of a smile on her stern lips.

For a brief moment or two I closed my eyes and allowed the silence to soothe my aching arm. Then I felt a hand on my forehead, and I blinked my eyes open and stared up at Tom Shea.

"Got yourself Sioux shot," he told me. "Lucky to still have your hair and hide."

"Luckier than some," I mumbled, thinking of Iron Heart.

"Yes," he agreed. "You boys were fools to take on that whole batch yourselves. What crazed notion caused you to stay back with Iron Heart?"

"He asked me to be his brother-friend. He said they always stand at each other's side, so I didn't see how I could leave him to stay behind all alone. I'm seventeen now."

"Kind of be nice to be eighteen," Shea noted. "Lucky an

139

army doctor didn't take a knife to that arm. You'd only have an elbow to scratch on summer afternoons."

"Yes, lucky," I agreed.

"Well, I always did believe the Lord gives a special look after to young fools. Was a brave thing to do, makin' that stand, Darby. But bein' brave's not enough sometimes."

He passed into my hand a slightly misshapen flint arrowhead, lying atop a small pouch marked by the sign of a bear's claws.

"A medicine pouch," he told me. "Yellow Grass Woman made it. She said a warrior with a brave heart ought to have strong medicine to keep him safe."

I glanced at the old woman, and she grinned bashfully.

"Other gifts've come, too. Food, blankets."

"Why? "

"They honor you. Nothin' earns a man so much credit as guardin' the body of a fallen friend. And for a white man to do it, well, that's somethin' unexpected. There's more, too."

"What?" I asked.

"Running Elk and Tall Bear brought in close to forty ponies. Your share is ten, and the boys insisted I choose the best ones. Snow's got himself a little herd to run with now. You're a wealthy Crow, Darby Prescott."

"What do I do with all those horses?"

"Well, there are some things you could consider. Fine mounts are always good for tradin'. You could get most anything you care for. We could even get you cash down at the Green River tradin' posts or up on the Missouri."

"I'll think on it," I said, yawning.

I had time to rest. For three days the camp remained in the hills overlooking the Big Horn River. Iron Heart was mourned deeply. His father and mother cut fingers, as did Little Heart, who was but fourteen and thought too young for the ritual.

Iron Heart was laid with his finest clothes on a scaffold in the branches of a tall cottonwood. Shea assured me the body bore no marks save those that had brought death, but I didn't find the same comfort in that fact the Crows did. Dead was dead, after all, and I'd miss my friend.

I didn't stay long in my bed. The swelling soon abated,

140

and the pain passed. The camp moved along after the buffalo, and though Shea insisted I was not strong enough to ride to the hunt, I did begin taking a turn at watching the pony herd.

No time was as busy in a Crow village as the buffalo hunt. Even the smallest children worked at cutting away hides and butchering meat. The women, even the old ones like Yellow Grass Woman, slaved away dawn to dusk smoking and drying the meat. I began to suspect the scouts had the easiest lot of all.

It was during this time that I began to notice Fox Woman. She rarely spoke to me, but her eyes followed me whenever I walked about the camp, and she managed more often than not to be at the creeks or rivers whenever I went to wash.

"You have many ponies," Shea said as the whole band gathered to celebrate the success of the hunt. "Fox Woman's father, Walking Horse, says he would accept three for her."

"She was to marry Iron Heart," I said. "I saw them together. Her heart will always be his. I don't even know her."

"To refuse would seem an insult."

"She's pretty, I'll admit, and I'm certain she'd be a better cook than our old hag. I always figured to be a bit older before taking a wife, though. Still, I don't want to insult anybody."

"There's a solution to it, if you care to take it," Shea said, grinning. I'd grown to appreciate his shrewd way of dealing with Indians, and I urged him to explain. "There's a young man, Hunts at Night, who has the eye for Fox Woman. His father's been long dead, and he lives with his grandfather. They're poor, but the boy has the mark of a good man. If you were to give him the three horses, he'd be able to wed Fox Woman."

"Wouldn't that wound his pride?" I asked.

"Not if it was in honor of Iron Heart. There'll be a feast tonight, with dancing and many songs. Two Blows will give away horses to honor his son. Your doing so, too, will earn you even more credit."

"And save me from marriage," I added, grinning.

"Come winter you may wish you had somethin' soft in your lodge," he warned. "But I expect you've got too much wayfarin' in your heart just now."

"I'll still have plenty of horses."

"Price may rise."

I couldn't help grinning at the thought of men bartering their daughters for horses. I could imagine Mary's face at the thought of some old man buying her for a few ponies! The Crows accepted it as quite natural, though, and when I sat with Two Blows's family that night at the feast, Little Heart told me it was a fair way of insuring a man was serious about providing a good home for a wife.

Then again some of the older men had close to as many wives as horses. I trusted they were not as much trouble as Yellow Grass Woman. Now that I was regaining my strength, she'd resumed her badgering.

Once everyone had eaten his fill, Two Blows and the other men told of the great buffalo hunts of the past. Then they spoke prayers and offered thanks for the gift of meat. There was a great deal of dancing and singing afterward, followed at length by several ceremonies.

First, Two Blows gave away horses in the memory of his son. Little Heart then stood at his father's side, and Two Blows renamed his younger son for the fallen elder boy. More horses were given away. Finally Bluebird and Farseeing Hawk stood and presented me with a beautiful beaded warrior shirt. I knew Bluebird had devoted many hours to that shirt. Iron Heart was to have worn it upon his wedding day.

"I, too, have gifts," I announced, nodding to Shea. "In honor of my friend, Iron Heart, and his family, I would give three ponies to Hunts at Night, for he must now lead the young men. I would also give to my friend, now called Iron Heart also, a fast horse to speed him on his path." I gave two other mounts to smaller boys who walked with the women for lack of horses.

The Crows raised a great howl, and Bluebird insisted I exchange my rags for her shirt that very moment. I did so, and with my hair now grown long and dark, falling over my ears and across my forehead, I took on the appearance of a Crow.

142

I left the council fire shortly thereafter, for my strength had not altogether returned, and I grew weary of the celebrating. I followed Shea to a small pond, and we bathed our foreheads and stared at the stars overhead. Hunts at Night joined us a moment, and though he spoke but little English, his solemn eyes and firm grip of my hand relayed his feelings.

"He asks you to think yourself his brother," Shea translated as the young warrior spoke soberly. "You are always welcome in his lodge, for you have brought great happiness to his heart."

"I'm glad," I told him. "And I know Iron Heart's courage will pass to the sons Fox Woman will give you."

He clasped my shoulders, and for a moment I thought he might throw me bodily into the pond. It was only his way of showing me his strength, and thus his worthiness, Shea explained afterward. Hunts at Night then returned to the feast, and Shea and I took to our lodge.

The next morning Shea had me out early gathering buffalo chips for our cook fire. He insisted I work the arm, lest the muscles tighten. It hurt considerably, but there was no arguing with him about such things. He declared he knew best, and I bit my lip and remained silent. He was, after all, experienced with wounds.

As midsummer passed into memory, I devoted more of my time to describing my adventures in the journal which had now lost track of the days. Shea considered that foolishness, but I insisted a man's memory could only be counted on to recall so many details before faltering.

"That's for the best," he argued. "Some of it's best forgotten. Pain and heartache. The good things stay with you."

So does the pain, I thought.

We continued hunting buffalo along the Big Horn, but more and more we found ourselves in conflict with the Sioux. Often pairs of warriors shadowed our movements, and a guard was kept about the camp. Twice bands of Sioux boys struck the pony herd, but both times our guards brushed them away like pesky insects.

Finally, though, as we made camp in a bend of the river, the Sioux struck in earnest, setting three lodges afire and stealing two women and three small children. One, a boy of seven, was later found hiding in a willow grove. The others were carried to the Sioux encampment.

Two Blows spoke angrily of the Sioux demons who had violated his camp, and warriors raised their voices, calling for a war party.

"The fires of vengeance," Shea called it. "Many a man's fallen on account of it. More will this time."

"Iron Heart said the Sioux caused the trouble," I said, remembering. "They've come north into Crow hunting ground."

"Well, I don't know any of the tribes really hold they own the earth," Shea explained. "Only the strong prevail. So there's sure to be more killing since the whites push everybody out onto the plain."

I nodded sadly. Early the next morning Two Blows and eight others rode out to punish the Sioux raiders. They brought back the captives, together with the scalps of two unfortunate Sioux. Two Crows returned tied to their ponies, though, and again a great wailing filled the camp.

The Sioux wasted no time in striking back. Two boys tending horses were struck down and a dozen animals made off with. Two belonged to me, though fortunately I'd had Snow upstream.

"We must find their camp and strike them hard this time," Two Blows argued. "We must wash them from this valley with blood."

I knew Iron Heart's death still weighed heavily upon him, and the sight of the two boys' scalped bodies stirred the other men to action. A war party of thirty men quickly formed. When the boy now known as Young Iron Heart asked me to accompany Hunts at Night and the other young men, I hesitated.

"I've got no heart for this," I told Shea. "I've seen friends die before. I think I killed a man fighting the Sioux. It's a heavy burden, that recollection."

"Those raiders took your horses," Shea reminded me.

"And I took them before that. I have no need of them."

"Not the point to it, son. A man protects what's his up here. If you won't ride, you'd best consider leavin'."

"I've been happy here."

144

"Then you share their trials, Darby. May not be pleasant, but it's the way life runs."

"Killing?" I asked. "I don't think I have it in me."

"You never backed down from a hard turn in the trail that I can remember. Shoot, you've battled grizzlies, and you stood with Iron Heart."

"He's dead," I said, sighing. "Ma and Pa, Jamie McNamara back on the trail, so many friends . . ."

"I know your heart," Shea said, resting a hand on my shoulder as he might have when I was a boy of fourteen heading to Oregon. "You counted the years and found yourself seventeen, a man. I count the scars, the tears, and I say the same thing. It's hard, this life. Warned you so. Good comes with the bad, though."

"Will you come as well?"

"I haven't moved my lodge from the circle, have I? I'll be along."

"Then I suppose I'm to go as well," I reluctantly agreed.

Young Iron Heart grinned at the news, and after the appropriate prayers were made, I rode out with the others early that next morning. I accompanied Hunts at Night. His dark, brooding eyes promised dark times for the Sioux. But as we tracked the Sioux trail, I grew more and more uneasy.

My companions showed no such concern. Young Iron Heart, in particular, was filled with an eagerness for adventure. I was reminded of my own enthusiasm for heading west three long years before. I knew nothing of the death and sadness awaiting me on the trail.

"Stay close," I urged the boy. "Watch for trouble."

He flashed me a confused look, then rode ahead to where his father galloped along. I, in turn, joined Shea on the far left flank.

"I don't understand," I told him. "The trail heads out into open country, and there's no effort to hide it. I'd use these hills or the river maybe to hide my tracks."

"Worries me some, too," Shea admitted. "If it keeps up this way much longer, I'll speak to Two Blows. I smell a trap."

I nodded my agreement. Soon, though, we found ourselves approaching a series of ravines alongside the Big

Horn. Shea explained downstream the river cut a deep canyon in the rocky ground, and I grew more nervous than ever. Two Blows now became cautious. He sent two men up ahead to examine the first ravine, but they found nothing unusual. We passed the gorge safely. Now, nearing the river, we spotted an encampment. A dozen tipis formed a small circle. Nearby a small pony herd grazed beside the river.

Shea rode forward to suggest caution, but the younger Crows were hot for blood and charged recklessly. I readied my rifle and gazed warily at the surrounding hills. It wasn't until Hunts at Night and the other young men reached the deserted camp, though, that the Sioux sprang forth from their hiding places.

"I knew it was too easy," Shea grumbled as he waved me back toward the ravine. Already it was filling with Sioux. The rim formed a natural trench, and arrows and musket balls aplenty began striking our companions.

"Lord help us," I prayed as Tall Bear slumped in his saddle. Arrows and lead struck others, and our entire band was forced back toward the river.

"Stay with me," Shea instructed as he joined Two Blows and a half dozen others on a rocky rise near the mouth of the ravine. "We'll wait our chance, then ride hard."

Suddenly two dozen Sioux horsemen surged toward us, shrieking and waving lances or hatchets. The younger Crows melted away toward the river, but their elders stunted the charge with accurate riflery and three rapid volleys of arrows.

"Now!" Shea told me as Two Blows waved his bow arm toward the ravine. I nudged Snow into a gallop, and we raced into the ravine, passed the startled Sioux archers, and continued up the steeper far bank and out onto the plain. Behind us friends fell to the pursuing Sioux. Two Blows took an arrow in his thigh, and Hunts at Night barely escaped a hatchet when Shea dropped an attacker at two hundred feet.

The Sioux rushed the fallen Crows like a swarm of angry hornets, and I cried inside for the mothers and daughters and wives of the slain. There would be no honored burial for these Crows.

I was soon too busy to mourn for the dead, though. One party of Sioux kept up the pursuit, and those of us most able formed a line to shield the retreat of the wounded. The Sioux horsemen seemed reluctant to test our rifles, and they hung back awaiting encouragement.

"Maybe it's over," I told Shea. "They've killed enough."

"They're only catchin' their breath," Shea told me with cold eyes. "They'll come soon enough."

He was right. A tall warrior wearing eagle feathers in his hair raised a lance and rode furiously toward our thin line. A rifle barked, and the Sioux toppled from his saddle as if struck down by a lightning bolt.

Another tried the same tactic, only to meet the same end. The display of courage put the others to shame, I suppose, and when a third warrior led his horse out from the band, he was followed by most of the others. They surged forward, and Shea raised his rifle and dropped one. Another rifle down the line felled a fourth.

"Boy, use that gun!" Shea shouted, and I raised my rifle, steadied the barrel, and fired. A bronze figure twenty yards away screamed out in pain and rolled off his horse. The remaining Sioux hit our line with rare fury, and the fighting grew heated. Crow shields were no match for steel axes, and the Sioux held no greater luck when confronted by lance points or pistol balls. I fired off all my chambers without thinking, and Shea shielded me as I stashed my rifle in its scabbard and fought to reload the pistol. I swapped mine for his and repeated the project. With six shots apiece, we then awaited the Sioux.

None came. Our line held, though at a cost. Two more fallen warriors were tied to their horses and led away. Others, wounded, followed. As the Sioux retreated, a single warrior shouted out in contempt. He waved a newly taken scalp, and Young Iron Heart answered in his shrill young voice. The boy rushed out to meet his older enemy, and I was shaken to the bone. The Sioux tossed the scalp aside and raced forward to meet his boyish challenger. The two met, blows were exchanged, and Young Iron Heart's horse collapsed, pinning him to the ground.

"No!" Shea called as I kicked Snow into a hard gallop. The Sioux turned abruptly as I bore down on him, but his shield did nothing to blunt the three shots I fired at him. The Colt was deadly at close range, and the Sioux flew backward from his horse.

"Climb up!" I shouted as Young Iron Heart worked himself free of his horse's lifeless form. "Hurry!"

The boy clawed at my leg with weary fingers, and I reached down and lifted him up onto the horse behind me. Then I raced back to the rest of the Crows.

The Sioux glared as we withdrew. Some of the younger Crows had taken time to count coup on their slain enemies, and scalps were taken. I tried to ignore the bloody goings-on as my stomach revolted at the horrid smells of powder and death that hung like a funeral pall over the Big Horn Valley. Shea located a riderless horse for Young Iron Heart, and the boy wearily abandoned his precarious perch behind me for the captured horse.

"I owe you my life, Bearkiller," the boy said, his face no longer flush with adventure."

"You owe it to yourself," I answered. "Don't hurry to die."

"As you did?" he asked. "I carry a brave name."

"Live to pass it on to your grandsons," I urged. Then I followed Shea and the others as we completed our retreat. The Sioux didn't follow this time. They had tasted enough blood as well.

148

Chapter 15

The Sioux did not leave the Big Horns, and as summer wore on, there were more skirmishes between Two Blows's band and their sworn enemies. Mostly combat was an individual affair—a pair of warriors facing each other with lances, or a few shots exchanged with rifles or bows. There were no more mass charges or large scale raids. Too many had died, it seemed, and both sides had learned the price of reckless bravado.

It suited me just fine. I had a nasty scar just below the elbow where the arrowhead had been dug from my arm, and I was still self-conscious about my ear. I was seventeen and already battlescarred and hardened from frontier life.

There were better days ahead. The conclusion of the buffalo hunt meant more time for games and casual hunting. Often I accompanied Young Iron Heart and his little brother, Far-seeing Hawk, into the mountains to shoot rabbits or an occasional deer. I rode with Hunts at Night along the river, learning Crow ways and enjoying the wonder of summer in the Big Horns. From me he learned some English. I admit he was far quicker to pick up my speech than I was to learn the complex Crow language. In time individual words came to me, but I failed to grasp the manner in which they joined and made sense.

My efforts drew alternating scowls and howls from my young friends.

"You will never make a Crow, Bearkiller," Far-seeing Hawk pronounced. "Your heart is good, but you talk like a white trader."

Well, in a sense that was what I was. I traded my nerve

and daring for what peace and belonging the mountains could afford. In the end I did well when it came to swimming or wrestling or hunting. I was rather a hopeless dancer, and I couldn't begin to sing the deep, moaning Crow songs.

"Perhaps we should have sent you to the Sioux camps alone," Two Blows suggested. "Your song must surely have driven them far away."

Afterward, I helped beat the drum, and I believe the whole camp was grateful.

It must have been near the end of July when the traders came. There were three of them, and they led half a dozen pack horses along. Two Shoshoni women traveled along to keep the camp, and a sad-faced half-breed Pawnee served as translator.

The Crows appeared wary, but Shea climbed atop his horse and rode out to meet the traders. I followed cautiously, but he was so at ease that I soon relaxed.

"Darby, this here's Tyler Sloan," Shea said, indicating a cleanshaven man in his mid-thirties with raven-black hair and piercing blue eyes. "Ty and I used to trap the Tetons. He's a good man who's thrown in with poor company, it appears."

"Watch your tongue, Shea," a bearded redhead growled. "There's Crows about who might get the wrong notions."

"More likely the right one," Shea said, laughing. "This one with all the hair on his chin's Burrell Ralston. He'd swap you out of a year's growth if given the chance and have you thankin' him for it in the end. Other fellow there's Chester Eldridge."

"Just Chet," a thin-faced young man with sandy hair said, offering me his hand. "I come out on a train toward Oregon, too, only I didn't get past Ft. Bridger. My folks went over a ledge with the wagon, and I paired up with Ty. You must be Illinois, I figure. Old Shea here's told us of a crazed boy 'bout your size and age who likes to tangle with grizzlies."

"We crossed paths last spring down along the Green River," Shea explained.

"Shea there swapped two teams of spent oxen for the best mules this side of Independence," Ralston grumbled.

"Most oxen'll come 'round with good grass, but those you left us, Shea, weren't worth tobacco spit. We ate 'em 'fore winter. Didn't taste like much, either."

"Should've found a better cook," Shea suggested.

"Did," Ty declared. "Got us a pair of Shoshonis. Hard workers, those two. I've half a mind to make the little one a proper wife next time we run across a preachin' man. I think Chet's got his cap set for th'other one."

"Leavin' Burrell the Pawnee," Chet said.

The redhead bristled, grabbed a sack of beans, and flung it within an inch of Chet's forehead. I couldn't help laughing and thus had to dodge a second sack sent my way.

"What you doin' way up here anyway, Tom Shea?" Ty asked.

I knew immediately they must, indeed, be close friends, for otherwise Ty would never have addressed Shea by his first name.

"Come to get clear of Blackfeet," Shea explained. "Found Sioux instead."

"So I see," Ty grumbled, turning my elbow so as to examine the fresh scar. "Wagon road's gotten too tame for you, has it?"

"You know I never guide trains two years runnin'," Shea remarked. " 'Sides, I promised Illinois here . . . Darby, I'd show him the Rockies."

"He's a fine guide, isn't he?" Ty said with raised eyebrows. "Nearly got me scalped first year we trapped the Tetons. Ran us plumb into a Shoshoni camp. Only thing saved us was we were nigh froze, and they thought we were spirits come out of the snow."

"Wasn't that at all," Shea argued, "and they were just a few Shoshonis, not a whole camp. As for the mountains, I know 'em well as anybody alive and better'n most."

"He does," I agreed. "He's kept me alive this summer when I've been fool enough to tackle thieves and grizzlies, not to mention Sioux raiders and Crow women."

"Women?" Ty asked, grinning. "Sounds like there's a tale or two here that needs sharin'."

Shea laughed heartily, and I began sharing the frightening ordeal of tolerating Yellow Grass Woman. I added a few words about the Nez Perce girl and Fox Woman. By the time I finished, the three traders were roaring. I grinned in triumph, and they welcomed me as a brother wayfarer.

I'm not altogether sure why I warmed so to the traders. As I soon learned, they swapped stale flour and worthless trinkets for the best elk and buffalo hides in the Crow camp, did their best to lure girls away from fathers, and even tempted boys to join their company and tend to the horses. I think perhaps it was hearing so much English. And to be fair, it was mostly Ralston did the cheating and the luring.

"If I had a suitable partner, I'd split trails with Ralston tomorrow," Ty declared when I complained of a worthless flintlock the bearded trader had swapped Far-seeing Hawk for a pair of soft moccasins. "He'll get us killed dealin' like that one of these days. Crows'll likely just grow sour. Sioux chase you down and cut pieces off you. You stick with Tom Shea, son, and he'll not lead you far wrong."

"I know."

"And if you tire of Crow life, tell old Tom we'll move along the Big Horn awhile before turnin' south toward Green River. Plenty of trade along the Sweetwater Road nowadays."

"I'll tell him," I promised.

The Crows were glad when the traders left, I think, and Shea was, too. I detected more than one Crow gazing sourly at Ralston, and afterward turning the same gaze on Shea. It wasn't his fault, though I suspect they judged it was Shea welcomed the traders to Two Blows's camp.

"I guess you never like to see friends take a wrong turn," I told Shea.

"Guess I see the future in 'em," he replied. "Ty and Chet are fair company, and wasn't so very long ago that Ralston ran a good trap line. Now what's there left to do? Turn scavenger or trader, hire out as army scout, or lead wagons of pilgrims to Oregon or California."

"Seems to me an honest trader could make out all right," I argued. "Emigrants need supplies, and the Indians can't always buy powder or lead. The traders at Ft. Hall and back at Boise both were fair people."

"Hudson Bay people. Jim Bridger's crew to the south are all right as well. These fellows like Ralston, though, they're a plague. And if they keep at it, someone's apt to lift their hair."

"They head south a bit, the Sioux sure will."

"Could be," Shea said glumly. "Hate to think Ty and Chet'll go the same way. They were friends not so long ago."

"Ty says he'd gladly part company with Ralston if you'd care to partner up."

"I'm no trader," Shea grumbled.

I thought to ask what he did consider himself, but a dark cloud crossed his brow, and I left him to his solitude. The Crow boys were enjoying a late afternoon swim, and it being hot as ever I recalled, I trotted to the creek, shed my clothes, and splashed into the water. Soon I was battling with Hunts at Night and Tall Bear over a buckskin-covered ball.

It proved a welcome relief, both from the heat and the serious talk. More and more every day I felt boyhood slipping away, and I envied the way the Crows didn't let age stand in the way of having a good time. Right in the middle of our game Two Blows himself shouted and plunged in among the rest of us. Soon he was romping about as a ten-year-old and carrying three or four boys along in the process.

I felt somewhat out of place just then, so I swam downstream and sat alone in the shallows, shaded by a cottonwood. Suddenly I felt a shadow. Looking up, I found myself facing Bright Owl, younger sister of Fox Woman.

She smiled shyly, then kicked off her moccasins and dipped her toes in the creek.

"Stay right there," I pleaded as I looked helplessly to where my clothes rested some twenty yards away.

"Bearkiller, it is hot," she said, grinning.

"Well, there's plenty of river left to you," I answered. "I don't need any company just now."

"You are alone," she pointed out. "My father says you have good horses. Two would be enough. I am younger than Fox Woman, but I work hard. I can cook and sew. My English is very good."

"Stop," I cried when she prepared to pull her dress over her head. "You don't understand. I'm still a stranger to many of your ways. I've gotten tall, sure, but I'm not ready to take on a family."

"No?" she asked.

"Isn't counting coup or having horses that makes a man," I told her. "I suppose it comes in his heart, when he knows he belongs. I don't—not here and now anyway. And before long I'm apt to ride away."

"I would follow," she explained.

"To what? I don't know myself. I don't even know you. You're pretty. You'll make a good wife and a fine mother, but not if you hitch yourself to me. You don't want to wind up like those Shoshoni girls, do you?"

She shook her head sadly, then stepped away. I swam through the shallows to where my clothes rested, watched her leave, then hurriedly dressed. Afterward, when I reached our lodge, Shea took me in hand.

"Heard you had some company at the creek," he whispered.

"I didn't do anything," I protested. "I wouldn't let her come in, nor take her clothes off either, Tom. Scared me close to death, if the truth be known."

"And this from the boy who used to spy on ladies bathin'," he said, laughing.

"That was a time back, though I admit I've got nothing against taking a look or two at Bright Owl or anybody else. It's them looking at me I'm none too in favor of."

"What about marryin' one?"

"We talked about that before," I reminded him. "Can you see me with a little one on each knee?"

"Your sister told me you were a fair uncle."

"She did? When was that?"

"When she tried to talk me out of takin' you to the high country. You've got the heart to be a fine papa, Darby."

"Maybe," I mumbled. "Only not here and now."

"Too many bears left to fight?"

"Guess so," I said, grinning.

"Well, from what Bright Owl told her papa, I'd say you handled it well enough. Well as anybody could, I guess. Must've been a sight, that little gal standin' over you, and

154

you bare bottom in the creek!"

"Scared to death."

"But keepin' your head. You're gettin' acquainted with mountain ways, Darby Prescott. A few years back you'd bolted for high ground, likely offended the girl and caused her papa to pay you a call."

"Strange thing is scared as I was and feeling like I was on the edge of a tall cliff, I was half of a mind to jump right in. Was that how it was when you took your wife?"

"No, that was different."

"Tell me," I pleaded.

"Well, to begin with, I knew her brother. We were off huntin', got in a tangle with some Sioux, and one of 'em opened me up some. She tended me, sewed me back together, and stood over me like a guardian angel. Wasn't any askin' or thinkin' about it. We were like two parts of the same rock. You couldn't tell where one began and t'other ended."

"You were happy?"

"Best time in my life, that was. Then our little boy came along. You'd liked him. The two of you are made from the same mold. He wasn't afraid of anythin', not even when the fever took him. Strange, but I cut my fingers, and the pain, well, I didn't even feel it. I already hurt worse'n God intended any man should."

"I felt like that when Mama died."

"No, Darby, it's not the same," he assured me. "You miss your mama, and the hurt's real, but losin' your heart's another thing. I mourned my own mama, and a sister dear as any you'll ever know. But it's not the same. No, sir, it's not."

I took him to know and sadly nodded my understanding. He gripped my shoulders, and I shuddered to feel his icy fingers. Here it was, hot as blazes, and he was near frozen with remembered grief.

That night I stood guard with Young Iron Heart over the ponies. I'd grown accustomed to having him around, but lately his eyes had begun to look on me as a big brother, and I grew uneasy. He expected a lot, and I worried I'd fail to prove equal to the task. I'd rescued him once, but how could anyone be sure to do the same next time?

Snow was particularly restless that night, and I paid special attention to him. That white stallion was my link with a past that seemed daily to fade away. I'd lost track of the days, and my journal was woefully neglected. Once I'd made a list of Crow words, but I hadn't added a new one in days.

"Easy, boy," I said, stroking Snow's nose. "Easy. I'm here."

Ordinarily Snow would have dipped his head onto my shoulder or given me a nip on the back. Instead he whined and stomped anxiously.

"What is it?" I asked, suddenly alarmed. "Is something out there?"

It was impossible to hear much surrounded by a hundred nervous horses, but seeing's another matter. The fire where Young Iron Heart had stood moments before now grew dim. No shadowy Crow boy stood alongside.

I thought to call out, but Snow's agitated movements hushed me. Instead I fingered the Colt on my hip and crept closer to the fire. Now I could see three figures moving among the horses. A dark shape lay beside the fire, and my heart nearly stopped. A man towered nearby.

I raised my pistol and started to fire, but I stopped. The shot would send the horses racing off in panic. They would be easy prey to Sioux raiders — or to whoever it was that had intruded upon the pony herd. My greater worry was Young Iron Heart.

I approached the fire with caution. Now I could detect the buckskin moccasins and breechclout of a Sioux hovering over Young Iron Heart. The Sioux spoke menacing words, punctuated by a gleaming knife. The warrior was slicing off handfuls of Young Iron Heart's hair and likely promising even worse.

"Let him go," I said, stepping out of the darkness into the light. My pistol aimed at his chest, the Sioux had little choice but to comply. Young Iron Heart scrambled to my side, and I angrily noted the blood flowing from slits cut in the boy's chest.

The Sioux made no effort to withdraw. His eyes blazed hatefully at the pistol which controlled the scene.

"Go fetch the others," I finally told Young Iron Heart, but he wouldn't leave my side. It was if something dark and terrible had frozen him to me.

The Sioux then laughed. He glanced as his companions began roping horses. There were perhaps five or six of them in all, and I clearly had scant chance of killing the whole batch. Still, I wasn't disposed to let them steal horses unhindered. Saddled with Young Iron Heart and fearful of stampeding the horses, I was seemingly helpless. Then, as if summoned by some friendly spirit, Tom Shea appeared.

"Raiders!" I called to him. The herd stirred, and two of the Sioux released their ropes and raced to their own waiting horses.

"Raiders!" Shea echoed, and the camp stirred to life. The Sioux across the fire no longer stood calm and sure of himself. He glanced at his fleeing companions, then stared at my pistol. He muttered something at me, then took a step back. I cocked my pistol and stepped closer. His eyes betrayed fear, though he refused to give way to it. I touched the pistol's barrel to his belly, then traced a line up to his breastbone.

"Now go!" I shouted, pointing to where his fleeing friends were collecting their own mounts. The Sioux glared at me hatefully, then raced after his comrades.

"He is nothing," Young Iron Heart declared, leaning against my quivering side. "You counted coup on him."

"I made an enemy," I declared.

"He is Sioux," the boy argued. "He was born our enemy."

I thought that was perhaps true, but it wasn't a comforting notion.

Two Blows moved his camp the next morning. The scouts found Sioux parties on three sides, so we set off northeastward where no enemies lurked. A small group split off from the main body. Angered at what they thought a coward's retreat, they were determined to punish the Sioux for their intrusion.

"Two Blows is right," Shea told me. "There aren't enough of us. Too many of the young men are already dead. We've got a good supply of meat for winter, and with luck, this band will grow strong."

"Yes, with luck," I echoed. "Doesn't seem to be a lot of that around these days."

That was true, for as we rode deeper into the thickly-wooded Big Horns, we came across more and more Sioux raiders. Often as not they made off with a few horses. Far-seeing Hawk was clubbed during one raid, and Hunts at Night was shot through the leg during another.

"I feel hounded," I told Shea.

"Yes," he agreed. "Only one thing to do now. Two Blows will keep moving fast and far, maybe head all the way to the Missouri. May not even be peace there."

"And what about us?" I asked.

"Well, we've got choices, I suppose. We could ride along, though I've no love for the country of the greasy grass, as it's called. Good buffalo range, but I can't see what other use God could have for that plain."

"And the other choice?"

"Choices. One, we could make our way south to the Sweetwater road, maybe hire ourselves out as hunters to some emigrant train. Or even as guides to some eastern dandy out to hunt the Great American West."

"Isn't much better," I grumbled.

"Then there's Ty Sloan."

"Be traders?"

"Well, for a time, we could be," Shea explained. "Good way to get fresh provisions, and it'd be a far sight better to have company cuttin' across Sioux country toward the Sweetwater."

"I figured every Sioux in tarnation was up here in the Big Horns."

"Not by a long shot, I fear," Shea declared. "They'll show you no love, Darby. We could happen across some you've fought. Maybe I ought to cut your hair back some."

"I'll find the clippers if you promise not to take too much."

"I'm not apt to take a quarter as much as a Sioux's scalpin' knife would."

"I've been doin' my best to avoid them, though," I reminded him. "I'm kind of fond of my hair, and what it's attached to."

He grinned, gave me a half-hearted shove, then frowned.

"Figure Yellow Grass Woman'll miss us?"

"Oh, she'll soon find another boy to torment, no doubt," I declared. "I'll leave some good friends behind, you know. I sure won't miss that awful corn mush, though."

"Nor I," he agreed, laughing heartily.

Chapter 16

We told Two Blows early the next morning of our decision. I said my good-byes solemnly. Only once did I give way to emotion, and that was when Young Iron Heart brought my horses from the pony herd.

"Watch yourself," I told him. "Don't let the Sioux sneak up on you again. And try not to forget Bearkiller too soon."

"You saved my life," he said, stiff-lipped. "I will remember." I knew it was a truth, for his sorrowful gaze was akin to mine the day we buried Mama.

We were three days riding south before we overtook Ty Sloan and his companions. Burrell Ralston met us with a hostile glare, and I judged surely he knew our purpose. Ty and Chet wasted no time at all in severing their partnership.

"Pure ungrateful, you boys!" Ralston declared. "You'd leave a man out in this barren country with only a Pawnee half-breed for company and half the Sioux nation hungry for scalps."

"Keep the younger Shoshoni," Ty suggested. "If you hurry along, you'll be among her people 'fore those Sioux find out the flints you sold 'em for their pistols won't raise a spark."

"Honest mistake," Ralston claimed. "How was I to know that St. Louis fellow sold poor goods?"

"Price should've hinted at it," Ty said, turning toward Shea. "Ralston knew well enough when Darby here brought that pistol back from Two Blows's camp. There's a bit of honor left in the tradin' business. Not much, mind you. Just a bit."

It took half a day to divide the goods. Ty and Chet did most of the work. Ralston just muttered about barren country and ungrateful partners. I looked around me at the distant shining peaks, at the grasses swaying in the wind, and I couldn't help wondering how anyone alive could imagine that place barren! Life was everywhere. Hawks turned circles in the cloudless sky, and buffalo no doubt plodded across the plain not far away.

"Thinkin' on the Crows?" Shea asked me as I sat in the tall grass and closed my eyes.

"No, I was remembering the Sweetwater country," I told him. "I've neglected my journal. I meant to write down everything, map out the country so I could recall it all."

"You'll remember what's important," he declared. "Don't need maps or journals."

He touched the scar on my arm, jiggled the bear claws around my neck, and patted the beadwork on my shirt. He was right. There were reminders. And I couldn't imagine forgetting the faces of the friends I'd made anymore than I could forget Mary back in Oregon or my brothers in far-off Illinois.

By late afternoon the goods had been repacked on the backs of horses, and Ty led the way southward. Before, in the Crow camp, I'd seen but a hint of the trade goods. Besides beads and frills, Ty and Chet carried twenty disassembled rifles, a small mountain of lead, and enough powder to blow us all to the Missouri River and back.

"Got to keep those guns hidden, Darby," Shea explained. "We'd have half the Indians west of Laramie after us if they knew we had 'em. A rifle's still a prize out here for the tribes. You saw yourself what a difference it can make in a fight."

"Yes," I agreed, remembering the shattered Sioux charge.

Ty and Chet joined us, and each wore a heavy frown.

"I've got some cotton shirts back there that might fit you better, son," Ty said, resting a hand on my shoulder. "That Crow beadwork's a wonder, but it's not apt to stand us in good stead with the folks we're likely to meet next."

"Sioux might recall you anyway, from what Tom here

says," Chet added. "Ridin' that white horse and all. Hard to forget, that animal, especially with a white man atop him."

"Not that I plan to trade anymore with the Sioux," Ty added. "I figure to ride south close to as fast as our animals'll take us. Trade with the Shoshonis'll fetch us better hides, and I'm none too easy bein' close to Ralston just now. Nobody's meaner than a cheated Sioux."

Shea readily agreed, and after making camp briefly beside a muddy creek, we started south toward the Wind River and the Shoshonis.

The Big Horn and Wind rivers form a vee of sorts south of the Big Horn Mountains. The Crow and Sioux know the stream that flows north into the Missouri as the Big Horn River, but upstream it's the Wind, according to the Shoshonis. As we cut through the gorge east of the rugged Owl Creek Mountains, I began to understand how the river got its name. The wind whined off the canyon walls like an army of shrieking phantoms. It was a haunted place, with the sun painting shadows of violet and red, amber and scarlet. Even at night the wind howled, and I couldn't help tossing in my blankets.

"It's always like that, first time down the canyon of the Wind," Shea assured me. "Just spirits, you know. Nothin' to cause you harm."

I knew that. But the sounds were beyond anything I'd ever heard, and no mountain of understanding could drive them away. I only slept by stuffing my ears with strips of cloth.

Once through the canyon, we began to encounter Shoshoni bands. They were a bit wary at first, but when they recognized Iris, as Ty had named our Shoshoni cook, they eased their suspicions. I was readily accepted, as I hadn't altogether forgotten the words learned in the winter camp of Two Knives.

The trading was fast and furious. Mostly we swapped rifles and ammunition for buffalo and elk hides. We also picked up fox and beaver pelts, beaded moccasins, and occasionally a prized elk hide robe. Ty was always careful to reveal only three rifles to any one band.

"Keeps the price up and our hair on," he explained.

I busied myself tending the horses and occasionally racing the older Shoshoni boys on foot or on horseback. Wagering was a favorite diversion, and Snow won often enough that I began to collect quite an assortment of beaded pouches, Shoshoni garments, and on rare occasions a piece of silver or two.

"Watch you never set the stakes so high it hurts 'em to lose," Shea warned, and I often turned down wagers, claiming I had nothing of equal value to match the bet. When I saw the loss weighed heavily on the loser, I offered a second challenge, most often afoot. I could never outrun those Shoshonis, and I think they warmed to me for my willingness to let them recapture lost esteem.

I filled half my journal during those long days beneath the blazing sun. Ty kept track of the days, and he soon had me back on a calendar. We camped on Sage Creek, in the village of the famed Shoshoni chief Washakie, the final day of August, 1851. We exchanged presents with the stern-faced, thick-waisted chief, and he welcomed us with feasting and dancing.

"He's a shrewd trader, this one," Shea warned. "I'll bet he talked Ty out of the last of the rifles sure. Watch yourself, Darby. I once knew Washakie to pick a Sweetwater trader clean, leave him bone naked and afoot."

I laughed at the notion, but as I settled around a fire that night and heard tales of the fierce Washakie, I doubted it not. There was a story that in his youth a band of Crows high upon a butte had taunted the Shoshonis.

"Come up and fight us," they'd called. Then their leader had bared his hindquarters at the Shoshonis, a severe insult. Washakie thereupon climbed the butte, slew the Crow, cut out his heart, and ate it. Afterward, the Crows stayed well clear of Washakie.

Another tale fascinated me near as much. It was the story of Sacajawea, the Shoshoni woman who had led Lewis and Clark to the Pacific. As Shea translated for me, I envisioned the girl, slight of build and no older than myself, carrying a newborn child and guiding the intrepid explorers through summer's demon heat and winter's frigid snows. The boy who spoke claimed to be a nephew of sorts to the brave woman, and had heard the whole story from Sacajawea herself. He'd painted her story on an elk hide, and I believed it to be as he said.

"Your turn, son," Ty said, nudging me when Sacajawea's tale concluded.

"Me?" I cried. "You and Shea have trapped this country since before I was born."

"Not that long," Ty insisted. "Tell 'em of the white horse."

I swallowed hard, then spoke in halting Shoshoni phrases of how I'd killed a bear and won the horse as a gift. I'd gotten so used to telling it that the bear had grown somewhat larger, as had the danger. I struggled to find the right words for my thoughts, though, and Shea suggested I turn to English and leave him to translate. I readily agreed.

I could tell the Shoshonis were used to grander tales, and though they nodded along good-naturedly, they were far from impressed by the skinny white man with the tall tale. The scars remained on my chest, though, and even old Washakie howled when I opened my shirt.

"How did you scratch the boy's chest?" the chief asked Shea "It's a good trick. Show me."

"Was the bear did it," Shea assured him.

A pair of Shoshoni elders drew me closer to the fire and examined the scars carefully. I felt like a horse at market under their critical gaze, but in the end they shook their heads and pronounced my story likely the truth. Doubters remained, but Bearkiller's tale was quickly taken to heart by the young, and I was never without a shadowing brood the remainder of our time along Sage Creek.

It passed all took quickly, though, for the old Washakie bartered us out of all but the most worthless of our trade goods.

"Now what?" I asked.

"We head south for the Green River ferry," Ty explained. "We've traded away the summer, and now it's time to swap our takin's for cash, do a bit of business among the pilgrims, and set off for winter camp."

"And us?" I asked Shea.

"We'll share the celebration," he said, "but I figure we might swing east down the Sweetwater, do some rememberin', and winter in the Medicine Bow country if the

Cheyennes aren't hungry for hair this year. I thought perhaps to take a train west next spring."

"It's a long ride to Independence."

"Not so long with good company," he told me, grinning in a way I'd almost forgotten. Then he bellowed like thunder and set to chasing me down the creek. The Shoshoni boys joined in the chase, and I found myself treed like a Pike County coon.

"South, huh?" I asked as my persecuters laughed wildly.

"South, then east," he said.

I shrugged my shoulders and leaped on him like a mountain cat. He merely tossed me to the Shoshonis, who quickly buried me under an avalanche of small arms and knees.

"I give up," I said, surrendering.

Shea explained, and the boys howled in triumph.

We swung south and east along the Wind River, then followed winding Beaver Creek toward the Sweetwater and the Oregon Trail. I deemed it late in the year for travelers, for the grass was thin from overgrazing, and the ruts dusty and deep. Even so, we spied a circle of wagons on the north bank of the river.

"Not movin', and it's midday," Shea grumbled. "No wonder they're late."

"Sickness?" I asked, gazing in surprise at the wagons. Not a soul was in sight.

"Never heard of sickness along the Sweetwater," Ty declared. "Not cholera anyway, nor the fevers."

"Likely pox," Chet suggested. "No one time over another for it to strike."

"You stay back," Shea warned. "I had a touch of it already, and they say you can't catch it twice. Fools! Ought to set out a black flag."

When Shea approached, though, a half dozen shotgun-toting women appeared to block his path. I instantly rode to his side. When I took off my hat, they saw I was young, and it softened their hard stares.

"We've had trouble," a sour-faced woman explained. "We have no need of renegades."

I gazed at their plain manner of dress, at the prayer books clutched in their hands, and I recalled how Shea

165

had told me Mormons traveled the north bank of the Platte. Maybe they did the same along the Sweetwater.

"We're traders, ma'am," I explained. "Headed for the Green River ferry. You folks are Saints?"

"Yes," she said, touching the hammers of the shotgun.

"I met some boys in the Platte headed west back in '48. They were Saints. Weren't much on talking. I guess you folks'd rather keep to yourselves."

"We're much the same ourselves," Shea confessed. "We thought maybe you were in need, from sickness or such. If you're farin' well enough, we'll head on along."

"We're not!" a slender woman on the left cried. "Lord, believe me, we're not."

"Charity!" the stern-faced leader scolded.

"I can't help myself, Esther. They're my own boys. Am I to turn away men who might save them?"

"You can't trust renegades," the leader argued. "The men are out looking. Likely Joshua and Joseph wandered off and will soon be found."

"How old?" Shea asked.

"Joshua's twelve," the boys' mother explained. "Joe's just ten. They wouldn't wander far, not out here. There were tracks near the river—horses. Indians stole them. I know it!"

"The men've gone to look?" Shea asked.

"Since mornin'," another of the women answered. "Boys are forever up to nonsense. They'll turn up."

"Let's have a look," Shea said, motioning me toward the river. We splashed our way through the shallows until we spotted tracks in the sandy bank. There were moccasin tracks as well. Then, a few yards away, I spotted a boy's cap.

"It's Joshua's," his mother said when we returned to the women.

"Then you're right," Shea declared. "There are moccasin tracks nearby. Likely Sioux. Shoshonis'd been more likely to trade with you."

"Lord, no," the distraught woman cried. "My little boys!"

"We'll have a look," I promised.

"Darby, this isn't our business," Shea argued.

"No, it's not," the sour-faced leader insisted. "Be along with you."

"I'll pay them . . . give them anything," the mother pleaded. "I have a hundred dollars."

"Don't be a fool, Charity!" one of her companions warned. "Men like these . . ."

"Keep your money," I said, gazing at Shea. "We'll have a look, won't we, Tom?"

"Guess so," Shea grumbled, turning back toward our companions.

Ty and Chet voiced no like sentiments. Iris shrank back at the mention of Sioux.

"We've got a summer's work on these horses," Ty explained. "Tom, tell the boy. Sioux might keep 'em, it's true, but more likely they've been robbed and killed. You'll do those boys no good, and surely get yourself scalped in the bargain. A man doesn't survive up here by makin' bad wagers with his hide, Darby."

"I guess not," I admitted. "Tom, you remember those wild boys up in the Tetons? I never could get them out of my dreams. I worry that these two might wind up the same way. Can't we at least ride out and have a look? We've got goods to trade. That woman pledged a hundred dollars."

"Your hide's worth considerably more," Chet argued.

"I'm sure you'll ride up with your Crow shirt on that white horse and bargain with Sioux ridin' well south of their huntin' grounds," Ty complained. "Only reason to be this near to the Sweetwater's that they're raidin'."

"I'll wear this cotton shirt, and I'll ride one of my other horses," I told them.

"Sure, the brown mare with the Sioux markings," Chet said, laughing. "Darby, this is plain crazy."

"It's been said of me before," I confessed. "You figure those Mormons'll find the boys? Not a chance. Another day, and the raiders could be halfway to the Big Horns. Got to be."

"Take my black," Ty said, nodding to the broad-backed mare he preferred for hard country. "I'll give you some trade beads, lead, and a horn of powder. You watch yourself, though."

"He won't have to," Shea explained. "I'll be along."

167

I grinned at him. I then swapped horses with Ty, packed the trade goods behind me, and set off with Tom Shea. Ty and Chet promised to remain a day encamped across the river from the wagon train. It was the best bargain I could manage and was thus grateful.

"I've done fool things in my life, Darby Prescott," Shea complained as we rode, "but I never stuck my neck out this far for a bunch of tenderfoot Saints. Must be the crazed dog-struck moon's got to you."

"What?"

"Full moon last night. Drives wolves and dogs to distraction. Must work on white boys, too."

"Maybe," I said, grinning at his effort to lighten the mood.

My smile faded as we picked up the trail of three horses headed north from the river. None were shod, and we moved ahead with caution. I figured the Sioux couldn't be too far, and in truth they weren't. A small encampment of three lodges circled a spring just five miles distant. As we approached, a band of twenty riders joined us.

"Who'd you be?" their leader, a bespectacled man of perhaps forty with flaming red hair, demanded.

"Darby Prescott," I answered. "This is Tom Shea. We tracked some horses out here from the river. You'd likely be the men of the wagon train sent us."

"Sent you?" the man asked angrily.

"We come across your womenfolk," Shea explained. "Told us of the boys. Likely they're down there."

The Mormons seemed eager to rush toward the camp, but Shea held his hand up and urged restraint.

"Any of you men ever fight a war?" he asked.

They shook their heads, and Shea frowned.

"Those Sioux down there'd ride through you in ten minutes, even though I'd guess there's but a dozen of 'em. You want those boys back? Well, follow me down there. Numbers'll have an effect, and I'll know what's best done."

They reluctantly nodded, and Shea led the way toward the Sioux lodges. The Indians quickly grabbed rifles and bows. There were no women in view, and I knew Ty'd been right about them being a raiding party. Shea rode out ahead, raising his hand in peace. The Sioux leader, a tall sort with braided hair and a jagged knife scar across his bare chest, strode out to block Shea's progress.

For a few minutes they spoke. The Sioux responded angrily, they turned toward the Mormons.

"I know nothing of whites!" he shouted. "Not here!"

I gazed into his eyes and saw only hatred. Then, glancing among the other Indians, I spied a young man wearing a pair of leather suspenders as a belt. Shea saw it, too, and we exchanged nervous looks.

"They're not here," Shea said, shrugging his shoulders and turning back toward the Mormons. "Best we look elsewhere."

The Mormons grumbled, called Shea a few names, and rode off toward the north. Shea led me southward. Once on the other side of a low hill, he halted.

"You saw the suspenders?" I asked.

"Saw a young one with buckled shoes on his feet, too. Most likely that means they've been killed, you know."

"Maybe," I admitted, "but wouldn't we've seen the bodies? Why carry 'em back to the camp just to strip their clothes? In this heat you'd smell 'em fast enough if they were close by. I'd guess they're hidden in one of those tipis."

"It's a thought," Shea admitted. "Guess maybe we ought to watch a bit."

I nodded, and we hid the horses in a ravine and crept closer to the camp. The Sioux made no effort to move along. They were in fine spirits, laughing and no doubt boasting of how they had fooled the white men. Then the scarred one shouted, and a young man darted into a lodge and drove two bare, sunscorched wretches out into the open.

"Lord," I gasped as the younger Sioux tormented their captives. A powerful hatred must have driven that scarred warrior. Well, why not? The plains tribes had suffered, true enough. But as I watched those friendless boys toting water or carrying firewood, all the while trembling and dodging toes or leather straps, I was determined to be their rescuer.

"Dog-crazed moon," Shea grumbled. "How you figure to do it, Darby?"

"Can't just make a grab for 'em" I muttered.

"Get 'em killed sure, and us likely, too. Better to wait for nightfall. Chance'll come."

"You've got a plan?"

"Pony herd's on down a ways, with just a couple of boys on guard. They're not liable to think much on their captives if their horses are headed for the open plain. I'll run 'em some, then circle back. You got to watch those boys, make sure you notice which lodge they take to. Cut the back of the tipi, get 'em atop my horse, and meet me at the river."

"I'm better at raiding horses than stealing captives, you know."

"You figure those two'd trade a Sioux prison for the likes of me?" Shea asked, running his fingers through his crusty beard. "You're almost human, Darby. They'd go with you."

I nodded, and the plan was set. As dusk settled over the camp, Shea set off on foot toward the pony herd. I led the horses close, then secured them to a scrub tree and crept onward. Soon there was a loud cry from the pony herd, and Shea fired his pistol in the air and chased the horses off onto the plain.

Shea predicted chaos in the Sioux camp, and chaos it was. Men ran in every direction. The scarred warrior soon restored order, though, and set off with his companions toward the horses. I was crawling toward the center lodge all this time, and when the Indians headed off, I slashed the tough buffalo hide covering and stared inside at the pair of huddling Saints.

"Come on," I whispered. "I'm taking you home."

They hesitated a moment, and I thought to myself I'd hardly care to return home bare as they were. Hides were scattered around the lodge, though, and I cut a slit through the center of two of them. I showed the boys how to slip the hides over their heads. When they did so, I nodded my satisfaction.

"Hurry," I urged. "They'll be back in a minute, and then we're all in for a time of it."

The fear creeping into my eyes persuaded them. They popped through the gap in the tipi and followed me toward the ravine.

"You'll have to ride double," I explained when we reached the horses. "You can ride, can't you?"

They seemed confused, but when I helped the older one up onto the saddle and handed him the reins, he took them as if he knew what to do. The younger one climbed up behind his brother, and I escorted them toward the river.

"Joshua and Joe," I whispered. "That's what your mama said your names were."

The first glimmer of recognition brightened their eyes, and I quickened the pace. The moon rose bright and high overhead, but the Sioux were safely to the northwest, hunting scattered ponies. I hoped to be rid of them for a time. That scarred one looked the type to hold a grudge, and the treatment afforded the young Saints would be nothing to that given a scrawny white man who'd dared to steal captives!

I rejoined Shea at the river, and we paused only long enough to let the boys wash away some of the accumulated grime before conducting them to their camp. All the while they said nothing. Shea joked, and I revealed my bear scars, but the youngsters merely shrank back in terror.

"Guess the Saints don't teach their kids to talk," I told Shea.

"That it, boys?" Shea asked, making a face or two at them as he rode bareback on a spotted Sioux pony. Maybe we should take 'em back."

The young eyes filled with fright, and they shuddered. Shea was instantly sorry, but the damage had been done. We made no more jests, just galloped along toward the wagon train.

The Mormon camp was already astir when we arrived. It seemed certain they'd given up their search, for men were harnessing mules to wagons, and women were packing up belongings.

"Ma!" Joshua suddenly cried, leaping from his horse and hurrying toward his dazed mother. Joe followed, and the woman wrapped her arms around her stray youngsters and drew them near.

The other Saints stared up at us in surprise. The

redheaded leader scratched his chin and said, "I thought you said . . ."

"I know," Shea replied. "Excuse the lie, if you will. I didn't see any way to get those boys out alive, nor us either, if you rode down on that camp. This way you're fit to head on down the trail, though I'd suggest you hurry else you'll winter in the Rockies."

"Thank you," the boys' mother said, holding up a handful of frayed banknotes. "It'll never be enough to thank you."

I turned to Shea, but he only laughed, grabbed his horse, and rode off toward Ty and Chet's camp.

"I had my reward," I said, smiling back at her. "You two don't do any wandering. Next time old Bearkiller might not be around to fetch you back."

I laughed at myself, then headed after Shea. The faces of the Saints gazed in wonderment, and I figured I'd likely spawned another tale or two, if such were permitted.

"Wait!" I heard someone cry, and I turned in time to see a weary Joshua rush forward holding something in his hand. It was a mouth organ, and he handed it up to me. I took it, noticing no gratitude in his eyes. No, there was something else. It was a kind of kinship perhaps, a would-be trail orphan greeting a true one. I blew a tune through the instrument and grinned.

"Thanks," I said, waving farewell. Then I continued along.

Chapter 17

When we splashed across the river to where Ty and Chet were camped, we received a warmer reception.

"Never thought we'd set eyes on you two again!" Chet hollered.

"Well, Tom knows his way around trouble," Ty admitted. "Even so, I didn't figure you'd have all your hair if we saw you again. Good Lord must be awful fond of you two."

"Well, I guess he had a soft spot for those Mormon boys," I said, fingering the mouth organ. "Sure couldn't've been an inclination toward such wayward souls as us."

"Truth is, Darby there's got too sour a voice for any angel's choir, and I'm too ornery for the devil," Shea argued.

We shared a bit of laughter. Then Shea dismounted and began discussing the journey across South Pass on toward Green River.

I left them to their plans. Me, I climbed down from the saddle and rushed to where Snow restlessly paced the ground. The black mare never did take me to heart, and I looked forward to having Snow beneath me as we resumed our wanderings.

Iris threw more slabs of bacon on the fire and passed out biscuits, and I satisfied my hunger. Then we packed up and readied ourselves for the trail. We couldn't afford to waste time when breaking camp. Those Mormon wagons would take forever lumbering up the pass, and all of us were eager to reach the ferry ahead of them.

"Best corn liquor to be found south of the Missouri," Ty

declared. "Good chance to unload our hides for some cash and have a time of it when we do it."

I recalled Shea had friends at the ferry. They'd had a reunion of sorts when the wagon train made its crossing. When I reminded him of it, he frowned.

"New outfit works the ferry now," Ty explained. "Mormons. Serious folk, I'm afraid, but Jed Burkett still operates his store on the west bank. You can satisfy your every desire there, Darby."

I nodded, though in truth I had what I needed already—a fine day, a full belly, and good company.

We were five days making our way through the South Pass, down Sandy Creek, and along to the Green River. It was dry, sandy country compared to the Big Horn and Wind River country. The Green River was a broad stream, though, and the surrounding land benefited from its waters. We paid the ferrymen to carry the pack horses and swam the rest of the stock across. Once on the far side, the sounds of music and devilments drew us to Burkett's store.

I began to understand what Ty meant when he said Burkett had everything a man could need. Canvas tents housed gaming tables, a saloon, even a doctor of sorts, though by the look of him he devoted more time to Green River corn than to patients. A motley collection of girls coaxed off emigrant trains and Indian girls taken in trade offered a different sort of entertainment in tents farther back.

Summer being over, a fair number of traders huddled around Burkett's place. There was also a wagon train camped a hundred yards north, so Burkett's customers were a wild assortment indeed.

"So, Shea, you old fool," Burkett declared when we tied our horses out front. "Thought you dead for sure. See you joined up with old Ty. Too bad about Burrell Ralston. A bad sort, I'll admit, but he brought in a fair share of trade."

"You got news of Ralston?" Ty asked.

"You don't know?" Burkett asked in turn. "Well, I'm sorry to be the one to share ill news, you boys bein' partnered and all, but Amos Hillary was in a few days back sayin' he buried Ralston in the Big Horns. Sioux took after him and a Pawnee, a Shoshoni girl . . . cut 'em up considerable 'fore finishin'. Hillary said the whole camp was full of bad flints. Only a fool'd trade such to Sioux. They got no patience for bad dealin's."

"Well, can't say I'm surprised," Ty confessed. "All the same, Iris'll take it hard, the girl bein' a sister or some such. Pawnee knew the risks ridin' in Sioux country."

"Let's not have a funeral here now," Burkett complained as Chet dropped his head, and Shea muttered to himself. "Man's dead. Time to raise a cup to his memory and get along with business. I'll get a jug. Why don't you fetch what you've picked up all these months in the high country? Got some elk robes, do you? Buffalo hides?"

I could tell Burkett was above all things a man of commerce. As we unloaded the hides and pelts from the pack animals, first one jug and then a second were brought out for our enjoyment. I only took a sip of the stuff myself. It near burned my throat down into my belly!

"Best keep that away from Darby," Chet said, slapping me on the back to help me recover my sense. "He's growin' still."

"Why, that corn o' mine'll put hair on the lad's chest," Burkett boasted.

"More like to burn it off," Ty argued. "I hear somebody lit a match to a jug of it once, and that jug did a dance 'round the moon and come back still half full."

"Was just a quarter full." Burkett said, laughing.

"I think I need to walk a bit," I told them, setting off toward the river. My chest rose and fell as always, but my lungs weren't taking much in. I coughed, leaned against a tree, and finally recovered feeling in my fingers. It was a far cry from Papa's apple wine, that Green River corn.

I sat for a time on the riverbank, skipping stones and listening to the laughter of the emigrant children as they splashed about in the shallows nearby. Women washed clothes or scrubbed youngsters upstream a bit. Burkett's ladies waltzed about downstream under the protective eye of a shotgun-toting giant.

"Had your fill of corn liquor, eh?" Shea asked as he sat beside me.

"No need for you to cut short your celebrating. I'll get

accustomed to such things in time."

"Likely, you will," he agreed. "Doesn't do a man much good, hard drink. Helps to forget sometimes."

"Last time we were here you got pretty drunk. It's because I made you talk about the fingers . . . and your family."

"Needed to be talked out, you know. I wasn't so sure then, but I am now. You can't carry sadness with you forever. Eats up so much of you there's nothin' left to look for the good out there."

"Sometimes I wonder if there is any good. Boys getting snatched by Sioux. Traders cheating and then getting scalped. A boy no older'n me killed! It's all craziness. Makes no sense."

"I warned you 'fore we set out life's hard in the high country, son. You had enough of a taste of it comin' up the trail from Missouri to guess it'd be a rough road. But the man walks it can stand tall, for he's done somethin' with his days."

"What've I done?"

"Survived. Sometimes that takes a lot of doin'. You brought those two Mormon boys back to their mama. You saved Young Iron Heart, helped those snowbound folks to Ft. Hall. There's people alive because you came their way."

"You sure?" I asked. "Tom, how can you be sure any of Two Blows's band still live? Those boys may drown crossing the next river, or get snakebit, or maybe catch fever. Who knows if those snowbound folks ever got to Oregon? They had no supplies, their wagons were next to worthless, and their stock was thin as death."

"I figure they got on, Darby," he said, managing a faint smile. "Fools and pilgrims always do, it seems."

"That why there are so many crosses on the trail?"

"Oh, there's dyin', true enough, but that's the way of things. You eat a trout. Well, it died, didn't it, but you're livin' on account of it. I'm no preacher, but I know there's a pattern to things."

"To Jamie? To your son?"

"That's bitter hard, buryin' the young ones," he said, shuddering. I saw his hands quiver, and I was sorry to have spoken of it. He stared sadly northward a moment, then rubbed his eyes.

"There's no answer to that, is there?" I asked.

"None I ever come by. Done my share of searchin', too. Thought the Lord heartless when He took your mama, Darby. She was needed yet, but that's how it was. My boy, too. But the trail winds here and there, and it matched us two up."

"Yeah," I agreed. "Me needing a father, and you without a son."

"So there's some good for you, true enough."

"True enough," I agreed, skipping a flat stone five times in the river. The emigrant boys howled their appreciation, and I gave them a wave of my hat.

"Take you back to your own trail days?" Shea asked.

"Yes," I admitted. "It's strange. Everytime I gaze down at the river, I see myself. Younger and skinnier mostly, but just as eager to shirk chores and get into mischief. I see Mama, too, and Papa. Mary and Mitch. I remember playing Mr. Hogan's piano."

"That was a sadness, that piano crashin' like it did. Try to raise a tune on that mouth organ yet?"

"Every night," I confessed. "Tried to set off where the rest of you wouldn't hear. It's taking time to make the sounds harmonize."

"Play a bit."

"I warn you it's sour as an old crow."

"Do it," he pleaded. "I've got a hunger for a tune just now."

I pulled out the mouth organ and did my best to render "Sweet Betsy from Pike." There was only the faintest resemblance, but Shea hummed along, and I soon improved. The music soon drew an old woman to our side, and she sang a verse or two. Others followed, and before long half the wagon train and a goodly number of traders had assembled.

"Oh don't you remember Sweet Betsy from Pike?" a young woman sang particularly sweetly. "Who crossed the wide rivers for love of her Ike. She washed and she mended, she cooked and she cussed. All 'cause they had sworn it was Or'gon or Bust!"

It was a new version, and I couldn't help laughing.

177

There were a few other smiles, and the young woman blushed. Ty Sloan nudged me, and as I resumed the tune, he struck up in fine fashion a considerably bawdier verse. The women muttered, the men howled, and the children whispered among themselves.

I'd begun to get the hang of the mouth organ, so I tried a fresh melody. Mama had always been partial to "Shenandoah," and I struck up the tune. It seemed terribly sad just then, gathered with a company of strangers, with traders and trappers, watching the sun set over the ferry. But I guess everyone there was headed one direction or another, and as voices shared the song, some of the haunting loneliness of the country passed away.

I found myself closing my eyes and remembering. I didn't even notice the boy nestling in beside me. When I finished the final refrain, I opened my eyes and saw—Jamie McNamara. There he was, red hair and freckles, devil smile, and all.

"Jamie?" I asked.

"My name's Jeremiah, mister," he answered with a grin. "You play that just fine. I got one back in camp. Figure you could teach me that song? Ma liked it 'specially."

"Sure," I agreed, swallowing hard.

"Thanks for the tune, son," a tall man told me as he waved the emigrants toward their camp. "Time we had a kettle on."

The traders nodded to the departing women, then started back toward Burkett's tents. Shea rubbed my shoulder.

"Mister, eh?" he whispered, laughing.

"Well, maybe I am getting to be full-grown."

"He did look like the McNamara boy. Or else the sun's playin' tricks with my eyes."

"More likely that corn liquor," I suggested.

"You cheered 'em some, Darby, like with that piano. Music's a comfort on a quiet night."

"I suppose. Still, it's not like a mama."

"You got yourself grown now, Darby Prescott. That comfort won't be comin' along again. You'll come to find a woman if you're lucky, but it won't be the same. You'll share somethin' different, maybe better. But when you lace

178

up a man's boots, you can't go back to boys' ways."

"I'd guess not."

"Let's go see if we can talk Burkett out of a meal. He charges most travelers half a month's labor for a plate of venison and beans."

"Maybe we ought to then," I agreed.

But before we could get five feet from the river, red-haired Jeremiah returned with an invitation to his mother's table.

"She cook biscuits, boy?" Shea asked.

"Hot and flaky so they melt in your mouth," Jeremiah answered. "With honey and butter. We got a cow, you see. Tonight we got some meat, too. Pa got himself a duck down on the river."

"Lead on," I said, and Jeremiah reached out, gripped my hand, and pulled me along toward the camp. Shea followed, suggesting it was now I that was the captive. I couldn't argue.

Mrs. Elvira Hitch, Jeremiah's mother, proved as good a cook as the boy said, and I never enjoyed captivity as much. The boy's father, a scholarly sort from Indiana, questioned Shea at length on the trail ahead. I was more taken with the boy's two sisters, Jessica and Juliet. Both were tall, blond, and pretty.

"My name comes from a book," Juliet was quick to point out. "In the book, Juliet dies tragically for love."

"She's a bother," Jeremiah declared.

"What kind of name is Darby?" Mrs. Hitch asked.

"English or Irish, I think," I replied. "Belonged to an uncle before me. I think Papa hoped Uncle Darby might leave me some land, but he married late and had five kids."

"Five?" Mrs. Hitch gasped. "Poor woman who wed him! I have the devil's own trouble with my three."

They spoke of the trials of traveling the Sweetwater road, but I kept silent. Jeremiah produced his mouth organ, and I led the way down toward the river.

"You headin' west?" the boy said as I showed him how I held the organ.

"East," I said.

"Thought maybe you could come along with us. Don't

have any brothers, you know."

"Looks to me like there are a hundred boys on this train."

"Nobody who'll show me things," Jeremiah complained.

"Your father?"

"Keeps me at my lessons, but he doesn't even have a horse to ride."

"Well, I'll show you what I've figured out about this mouth organ. For the rest, you'll have to look around. Me, I pestered our scout when I came west."

"You rode in a wagon?"

"Mostly walked," I said, blowing an A chord, then showing him what I did.

"Our scout's drunk most times. Cap'n Daniels'd fire him if we could find somebody else to take us. I think that's why Pa asked your friend about the trail."

"Shea's the best, but he swears he won't guide wagons two years in a row."

"You been west."

"Me? I'm scarcely seventeen. I can't keep myself from trouble, much less spare others from hazard."

"Was just a notion," Jeremiah mumbled.

I grinned, then stuffed his mouth organ in his mouth and bid him play.

We passed close to three hours making some of the worst sounds ever to plague humanity. In time a melody of sorts came forth. Then Mrs. Hitch dragged Jeremiah off to bed, and I followed Shea back to Burkett's place.

"They wanted to hire us on as scouts," Shea explained. "I was half tempted. Best food I've had in three summers. But I figure there's mountains yet to climb to the east. Drew 'em a map of sorts so if their scout drinks himself to death, they ought to make it on all right."

"Tom, was I as wide-eyed as Jeremiah when you met me?" I asked.

"Green as a turnip. Wide-eyed? Well, no. You were kind of on the sour-eyed side. Your papa worked you with rough hands, and you didn't take to it much. You did have a way of pesterin' me with all manner of fool questions, I'll confess."

"And you didn't toss me straightaway in the river?"

180

"Wasn't but the Kansas River then, and muddy as you were, it'd surely dammed the fool stream up. Truth is, meddlesome or no, you've always been good company. Now, why don't you strike up a tune on that organ, and let's find ourselves a place to toss our blankets?"

I grinned, did just as he requested, and we hurried along to Burkett's store.

We passed the night in a storeroom. Ty and Chet snored noisily nearby. The next morning, as the wagon train rolled west, Ty apportioned out what monies he'd received for pelts and hides, then announced he and Chet would stay on to help Burkett manage his store.

"You'd be welcome here, too, Tom," Ty explained. "Burkett said as much. Darby could work the stock. He's got a way with horses."

"I don't take to walls and a roof," Shea countered, gazing at me.

"We've got mountains to see," I added.

"Well, see they've none of 'em got grizzlies or Sioux waitin' on 'em," Ty said. "We'll cross paths again, I figure."

"Sun's still risin', isn't it?" Shea asked. "World still turns."

Chapter 18

We headed north through the South Pass and on past the spring-fed creeks that flowed into the Sweetwater River. It was a country fresh and green even in September, and we made camp high atop a mountainside amid a nest of cottonwoods. Below us the Oregon Trail snaked its way south and west. Beyond, the mountains hid the Wind River with its Shoshoni villages and the Tetons past that.

"Not altogether a bad place to pass autumn," Shea observed. "Catches a world of snow come winter, but just now it's pleasant enough."

I nodded my agreement. The streams offered a welcome, if somewhat chill, relief from the afternoon sun, and there were trout to catch and elk to hunt. Best of all, we were troubled by no one.

"Puts me in mind of what the whole country was like when I first headed out from Independence," Shea told me. "Nobody but Indians and a few crusty old trappers about. Plains grew black with buffalo, and antelope raced across these hills like locusts. All a man could ever want was there if he knew how to reach for it."

"So what happened?" I asked.

"Oh, too many letter writers and journal keepers, I suspect. Talkin' 'bout shinin' mountains and rivers so clear you could see the rocks on the bottom. Whetted the appetites of pilgrims and adventurers. Now there's this talk of gold in California fillin' the trails! Too many horses and mules chewin' the grass down to a nub. Hunters shootin' buffalo for sport in some places. Indians dyin' of sickness or gettin' shot by folks that don't take the time to learn their languages or their beliefs."

"It's not easy, you know. I've spent half a year among

the Shoshonis and the Crows now, but I don't know that I understand either. Their words are hard, too."

"You try, Darby," Shea declared. "More'n most. It speaks well of you."

"Or you," I added. "Not everybody'd have the patience for a fool who makes so many mistakes."

"They'll happen to anybody. You learn from yours."

"I hope so," I said, laughing. "I've only got so many ears to get half shot off and chests to get clawed."

He laughed, then knelt beside the ground and began scratching for roots. Later he showed me how to set rabbit snares for what must have been the fiftieth time.

Another day passed quietly. Then, toward late afternoon, a wagon train encamped at the base of our mountain. Solitude had brought peace, but I couldn't resist the temptation to ride down and visit the emigrants. It was a small company, just twelve wagons in all, and the sorrowful state of both animals and wagons spoke of a difficult journey.

"I'm Darby Prescott," I told the train's captain, a round-faced Vermonter who introduced himself as Charles Elsworthy. "I'm camped hereabouts with my partner."

A pair of rifles watched me carefully, and I opened my coat to show there was just the one pistol on my hip.

"I mean you no harm," I insisted. "Not that I could cause you much. Just hungry for a little news, some conversation. Not a lot of English spoken in these mountains."

"Guess not," Elsworthy said warily. "Just back a ways we passed some folks had trouble with Sioux. We were raided ourselves by renegades a day out of Ft. Laramie. How far'd the South Pass be?"

"Half a day's ride," I answered. "Don't you have a scout?"

"Went off hunting two days ago," Elsworthy explained. "Didn't come back. We waited a day, but we're late as is."

"Sure are," I agreed. "Your stock looks worn down some, too. I helped pull a train out of snow three feet deep south of Ft. Hall last winter. You might look for a place to wait out the snows, then move on to Oregon afterward."

"We're bound for California," he told me. "Gold!"

"Can't say I know that road. There's high country to cross, though, and it's late. I'd be careful."

"Know of a guide to be hired?"

"Maybe at the Green River ferry," I suggested.

"You sound to know the country."

"I'm no scout," I told them. "I might could get an early outfit through to the Willamette, but I'd never be what you want. If you're short food, I could probably do some hunting for you, though."

"We'd pay you," Elsworthy promised. "Five dollars a buck, and you could keep the hides. You look to know what to do with them," he added, gazing at my buffalo hide boots.

"I'll be back before nightfall," I promised, turning Snow toward the mountain and making my way up the slope to tell Shea.

"Sounds to me like there's a fair profit to be turned huntin' for these pilgrims," Shea observed when I passed on the news. "Been considerin' sellin' off some horses, too. With that paint I picked up from that bunch of Sioux, we got a regular herd. All we need's a spare for each of us and another to pack our goods on. Five. As it is, we've got your three and my five. Close to twice our needs."

"I'll bet there's a price to be gotten for them in that camp," I told him. "Their stock's pitiful thin."

"Well, grab your rifle, and let's scare up some meat. I saw a pair of doe down past that spring toward midday. Three ought to do those folks just fine. We keep the hides, too, eh? Give you somethin' to do for a bit."

"Sure will," I muttered as I followed him toward the spring.

It seemed almost unfair to hunt that mountain. A Shoshoni armed with a bow had to stalk with great care, get in close enough to make the sure shot. With our rifles, we could drop a deer from more than a hundred yards out and be sure of a kill. True, reloading took a while, but we had among us three rifles, so the deer had but an instant to dart away.

Shea had a nose for game, and it took him no time to circle behind the pond and approach downwind of the deer. There were five in all nibbling the soft meadow grass beside the spring. Shea pointed to the one on the left, then aimed his own rifle at a buck to the right. He held up the five fingers of his right hand, and I silently counted down with him so that our two shots were as one. While I watched the deer fall, Shea took the third rifle and shot a buck in full flight.

As the powder smoke drifted away, I stood and gazed at our work. The three animals lay lifeless in the meadow, staining the grass with their blood. Once I would have shuddered at the sight, but I'd seen worse now. I followed Shea to the spring and dragged my deer into the trees, hung it in the notch of a small willow, and made the throat cut so that the blood would drain.

"Best go fetch a horse while I get to the butcherin'," Shea suggested. "That'll leave those pilgrims time to get a supper fire started."

"Sure," I agreed, heading back to our camp.

I returned with a pair of pack horses. I wrapped chunks of venison in the deer hides, then tied them atop the horses. The sun was beginning its westward plunge by the time I reappeared in the emigrant camp.

"You're most welcome," Elsworthy declared when I began untying my bundles." A regular godsend, Mr. Prescott."

"Darby," I told them.

"Well, Darby, I'll get your mony."

"Mr. Elsworthy," I called as he turned to leave. "My partner and I've got three horses we can sell you, too. These two here and an Indian pony. We'd make you a fair price, and they'd help you top the South Pass."

"Name the price," Elsworthy said, smiling at his company. "See there, folks? Here we are despairing that McDougal's gone and disappeared, and God sends us welcome aid. You fetch the other horse, Darby. I'll get my money box."

I went on with my work, then left a group of women to divide the meat among the company. I had no need to fetch the pony. Shea soon appeared with it in hand.

The sight of Shea, with his heavy beard and rough appearance, took the wagon train company aback. Children huddled beside mothers and fathers. One child

185

shrieked, and Elsworthy himself inched closer to a rifle.

"It's all right," I announced. "It's my partner, Tom Shea."

I wasn't such a known quantity myself, though, and no one took my word as cause for setting aside his caution. A tenseness filled the air. Shea noted it and drew to a halt twenty yards from the nearest wagon.

"I welcome or not?" he called.

I turned to Elsworthy, hands on my hips, and waited for the captain to reply. He seemed unable to decide. Finally, helpless to erase the suspicion, I drew the mouth organ from my hip pocket and started up a melody.

"Well, I'll be," a woman remarked. Two others sang along when I began "Shenandoah."

"He's all right, you know," I told them, pausing long enough to wave Shea along. "He's saved my life more times than I can recall, and he's brought you horses to help you on your way. If he meant you harm, he'd come by night."

"That's true enough," Elsworthy admitted. "Well, bring your friend along. We do need the horses, and after all, you've fed the hungry this day. Guess that earns you a bit of gratitude and perhaps some hospitality as well."

I nodded, then accepted the promised fifteen dollars, collected my hides, and tied them behind the saddle on Snow's back. Shea, meanwhile, attended to the terms of the horse sale. Afterward, with business behind us, we joined the company for venison steaks, stewed potatoes, and a bit of singing.

"Darby here says you've scouted the trail," Elsworthy said later as we warmed ourselves around a small campfire.

"Led a few pilgrims to the promised land," Shea explained. "Left a few along the way. You folks got a late jump on winter snows."

"We've had a hard time of it, yes, sir," Elsworthy confessed. "We started late, and the grass was poor along the Platte. The Sweetwater was little more than a mud wallow in places, and we caught fever, lost even more time."

"Best thing'd be to find a place to winter, put up some cabins, get meat and wood put by against the cold. Folks cross the desert to California this late find no grass nor water either, and the snows drown 'em in the passes."

"We'd pay you to show us the way," a stern-faced woman offered. "You and the boy, both."

"He hasn't been a boy since he killed his first buffalo," Shea told them. "I've got my eyes on a little cabin up in the Medicine Bow country, an easy winter 'fore takin' on pilgrims in the spring. I got money, so it doesn't much tempt me, you see."

"I warned you," I reminded Elsworthy. "Tom sets his mind to a thing and sticks to it. Do like he says, then head out again once the grass greens in April. California can wait."

"Not the goldfields," one of the men complained. "I left my wife and young ones back in Missouri. I'll not wait another year to make my fortune."

Others muttered the same sentiments.

"Well, you've got no one stoppin' you from gettin' buried in snow," Shea remarked. "We dug out folks thought the same up near Ft. Hall. Maybe you'll find fool's luck and get through. More likely not."

We sang a bit then, and I played "Sweet Betsy" for the children. Shea shared a story with the littlest ones. Then we left.

"They're the worst kind of fools," Shea told me that night as we lay in our blankets. "Got kids half-starved already. No food to be found in the barrens. Wind up dead, the lot of 'em."

I closed my eyes and tried to erase the faces I'd come to know. A pair of dark-haired boys put me in mind of myself, and there was a yellow-haired girl as pretty as any I'd ever seen. She sang like an angel, and she'd walked with me a bit after supper. I sat up and gazed at the stars overhead.

"Don't think of 'em too much," Shea warned. "Good way to break your heart."

I nodded, then closed my eyes and let sleep carry me away. No rest came, though, for I dreamed of hunger and blizzards and death. When I awoke, Shea already had breakfast sizzling on the griddle.

"You let me sleep," I gasped in surprise.

"You looked to need the rest. Cried out some last night, and you thrashed about. Guess the pilgrims bore heavy on you."

"Guess so," I said, straightening my blankets and pulling on my trousers.

"They're leavin', you know," he told me. "I could map out the route, and you could help 'em along."

"Me? Not you?"

"I got no heart to bury the little ones," he explained.

"Figure I do? I plan to winter in the Medicine Bow country with you, Tom Shea. You won't find me as easy to shake as some Sioux raiding party."

"Shake?" he asked, laughing. "Glad of the company."

Our next visitors weren't emigrants. A band of Shoshonis made camp beside the trail, no doubt hoping to trade hides for such as they could get. When we rode down to visit, they eyed us with caution until Shea called to them a Shoshoni greeting.

After we mentioned camping with Washakie and Two Knives, they welcomed us warmly.

"There's been sickness along the trail this year," Shea explained to me later. "It's got the tribes uneasy. Measles near killed off one whole band of Shoshonis th'other side of the pass, and smallpox hit the Pawnees again, so they say."

"Makes you think," I admitted.

"Merits consideration, all right. We'd best give a hard look to anybody travels through from here on."

It proved wise counsel. The very next day we spotted a short line of wagons plodding along the trail below. The Shoshonis wasted no time in breaking down their camp and moving off. The reason was clearly evident. A black flag flew beside the lead and trailing wagons.

"Plague train," Shea mumbled. "Best stay clear."

"Looks to me like they're moving along all right," I observed.

Later, as they made camp, I slipped down the mountain on foot and spied a band of children collecting firewood. Later, three boys dipped fishing poles in the water, and I stepped out of the trees twenty feet away and nodded to them.

"Best stay away, mister," they urged. "We've had sickness."

"Saw the flags," I replied. "Pox?"

"Of a sort," the younger answered. "Chicken pox."

"Oh," I said, laughing. "Had that when I was four. You can't get it but once."

"Yeah, we had it, too," the taller of the three said, waving me over. "Killed two babies, though, and an Indian who was helping our scout."

"Been hard on the men, too," the third boy told me. "We couldn't make so much as a mile along the trail for two weeks. Now it's mostly worked its way through us, but Sally Tilden and Ed Hale are still having a hard time."

"Sally's just five," the smallest explained. "Ed's eleven."

"Well, they'll likely fare all right," I declared. "Young ones usually do."

"Sure," the oldest declared. "They're about the only ones who haven't had it. We mostly fly the flags to warn the Indians. Pa says it could kill off a whole tribe, them not being used to it."

"Happens," I mumbled. "I'm Darby Prescott, once out of Pike County, Illinois."

"We're from Illinois, too," the youngest said with a grin. "Jeremy Walker's my name. That tall one there's my brother Lloyd, and this is Terris Mason, though everybody knows him as Terry."

I shook their hands and shared with them a bit of my history. Another time we might have a swum a bit, but there was a nip in the air, and they had supper to catch.

I told Shea later about the plague train, and he judged it folly to visit the company.

"I've had chicken pox," I explained.

"They look like doctors, those boys?" he asked. "What would they know of sickness? One set of spots isn't all that different from another. Best you stay clear."

I nodded. It was always best to practice caution, so I kept away from the camp that night in spite of the temptation to share a tale and play my mouth organ.

I was awakened early that next morning by singing. Shea snored away as always, so I got dressed and had a look. The company gathered on the hillside below, and for a

189

moment I thought it might be Sunday. Then I saw the twin crosses and realized the sick children must have passed over during the night.

Well, I was a fool to say they'd likely mend. You'd think I'd forgotten about Matthew and Jamie McNamara. Fate had a way of reaching out and snatching life from the young, and the trail was particular fond of doing it.

Another day I might have tried to play a melody for the mourners, but I didn't figure a wailing tune would cheer anybody. I sat on the slope and watched them drop the two bundles in shallow slits, then shovel dirt and rock over both.

The wagons pulled out shortly thereafter. I noticed the black flags had been put aside. They were no longer needed, for the plague had done its worst.

Or so I thought.

The Sioux came that same afternoon. I saw their dust from a mile and a half away, and I would have ridden down to greet them blindly if Shea hadn't held me back.

"Best you see who it is first," he warned. "They come from north and east."

"That a worry?"

"Might be," he said, grabbing his rifle. "But we'll wait and see."

I walked to where the horses were hobbled and made sure they were out of clear view. Then I grabbed my own rifle and joined Shea. We watched nervously as figures emerged from the dust. First came a pair of bare-chested boys. They were followed by a taller, older fellow with a dark, brooding brow and a jagged scar across his chest.

"Sioux," Shea whispered.

"It's the same bunch took the Mormon boys," I told him. "I recognize that one with the scar."

"Doesn't seem any too friendly."

He wasn't. I recall how roughly he'd treated those boys. I was unprepared for what he next turned his hand to, though. The younger Sioux rode around the creekbank, picking through the leavings of the wagon trains. Then one of them spied the crosses. The whole Sioux party galloped to the spot, then began digging at the ground with knives.

190

"Tom?" I appealed. My face betrayed my horror, and I raised my rifle.

"Can't hold it against 'em," he said, gripping my arm so that I relaxed my grip. "You recall how we covered young Jamie's grave with the wagon tracks? Those pilgrims should've done the same, or else not marked the spot so plain."

I tried to share his understanding, but it wasn't possible. The pitiful bodies were hauled out, and the raiders made a great show of pulling off the blankets and stripping the bodies.

"It's bitter hard, standing by and doing nothing," I told Shea. "Might not be so bad if they'd been older, but little children like that . . ."

"They don't feel it," he assured me. "Best watch no more. Let's have a look at the horses."

I followed him through the cottonwoods to where the horses grazed. The Sioux spent a bit more time down by the creek, then continued down the trail.

"Never knew Sioux to raid this far into Shoshoni country," Shea told me afterward. "Isn't any too smart."

"That scarred fellow lives on hatred," I said, kicking the ground in anger. "There's a tale there, no doubt, a reason for it, but I can't find any sympathy for him."

"You've grown a hard heart, have you?"

"Gets harder every day," I confessed.

"Time we left this place then."

"Got something to do first, I said, turning toward the disturbed graves. Shea held me back.

"Wait for the Sioux to leave," he advised.

"What? They've gone."

"South," he reminded me. "They won't enter the pass, not even if they're dog-struck crazed. Be back through here soon, and they're sure to wonder who mended the graves."

"Can't just leave the bodies out there in the open," I objected.

"Be best."

"I can't," I told him.

"Then you take a couple of blankets, wrap 'em up good, and bury 'em off a ways, in the trees. Afterward, you put rocks over the spots. Mind, don't be too neat about it, or

191

they'll be able to tell. Scatter the rocks, and see the ground's even."

"You're welcome to help," I told him.

"I've not had that pox," he said gravely. "You have a careful look yourself, Darby. It's not chicken pox, you stay clear of 'em."

I nodded. Then I grabbed a spade and set off toward the graves.

I examined the bodies, but they'd stiffened, and I could hardly see signs of any spots. I wrapped the small white lumps as gently as I could, then carried each in turn a quarter mile to a thick wood and dug a new grave.

Somehow I felt it proper they should lie alongside each other. Though the boy was near as old as Jamie'd been, the girl was small and needed company. I knew if burial eased the anguish suffered by the spirit, perhaps the two could comfort each other on that forlorn hillside.

The Sioux returned as Shea predicted, but they didn't bother passing the violated graves. Instead they rode briskly northward toward the Sweetwater. I, for one, was glad they left. I'd fought that tribe, and I'd found them honorable enough and more than clever. These riders were outcasts of a sort, a small band bent on murder. Well, who was I to judge the Sioux for their crimes? I'd seen white men as bad on the Barlow road.

That night I saw the scarred-chest Sioux in my dreams. He waved a blood red lance toward me, and I cried out in fear.

"What's troublin' you, boy?" Shea asked, rousing me. "You all right."

"Just having a nightmare," I explained, blinking the Sioux from my mind. "I'm all right."

"It's this place," he observed. "It troubles you. Well, it's best we were on our way. Time we started east."

"Sure," I whispered, rolling over and drawing the blankets tight against my chest.

When I closed my eyes, the dream returned. Only it was different this time. The clouds overhead split, and amid crashing thunder and brilliant lightning the white buffalo thundered down and trampled the scarred one underfoot.

"Have no fear, dreamer," a voice whispered to me. "He

will trouble you no more."

Indeed, a great peace settled over me, and I slept well past daybreak the next morning.

Shea was serious about leaving. I awoke to find him packing up our belongings and readying the horses.

"Those Sioux are up ahead," I reminded him.

"We'll keep our eyes open. I wouldn't guess they'd hug the trail too closely. Not enough of 'em to take on a wagon train."

No, I thought. Their way's to creep in at night and make war on children.

Two days east of our old camp we did indeed happen across the raiders. The white buffalo had been right. The scarred one would trouble me no more. He and his companions lay stretched out beside their lodgepoles, covered with red spots and guarded by two boys who gazed helplessly as we passed by. Death was already reaching out for them as it had the older ones.

"Well, looks like that band won't loot any more graves," Shea told me.

"It's a judgment," I declared. "Death struck them from the grave!"

"Seems so," Shea agreed. "Can't find any hard words for 'em now, Darby, especially not for those boys back there."

"No, but I don't have much pity, either," I said. "They brought it on themselves. And now they're dead, too."

"You don't plan to bury 'em, too, do you?"

"I don't think the ones left would look too kindly on that."

"No. Likely not," he agreed, kicking his horse into a trot. I followed, poking the pack horse and urging our spare mounts along. The sooner we put that place of death behind us, the better!

Chapter 19

It took us two weeks to ride eastward along the Sweetwater and southward up the headwaters of the North Platte into the Medicine Bow Range. The mountains were not grand and impressive like the Tetons, but with autumn transforming the willows and cottonwoods into wondrous shades of orange and scarlet, it was as awesome a sight as I could recall. Along the Sweetwater we had passed the last emigrant wagons bound west. In the Medicine Bow country, only occasional Cheyenne and Arapaho bands happened by, and they ignored the two crazed whites who seemed determined to lose themselves in the high wilderness.

For my part, I welcomed the windswept heights. The nightime chill often had me huddling beneath blankets and buffalo hides, but in the afternoons I gazed out at eagles drifting over the virgin plain, and I felt I'd discovered a private, untouched world.

The night we finally left the North Platte and climbed into the mountains themselves, Shea shared with me the legend of the Medicine Bow.

"Long time 'fore the people divided 'emselves into bands or tribes, they were truly one with the land," he explained. "As the Sky Father and the Earth Mother made the sun and the stars and the moon, so they molded the first man and woman. Children came to be born. Birds were placed in the heavens, and fish were given the waters. The elk held dominion over the mountains, and the buffalo thundered across the plain.

"All was not well, though. Man grew unhappy. 'Where is my place to be?' he asked the spirits. 'I, greatest of your creations, must run from the wolf and hide from the bear.'

The sky spirits wished man to stand tall, for he alone they had set upon but two legs. He alone was to walk the land with reverence and understandin'. So it was that a dream was sent to the youngest of man's sons, a boy whose eyes were wide enough to see all and listen. A great shining light called him to the high mountains, for here he was to receive a gift—the bow. Crafted from the trunk of sacred ash, its string the sinew of the doe, here was the tool which would raise man above all. And beside the bow rested the seven sacred arrows tipped by flints cut of Earth Mother's ribs, fletched of eagle feathers. The bodies of those arrows were shaped by Sky Father's own fingers from the sacred ash.

"Boy set out upon his quest with a warnin'. He must harm no creature in his path. He must neither eat nor drink nor rest until he came upon the bow. Only with it safely in his hands dare he rest. He realized the difficulty of the task, but he trusted the spirits would not send him a task he couldn't do. So he set out alone toward the high mountains.

"Days and days he walked. His belly ached, and his thirst grew. He was so weary he dropped to his knees. Still onward he struggled until, when he could move no more, he sat beneath the branches of a willow and prayed for the strength to go on. He felt hands upon his shoulders, and he rose upon his feet. There before him was the yellow light. Hands held out the bow, and he gripped it. The arrows lay around his feet, together with food and drink. Soft grass bid him rest upon it.

"So he ate and drank and slept. In his dreams an eagle spoke, bidding him listen well. The medicine bow would send its arrows into the heart of any living creature, the eagle explained, but only if the spirit of that creature gave itself freely to the hunter. Prayers must be made, and the pipe smoked before each hunt. If used in anger against the innocent, the medicine would be broken, and the bow would crack.

"Boy took the great bow and the sacred arrows back to his father and told of his quest. A feast was made, and Boy was given the name Long Walker, for he had journeyed to the mountain and returned. Soon he put the medicine bow to work. His arrows flew with the true aim, and he brought back deer and elk and buffalo for the people. Man grew strong. No longer did the wolf and the bear hunt him. Now they were the hunted.

"But Long Walker had a rival. Among his brothers was one called Snake, for he walked the earth low like a snake. He had no dreams, and he sought no vision. One day Snake stole the medicine bow and took it onto the plain. Long Walker, seein' the bow gone, went to search for his lost possession. An eagle flew above and saw Snake with the bow. Long Walker hurried after his brother, cryin' out that the bow must not be used. Snake had no ears for his brother's words, though, only envy and hatred. Snake notched an arrow and aimed at his own brother.

" 'I give my spirit,' Long Walker called so that the wonderful bow might not break. But Snake made no prayers, and as the sacred arrow left the string, the bow snapped. Sky Father saw all this, and he sent his son, Wind, to blow the arrow back at the foolish Snake. It buried itself in Snake's heart.

"Long Walker gazed upon his brother's body and wept that Snake had been so foolish. Then he held up the broken bow and prayed for Sky Father to mend it. 'You must bury the bow high upon the mountain,' Sky Father answered. 'One day, when man again has eyes to find it, the bow will become whole. Now there is too much hatred among the people.' And so the bow has remained in these mountains waitin'. Man fashioned other bows, and he killed the elk and the buffalo and his own brothers, too. But he's never known the perfect aim since the medicine bow was broken."

"And this is where it's buried?" I asked.

"Accordin' to some. Often Cheyenne and Arapaho boys climb these hills on a vision quest, hopin' to receive the medicine bow. Nobody ever has that I've heard of."

"Figure I ought to have a look?"

"You?" he asked, laughing. "I never knew you to go without eatin', much less sleepin', long enough to get far. But if some eagle takes to whisperin' in your ear, you might have a look."

I grew solemn a moment, then told him of how the

196

hite buffalo had appeared in my dream and trampled the
ar-chested Sioux.

"You know, Darby, mountains are places of strong spir-
s. I'm not sayin' what's real and what's dreams, mind
ou, but I've heard stranger tales'n yours. I got a great
espect for spirit dreams, as most do who've walked the
igh country. You tell me next time, though. Often as not,
ney're warnin's, and those are best paid mind to."

The first breath of winter was on the wind now, and
hea wasted no time in locating a sheltered slope on
hich to build a cabin.

"Thing to do," he explained, "is use the mountain itself
or part of the north wall. Keep the worst of the wind off
ou. You dig out some, then cut pines for the walls, strip
ne bark, and leave 'em to dry a bit. Meanwhile we can
nake a dugout shed for the horses and cut feed."

We set to doing just that.

In truth, it felt good to swing the heavy ax. As it bit into
ne soft white pine, stinging my fingers, I felt that oneness
vith the earth that Tom Shea spoke of so often. And when
ne first of the giant trees crashed to the ground, I stood
ill in the afterglow of triumph.

"Don't sit there admirin' the fool thing," Shea com-
lained. "Set her on the stump and get the bark stripped!"

I did, then started on the next one. Shea had carefully
ut an *x* in the side of the pines I was to fell, and I was
areful to cut only those. He wished to keep a protective
vindbreak around the cabin and shed. Later, when we
egan cutting firewood, he disdained the pines altogether
 favor of hardwood trees.

"Wood'll burn hotter and longer," he told me. It also
neant hauling trees up from the base of the mountain
ometimes.

As for the cabin, once the pine sap had done its running
nd the lengths were dried, we set to work making a
oundation of stone. Shea mixed straw and mud to make a
asty kind of mortar to hold the stones in place. We used a
imilar substance to build a chimney and to place between
ne pine logs to windproof the walls.

A far greater challenge was making windows. I'd helped
'apa frame windows for the house in Oregon, but we

lacked the tools I'd used. I found myself splitting pine logs and then whittling them into a flat shape. They were then squared as best we could. Three ash slats backed by buffalo hides made shutters to keep the cold out come first snow.

Our greatest challenge was setting the roof beams in place. The top logs on the walls had proven a challenge, but the beams had to be set at an angle. Twice we nearly had them pegged in place when one or the other fell. It took every bit of patience to hammer them in place. Then we added cross pieces and began slicing cedar shingles.

In all, it took nearly a month to complete the cabin and its neighboring dugout. In the end, it was a match for the cabin back in the Tetons. In a sense it was better, for there were no phantom wild boys or ghosts of old trappers to haunt me.

"Well, Darby?" Shea asked as we finished hanging the door. "How do you feel?"

"Close to perfect," I confessed. "I forgot what it felt like to build something. Feels good, putting your hands to a real purpose."

"Some'd find purpose to stayin' alive," he told me.

"I admit it's been a struggle sometimes. I felt good when those snowbound emigrants made it to Ft. Hall, and bringing those Mormon boys to their folks, well, that was better still. But once all that was done, there was nothing left to remind you of it. This cabin, well, it'll last a bit."

"Likely so," he grumbled. "If it was up to me, I'd burn it come spring. I'd have no sign of my passin' through here left behind at all. I'd come and leave like a hair of the wind."

"Don't you want to be remembered as Tom Shea, famed wagon scout and frontiersman?"

"What?" he asked, laughing. "Nonsense, that kind of talk. I'll be remembered by those that matter—the folks I've nudged along to better places, and those I've wintered with, hunted with, fought alongside."

"Those you've helped grow?"

"Not many of them, you know. But I expect one of these days you'll find a bright-eyed girl and make a family for yourselves. If I'm still around to spin a tale or two, I'd

are 'em with the little ones. If I'm not, you might do it
r me. Tell 'em about Three Fingers Shea, the old fool
at took you into the Medicine Bow country that winter
'51."

"I will," I promised.

"Know that, Darby," he said, swinging the door open
d peering inside. "Well, now all we need is to fell some
h trees and cut slats for a couple of beds. Need a table,
o, and some chairs. Wouldn't hurt to scare up some elk.
few hides on the floor would keep the cold off our feet."

"And here I thought we were through!" I cried.

"Work's never done up here. Always somethin' else
itin' for you. Got to cut feed for the horses, build up the
odpile, and then . . ."

"Yeah, I know," I said, scowling. "I'm getting the ax."
He laughed, then followed me outside.

We labored long and hard to cut grass, shoot and skin
, and get the slat beds constructed. We were still work-
g on the table, though, when the first snow flurries fell in
ovember. They weren't the last. By Christmas, at least
e day I determined was most likely Christmas, a foot
d a half of snow covered the mountainside. Thereafter,
cept for rare days exercising the horses, we were snow-
und through February.

I relished the mouth organ that hard, cruel winter. Its
tes flooded the little cabin with song and warmed me
most as much as the fire. It was a lonely time for the two
us, and long days kept inside by howling winds and
ifting snow gave time to reflect on life's disappoint-
ents.

"I never thought much on it, but I'd judge winter's the
rd's way of bringin' men to their knees in prayer," Shea
marked one morning. "A man may walk tall and pride
mself that he's holdin' the reins to his own fate, but it's
t true. A tree might fall on his cabin. Snow might block
s smoke hole. He might run smack into a grizzly back of
s woodpile or fall down a well. No, only a fool thinks
's got a hold on his life. Best he can do is wrestle it some
d try to hang on."

"That's a hard thought," I told him.

"Hard and true," he declared.

199

He had his proof soon enough. First a bitter freeze nea
killed us. The heat from our fire usually melted the sno
around the window and door, but it got so cold tha
melted snow froze into solid ice. It as good as nailed th
door and window closed. The cabin grew stuffy, and ha
Shea not poked a few holes through the snow on the roo
we might have suffocated. Even so, the confinemen
weighed on us both. I felt as if I were lying in a seale
coffin, and I fretted we'd burn all our wood, the fi
would go out, and snow would blow down the chimne
and bury us.

"Likely freeze us first," Shea declared.

I recalled old Palmer, and it was all I could manage t
keep from taking the ax to that door. Of course then w
would really freeze, but I was too irrational to think c
that.

After three days in our cabin coffin, the cold abated
and we managed to free the door. Then we dug a tunnel c
sorts through the snow and saw the horses had fresh wate
With all that snow about, you wouldn't think that to be
problem, but the dugout stable afforded the animals littl
access to the snow outside. There was plenty of forag
true enough, but the water troughs were near empty, an
the place stank of dung. It was my unpleasant chore t
collect the dung, fill the troughs, and carry logs from th
woodpile inside the cabin.

"Did a fine job on that," Shea told me when I finishe
"Now, why don't we see if we can scare up some fres
meat? This dried venison is mighty tiresome. A good el
steak would do my heart good."

I grinned and fetched my rifle. In truth, the hunt wa
almost as welcome as the fresh meat would be.

It was far from what I envisioned, though. We'd ha
snow back in Illinois, and the deep drifts last winter nort
of the American Falls had done their best to bury me
Snowdrifts in the Medicine Bow Range were near as tall a
I was, though, and twice they close to swallowed m
whole.

We came across the grandaddy of all elk just beyond th
frozen spring that had once been our water source. Tha
elk had more prongs on its antlers than I'd ever seen, an

s great strong neck bulged with muscle. I was half tempted to pass it by, such a grand sight it was, but I was so cold and hungry. I took out my rifle instead.

That elk must have thought us apparitions. We came out of thick flurries painted white with snow. Ice froze our whiskers white, too, and if not for the long black barrels of our rifles, we might have been thought snow beasts.

Shea tapped my back to let me know I had the first shot. I checked my powder charge, then placed a percussion cap on the nub below the hammer, took aim, and fired. The rifle sent a whirl of black smoke out into the ivory white universe, and the elk leaped high into the air and fell gracefully into a blanket of snow, its eyes frozen in death.

"Fine shot," Shea declared as we trudged through the deep drifts toward the fallen elk. Together we dragged the giant back to the cabin, then skinned it, butchered the meat, and dragged the carcass off for such wolves as still moved upon the frozen world.

It was early the following morning when I met with misfortune. The sun had come out for the first time in memory, and I had in mind to give the horses a bit of a ride. As it happened, the drifts prevented me even getting them out of the stable. Instead I walked uphill a way and stared out at the valley below. The sparkling blue thread of the North Platte glimmered beneath its icy coat, and snow draped the pines and spruces like long white shawls. If I hadn't been so cold and wet, I would have deemed it beautiful.

I caught sight of something glinting in the sunlight off to my left. A large boulder stood nearby, and I couldn't help recalling Shea's tale of the magical medicine bow. It couldn't be true, of course. It was a tale designed to mold character as most Indian legends do. Still, my curiosity was aroused, and I waded through the deep snow toward the boulder. The closer I got, the brighter the light. Then, as I stepped toward it, the earth beneath me seemed to explode. My leg buckled, and my foot grew momentarily numb. Then it erupted in pain, and I howled to high heaven.

"Lord, Shea, I'm killed sure!" I shouted.

He'd never been one to move quickly when there was a choice, but right then he flew across the mountainside like a snow eagle. When he approached the boulder, he slowed.

"What's got you, Darby?" he asked.

"Feels like a bear's teeth," I told him.

"Worse," he declared. "If it's what I think, you've got yourself a world of trouble. Can you feel your toes?"

"I can't even feel my knee just now," I told him. "When I do feel something, I wish I couldn't."

"Well, it's my fault," he muttered. "Should've thought to look around good before the snows came. I'd spotted it sure."

"What?" I cried.

"Traps," he grumbled, skillfully digging out a chain tied to a pine just back of the boulder. As he dug deeper, my eyes followed the chain down toward my aching left leg. Finally Shea reached snow stained red with my blood.

"Good Lord!" I cried.

"Hold still," he urged as he dug out my foot. It was held in the wicked jaws of a bear trap.

"Tom?" I whimpered.

"Hold still," he repeated. "Consider yourself lucky. The snow likely slowed it some. Ordinarily a trap like this one'd take the leg off a skinny fellow like you. Now I want you to take a deep breath and ready yourself for some pain. Then when I open up the jaws, you got to pull out that foot. Understand?"

"Sure," I said, trembling.

He counted aloud to three, then jerked open the jaws of the trap. A wave of pain mixed with nausea swept over me, and I almost fainted.

"Pull your fool leg out!" Shea shouted. "I can't hold the thing forever."

I tried to lift the foot, but it felt as if it were made of lead. I tugged and tugged, then finally fell backward. That motion freed my leg, and Shea was able to release his grip on the trap. The jaws clamped shut with a clang, and I was glad not to have received that force upon my leg.

"Pack it with snow," Shea suggested, and I took off the worn woolen scarf brought west from Illinois and filled it with snow. Then I tied the scarf around my leg. Finally

Shea lifted me in his iron-like arms and bore me back to the cabin.

"You've gotten too old to carry about," he declared when he set me in my bed. "Won't ever complain about you bein' skinny again. That's for certain. Now, let's have a look."

I wasn't half ready for what I saw. The jagged teeth of the trap had near torn the flesh from my ankle in places, but the snow had kept the bleeding light, and Shea now fashioned a binding of cloth and buckskin. Afterward, he again packed it in snow and left me to rest.

Next morning he snared a pair of rabbits and made a medicine poultice to draw out the festering. He splinted my leg, and pronounced me as fit as could be expected.

"Might as well find that journal of yours," he told me. "You'll be a month off that leg."

"But the horses need exercise," I objected.

"I'll do what I can for 'em," he answered. "You stay off that leg, hear? It gets to festerin', you'll lose it. A man can walk the mountain with half a hand, but he's little good with one leg."

I nodded, and thereafter I was limited to cooking and writing. Perhaps it was a punishment of sorts, for in all the time I'd been gone, I'd not written Mary once. I now jotted down the particulars of my adventure, leaving out the parts which would have made her worry, and suggested next fall I might again reach Oregon. It would be a time being delivered, of course, but we were close to Ft. Laramie, and I hoped the mails might move west from there.

That night I stared through a crack in the shutters at a particularly bright star in the sky outside. It took me back to an old tale of Papa's, of how sailors had relied on stars to guide them across the Atlantic to the New World.

"You've brought me to a better place, too," I told the star. "I'll mend, and the snow will melt."

Winter, after all, was a season to outlast, to survive. I'd done it before and would again.

Chapter 20

I did survive, and my leg mended as well. In fact, there was only a thin scar to remind me of my misfortune. By first thaw, I was hobbling around, and when the cotton-woods began to sprout their new leaves, I was fit as ever and anxious to set out onto the plain once again.

"It's been a good winter after all," I told Shea.

"But you're gettin' the wayfarer's itch, eh?" he asked.

"Well, I confess it's struck me, too. There's yet snow to ride through, and the nights'll be cool. Cabin's taken on a softness, you know."

"If we're going to get to Independence in time to take on a train, we'd best hurry."

"Eager to try your hand at scoutin', are you?"

"Well, we've wintered with the Shoshonis a bit, ridden with the Crows, been chased about by Sioux, and done our fair share of trading. Seems like we're entitled to a bit of peace."

"That what you remember of the trail?" he asked, shaking his head. "Well, seems like you've got somethin' left to learn after all."

And so we put the horses out to fatten themselves on new grass while we packed up belongings and gathered food for the journey eastward. Hungry deer and elk eagerly nibbled at the mountain plants pushing their way up through the lingering snow, and they were slow to react to our sudden appearance. We ate well, and I busied myself afterward curing the hides or drying meat.

"You've done a fair job of it," Shea observed when I'd finished the last of the elk hides. "Ready for some ridin'?"

"Don't know if I am or not," I said, "but Snow's about to break his hobbles for want of a good run along the river. We leaving soon?"

"Dawn tomorrow," Shea announced. "Regrets?"

"Well, I'll miss the cabin some. Never did find that bow you talked about, either. But I suspect my rifle'll stand me in good stead awhile yet."

"I'd say so," he said, grinning. "You know, son, you've got the makin's of a good man. Always thought so, and here lately you look the part as well."

I walked to the spring and stared down at the reflection forming in the pool there. The boyishness had departed. Winter had swept it away. Before me gazed a shaggy-haired renegade. If not for the brightness in my eyes, I might have suspected the mountains of casting a spell, for my beard had finally grown to cover my chin and cheeks. My hips and shoulders had broadened. Why not? I'd come to be eighteen now, or soon would be. It was fitting I should look the part.

"Pleased with what you see?" Shea asked.

"Well, I've seen prettier faces," I replied. "Lots, in fact. But the boy's fast fadin', and I'm not altogether dissatisfied with what's come to take his place."

"Nor am I," he said, grinning. "Now come along. There's work waitin'."

We headed out early that next morning, bathed in dawn's golden glow. Our path through the mountains would carry us close to two hundred miles before reaching Ft. Laramie where the Laramie River flowed into the North Platte. There, Shea had explained, we would purchase provisions, especially shot and powder, before beginning the long trek across the high plains to Independence.

An ordinary man might spend half a year getting through the Medicine Bow country and on to Laramie, but our horses, weary of winter confinement, surged forward with rare energy, and we were on the North Platte in two weeks. Along the way we'd managed to mend tears in buckskins and sew new garments as needed. I'd split the seams of most every pair of trousers, and I devoted a fair share of each night to converting deer hides into pants.

There was time as well for an occasional swim, which also served to remove a considerable layer of winter grime. Twice we shot buffalo to replenish our foodstocks.

Once on the North Platte, we ran across numerous bands of Sioux and Cheyenne Indians. We kept a weather eye on them, but they didn't bother us. We learned from a passing trader the plains tribes had signed a new treaty the year before, promising to allow safe passage of the Oregon Trail.

"Explains why the Sioux were so far west and south last summer," Shea remarked. "I guess our scarred friend didn't get the word."

"Or didn't care to abide by it," I added.

"You're learnin'," Shea told me. "Well, I'd expect as much."

I laughed, then rode past him along the river toward the fort.

We appeared at Ft. Laramie the middle of April, 1852. The post sutler provided the date, and I eagerly noted that fact in my weathered journal. I'd been there before, in the summer of '48, but the years had transformed the little post on the North Platte into a sprawling collection of two-storied barracks with white-painted columns supporting wooden porches. Field pieces stood outside the fort headquarters, and a dozen Indian lodges clustered beside the river.

There weren't all that many soldiers. The ones I saw were blue-coated cavalrymen sauntering about in their short caps, idly passing time between drills while alternately watching the Indian women bathe at the river or chasing children, red and white, from the post stables.

It was early still for the first emigrant trains, but the traders had begun hauling supplies westward. One collection of wagons bound for our old friend Burkett had made a temporary stop at the fort, and I entrusted my letter to Mary with one of the freighters, Lucas Bernard.

"I'll see it gets sent along, son," the crusty driver promised.

"Give our regards to Ty Sloan while you're there," Shea added. "Tell him to save a jug for me come summer. Likely I'll need it if I'm shepherdin' pilgrims along the trail again."

"Scoutin'?" Bernard asked. "I'd as soon be scalped by Cheyenne as herd a bunch of tenderfeet west."

"Well, they're not all bad company," Shea said, leading me on toward the sutler's. "And I've got to where I can mostly tolerate their ways."

"Not me!" Bernard barked. "I leave 'em to you."

I couldn't help laughing as he embraced his mules and bid a boy of fifteen or so help harness the animals to a waiting wagon. Once inside the sutler's store, I quickly forgot Lucas Bernard. The sutler, an amiable fellow named Jesse Borden, strode toward us.

"Forgotten the date so soon, son?" he asked.

"No, brought my partner along to do some business," I explained. "We're near out of everything."

"Well, as you can see, we've got most anything you could desire," Borden boasted, pointing to the neat shelves bulging with everything from flour and patent medicines to powder and lead.

"Give him your list, Darby," Shea urged, and I drew out the paper on which I'd scrawled what supplies Shea judged were needed to get us safely to Independence. The sutler danced down the list, smiled at the prospect of such good trade, and picked up a wooden box.

"I think we can fill your needs easily enough," he assured us. "Let me put you in Laveda's hands."

Laveda, I was soon to discover, happened to be Borden's sharp-tongued seventeen-year-old daughter. She was as haughty as she was pretty. Laveda motioned for me to take the box. Then she began moving about the store, filling the box with one item after another. Soon the box weighed near as much as I did, and I strained under the weight.

"You want me to carry it?" she asked with disdain. "Or perhaps I should call my young brother Laurence out to help."

"You might put some of the goods in another box," I

suggested. "I wouldn't overburden a horse."

"Well, I've known horses to bathe," she complained. "The worst on the post isn't a match for you. Where've you been of late, a Cheyenne dung heap?"

Her sharp eyes bored through me like blazing embers, and I dropped my chin. She pointed to the counter, and I set the overfilled box there, then took a second, empty one.

"Shame is," she went on, "there aren't many young men come through here. Those who do are usually dragged along west with mothers and wouldn't prove worth the effort to ask their names. You might be fair company, on the other hand, if tamed some."

"You plan to try?" I asked, raising my eyebrows.

"Anybody else around to do it?" she asked. "What's your name, anyway?"

"Darby, Darby Prescott," I growled. "Out of Pike County, Illinois, by way of Oregon and the Rocky Mountains."

"Well, Mr. Pike County, if you'd care to get washed some and cut back a bit of that bird's nest you've grown as a beard, I might permit you to escort me to Colonel Randolph's midafternoon tea. The colonel's lady, Mrs. Ernestine, plans to play her pianoforte for the post's entertainment."

"You figure I can tame myself enough by then?" I asked sourly.

"Possible," she muttered. "Unlikely, but possible."

I frowned, then lugged the box over and let her dump two sacks of flour in. Powder and shot followed. Then percussion caps. Finally she added a tin of coffee, totaled the bill, and set before me the figure.

"Shea?" I called, marveling at the small fortune she wanted for the goods. Shea gazed at the figure, laughed, and handed it back.

"Fetch your papa," he suggested.

"That won't change the price," she insisted. Shea didn't budge, though, so Laveda stepped into the back room and summoned Jesse Borden. The sutler appeared, arms crossed on his chest, but Shea merely grinned and tore up the bill.

"Now, let's set to doin' business," Shea said. "Darby, fetch a couple of those elk hides from the horses."

I turned and trotted out the doors. I stepped to the horses, collected three elk hides, together with four buffalo hides, and returned, near overwhelmed by my burden.

"Well," Borden said, touching the soft hair on one of the elk hides. "Nice work. Cheyenne?"

"Darby here worked 'em himself," Shea explained. "Won't find half the quality anywhere. I sold a couple like that for twenty-five dollars in Missouri a couple years back."

"This isn't Missouri," Borden said, pretending to ignore the hides. "We trade a bit of tobacco to the Crows for buffalo hides."

"Like these?" I asked, passing one of the hides to Laveda.

Her hardness fell away as she touched the hide. I'd combed it myself, working the tangles out so that it was soft as a blanket yet three times as warm.

"Good seamstress could make a fine coat out of that hide," Shea declared. "The lot of 'em's worth a hundred fifty dollars, but I'll settle for the goods and fifty in coin."

"I'd say you would," Borden answered. "I never pay more than ten dollars a hide to anyone."

"Then that explains the poor quality hangin' on yon wall," Shea said, pointing to the buckskins and wolf pelts decorating the store. "You'll make a profit when you sell 'em, and you know it. Entitled to it, I'd say. But I don't plan to let you gouge me on both ends of this deal, Borden. I don't look like a fool, do I?"

Borden laughed. He examined the hides again, then turned to Laveda.

"Well, Daughter?" he asked. "Think they're worth his price?"

"I could sell the elk hides at a profit to the officers' wives tomorrow," she said. "The buffalo, well, I'd have to fashion coats of them. Shouldn't be hard to sell them once the wagon trains start rolling."

"Then do we have a bargain?" Shea asked.

"Appears so," Borden agreed. "You know, I buy pelts for the American Fur Company here, too," he explained. "You plan to hunt and trap this spring?"

"Headin' east," Shea explained. "Plan to take a wagon train across to Oregon."

"Do you now?" Borden said, brightening. "Well, we might have other business for you as well. Plan to go by way of Scott's Bluff?"

"Don't know a better way, 'less a man was to want his scalp lifted by Kiowas or Sioux," Shea answered. " 'Sides, my partner here's partial to the Platte River road. Been up it before, you see."

"Well, it's fifty miles of hard traveling in a wagon to Jonah Redding's new trading post beside the Platte," Borden explained. "I've got a fair-sized fortune in pelts I need to get there before his St. Louis freighters arrive to cart them back east. I can't leave the store to do it, and the man I hired got himself shot last week gambling with some Crow scouts. I'd pay a man I could trust a hundred dollars to deliver the goods to Redding. Well?"

"Be a fair amount of trust to put in a man you just met," Shea pointed out.

"Well, I confess that I've heard some of you. The three fingers on your left hand are a fair calling card. Tom Fitzpatrick's spoken some of you."

"Oh?"

"If you're bound that way, it would be a favor to me and profitable to you. Well, Mr. Shea, have we a deal?"

"Darby?" he asked.

"Sounds fair enough," I said. "Hard country part of the way, but we've crossed worse."

"Agreed then," Shea said, shaking Borden's hand.

"Don't turn toward the high pass and deal with that old fox Robidoux, mind you," Borden warned. "Deliver the whole batch to Redding, with the letter I'll send along, and he'll pay you then."

I frowned. It seemed a fine way to be cheated, but Shea

readily agreed to the plan.

"Best way," he told me. "No point to carryin' the extra cash with all those pelts, and I don't figure him to cheat us, not with all these goods here at risk. He knows we'll be back through, don't you, Borden?"

"You can depend on my father's word," Laveda insisted. "You just see you keep your part."

"We will," I said, giving her a hard stare.

"And don't forget the colonel's tea," she whispered to me. "Provided you scrub first."

I was half of a mind to start the scrubbing with her mouth, but she gave me a pleasant sort of grin then, and my anger faded. Laveda, for all her sharp words, cut a fair figure, and I found the notion of sitting with her a bit most appealing.

"Time we made camp," Shea said then, leading me toward the door. I gave Laveda a final nod, then headed out the door.

We pitched camp just upstream from the Indians. A warm spring provided a natural bathtub, and I readily availed myself of it. Laveda had included among the supplies a cake of lye soap and a box of shaving powder. As I sat soaking in the warm water, I made a lather of the powder and rubbed it into my whiskers. Then, using a small looking glass supplied by Shea and Papa's old razor, I erased the beard.

"Figure you could clip my hair some?" I asked when I rubbed the lather residue from my chin. "Awful tangle as it is."

"I'll get the shears," Shea said, rummaging among his belongings. He then waved me out of the pool and clipped six months' growth of hair from my head. I then managed to comb out near all the tangles, trim the last stray hairs, and make myself almost human.

"Got to admit it's an improvement," Shea observed as he handed me the looking glass again. "Skin's awful pale."

"You expected me Crow brown after wintering in the Medicine Bow?" I asked, rubbing the scar on my ankle.

"No," he said, laughing. "Never saw anything as white

211

as you, though."

I peered down at my pale chest and shook my head. True enough, I looked half ghost. I'd nearly scrubbed the hide off my bones. But cleanshaven and fresh-clipped, I felt twenty pounds lighter and quick of step.

"You know," I told Shea, "you might be more pleasant company yourself if you scrubbed some."

"Maybe I ought to've sprinkled some sage over my ears?"

"Wouldn't hurt the scent hereabouts."

"Lord, how a pretty girl's smile can turn a man's senses!" he grumbled.

"Sorry you didn't winter with the Crows?"

"No," he said, laughing. "The company was fine, as it happened."

I tossed him the soap, and he muttered to himself as he kicked off his boots. He took his bath, though, and he even trimmed his beard some.

"Coming to the colonel's tea?" I asked.

"Don't press a point, boy!" he growled.

I didn't. Instead I spread out my clothes and tried to find something suitable for attending tea with the finer folk of Ft. Laramie. Every shirt was threadbare save the beaded Crow garment, and I thought that less than likely to draw applause from a bunch of soldiers.

"Should've thought to buy you some pilgrim clothes," Shea said as he watched me stick my fingers through several holes in a threadbare gingham shirt.

"There's time yet," I told him. "Trail's hard on knees and elbows."

"Not to mention bottoms," he added, tossing me a set of union drawers worn clean through in the seat. "Want I should go on down to Borden's place, fetch you somethin'?"

"No, I'll make do," I said. "We'll be leaving soon anyway. Wouldn't want to get the girl's hopes up."

He laughed, and I grinned. Then I rushed to get myself dressed and hurried back to the fort.

I may not have been the best dressed man in the territory, but then there weren't all that many under twenty to choose from, and Laveda seemed pleased enough to take my arm.

"If you've got a day or two, I'll mend your shirt," she offered as we headed toward the colonel's house.

"I could keep you busy all year patching things," I told her. "What I haven't outgrown, that is."

"When we finish, come by and have a look through the trunks in the storeroom. We're always buying up odds and ends from the emigrant trains. Folks die, and there are clothes to be had for a few pennies."

"Sure," I said soberly.

We sat on one side of a small parlor amid a sea of uniform coats and fine dresses. I paid little attention to the faces of the officers and their ladies. A few children crowded up front. Otherwise, we were the sole civilians.

Mrs. Randolph stepped up to the pianoforte, sat down, and began playing. In truth, only a kind-hearted soul would have praised the playing much. She rarely hit three right notes in a row, and after two selections, some of the audience made excuses to retire. For me, any music was strangely welcome, though.

Later, when the colonel announced the performance concluded and motioned orderlies in to serve tea and small cakes, I led Laveda to the pianoforte and gazed longingly at the keys.

"Well, young man, did you enjoy the music?" Colonel Randolph asked.

"Yes, sir," I said, running my fingers along the polished mahogany. "I miss the music, being out in the wilds."

"Hear that, Sam?" Mrs. Randolph asked. "The wilds?"

"Darby's been wintering in the mountains, Mrs. Ernestine," Laveda explained. "He's a hunter and trapper of sorts. He and his partner are headed east to guide an emigrant train."

"Indeed?" Mrs. Randolph asked. "Well, an intrepid explorer. I don't suppose you've had much occasion to hear a concerto then."

"Oh, yes, ma'am," I told her. "My grandmother played

rather well, and she taught me soon as my feet touched the foot pedals."

"Well, well," the colonel declared. "Care to play something for us?"

"It's, well, Mrs. Randolph's day," I said, nervously shying away from them.

"Nonsense," the colonel's lady argued. "Have a try."

I could tell what was on her mind. Let this half-savage in his buckskin trousers and moccasins play for a time. Then her own performance would be appreciated!

"Go on," Laveda urged.

I swallowed hard, then sat down and fingered the keys. "I mostly know folk tunes," I declared. "Trail songs."

"Play us one," Colonel Randolph suggested.

I sighed, scratched my ear, and closed my eyes a moment. All I could think of was "Shenandoah," so I began. The sad, somber refrain flooded the room, and a hush settled over the company. I touched off each note with a tenderness built up over months of separation from the piano at the Willamette church. The melody drew me back along the hard trail west, then east through snowdrift and peril. I played a second verse, and some of the ladies took up singing. Mrs. Randolph, in fact, led them. Her fingers might have betrayed her with the pianoforte, but her voice was astoundingly lovely. Laveda sang, too, and I warmed in the glow of her smile.

When I finished, I received a rather polite applause. I stepped away from the instrument, and Laveda led me to the cakes.

"Did you have to show Mrs. Randolph up in front of her own husband?" she asked through clenched teeth.

"Couldn't help it," I said somberly. "It's been forever since I played. Year and a half, at least. Just couldn't help it."

"Well, it was pleasant," she said as I handed her a small plate with a slice of lemon cake on it. We sipped tea, then made our escape.

"However did a pale, thin, piano-player from Illinois come into the company of a rough character like Shea?"

214

she asked as we strolled beside the river.

"Don't know," I confessed. "Just lucky, I suppose."

"You don't belong out there on the plain," she insisted.

"You don't know me," I replied. "It's the only place I do belong."

Chapter 21

We passed ten full days at Ft. Laramie before Shea determined it was time to carry Borden's pelts east to Scott's Bluff. I got rather fond of Laveda's company in that time, and my appearance benefited considerably. For one thing, she dragged me to the post barber for a proper hair clipping. She located a leather strap so I could put an edge on Papa's old razor. Best of all, we sifted through four trunks of clothing and managed to put together a fair-sized collection of proper clothing.

When she and I attended a post social the night before I left for Scott's Bluff, I was rather a changed man. Not a hint of stubble clung to my chin, and a white muslin shirt, brown woolen trousers kept up with black suspenders, and a pair of polished black soldier boots gave me the appearance of a civilized young man. Only my bone and bearclaw choker hinted otherwise, and Laveda removed that and my floppy deerskin hat before permitting me to escort her across the parade ground.

When I bid her farewell next morning, she didn't say much. She rested her head on my shoulder a moment, stroked my chest, and wished me well.

"We're on the way west, remember?" she whispered.

"Sure," I said, turning away. By midday Shea and I were a quarter of the way to Scott's Bluff.

The high plain that stretches north and south from the North Platte is a whitish, yellow-green land come April. In 1852 the buffalo herds sometimes blocked the river road for miles, stopping all travelers in their tracks. Shea didn't trust the sluggish Platte's waters, and we kept to the high ground, relying on springs or digging wells. Our horses strained under the weight of their cargo, and Shea was wary of strangers.

It was only fifty miles to Scott's Bluff, that strange, white-yellow sentinel that stood watch over the trial. Back in '48 he'd led our train away from the river through Robidoux's pass, where the Frenchman had operated his first trading post. Now Shea explained the wagons preferred the river. So it was that Jonah Redding had located his trading post on the North Platte.

When we appeared with our load of pelts, the trader eyed us somewhat suspiciously. Borden's letter set him at ease, though, and Redding promptly paid us the promised money.

"In a hurry east, or would you care to earn a few more dollars?" he asked us.

"Depends what we'd have to do," Shea answered.

"Well, a boy rode in yesterday from a wagon train. Wanted some medicine for a fever and some blankets. I gave him a bit of tonic Doc Hardesty swears by, but I didn't have blankets. I told the boy to see Robidoux, but the lad was in a hurry. He left me some money, and I promised to find the blankets. Well, I got 'em, only I can't very well abandon my place and set off down the trail."

"We'll take them," I promised. "We're bound that direction anyway."

Shea frowned, then sadly shook his head. Once we were outside, he scolded me for being foolish.

"You forget your senses?" he asked as I tied the blankets on a pack horse. "Train's got fever. You forget about those Sioux back on the Sweetwater?"

"No," I told him. "Didn't forget it was along here that Jamie died, either. I'll bet it's the same swamp fever. Likely they didn't have a scout wise like you. After all, they're early on the trail."

He saw right through my flattery, though, and as we rode along, he urged caution.

We came upon the wagons circled on the south bank of the river halfway between Chimney Rock and Scott's Bluff. Black strips of cloth warned of their trail, and Shea bid me stay with the animals while he took the blankets closer.

"Hello, the train!" he called.

A slender young woman stepped out from a nearby wagon, saw the blankets, and started for Shea with a great smile on her face.

"Thank God!" she exclaimed. "You're most welcome, sir. We've half the company eaten up with fever!"

Shea spoke a bit more with her. Then he yelled for me to stay put and continued along toward the closest wagon. Half an hour later a yellow-haired boy of about twelve departed the camp and marched briskly toward me.

"Mr. Shea says it's all right for you to come along," the youngster said, tugging on my sleeve. "Says it's what you thought. I'm supposed to help you dig a well."

I nodded, then collected the reins of the horses, and followed the boy toward the wagons. There were close to thirty of the sway-backed long-bedded Conestogas, and better than a hundred people in that company. Close to eighty of them were abed with fever.

"Why not you?" I asked the boy.

"Don't know," he answered with a shrug. " 'Cept maybe it's the water, like Mr. Shea says. There's just me and Marietta, Ma and Pa. We didn't fill up our water barrels when everybody else did."

"Sure, that saved you," I told him. "I lost my best friend to this fever when I came west."

"When was that?" he asked.

"Back in '48," I explained, tying the horses to a wagon tongue, then taking a spade. "Now find a shovel and help me dig. You're able, aren't you? I mean there's not much more'n hayseed and vinegar to you."

"Is to," he boasted, doubling up his fists and preparing for war. "Try me and find out!"

218

I reached over, slung him over my hip, and dragged him along to a heap of garbage. There I left him while I started digging the well a few yards away.

"Marty, no!" a voice called out. I looked around just in time to dodge a shovel swung by the youngster at my head.

"Going to dig or bash my head in?" I asked, shoveling a bit of dirt toward him.

"Dig," he said, grinning.

By the time we'd completed our shallow well, I was rather well acquainted with Martin Martinson. He put me in mind of my brother Jeff, who was forever in one bit of mischief or another. Marty wasn't much more than seventy pounds of ornery bone and gristle, but I took a liking to him straight away.

Partly it was on account of his sister Marietta. She was a hair younger than Laveda Borden, but prettier and a whale of a lot easier to tolerate. She was a worker, too. Her father was the captain of the company, and her mother supervised the sick camp while Captain Martinson oversaw the stock. Marietta cooked, or mended, or prayed, or tended children, or nursed the sick near every minute of that entire day.

"She's got backbone enough to be a Crow," Shea remarked later as we emptied water barrels and refilled them with well water. "Haven't seen many white girls with that kind of grit."

"You don't make it down the trail without it," I told him. "You look hard enough, you'll find most of them have it."

"Seems to me they mostly whine and pray."

"Oh, you just don't remember," I complained.

"Maybe so," he said, scratching his head. "Still, I think you caught her eye."

"Whose eye?" I asked, trying not to display my interest.

"You know whose," he said, grinning. "Marietta's smart enough to notice your gaze, too, Darby Prescott.

'Course, if you're bound to go huntin' white women, you could do worse."

I laughed and continued with the work. He slapped my shoulder and howled.

The warm weather and fresh water soon put an end to the fever outbreak. It was half a week before the Martinson company was strong enough to consider continuing their journey, though. The fever had taken a toll, too. Four graves were dug, two of them for babies.

"To think it's all on account of the water!" Captain Martinson cried. "We never heard of such."

"That's what scouts are for," I grumbled as Shea and I prepared to leave. "If they're listened to, that is."

"I listen to those who know," Martinson insisted. "But you rely on a scout to know, and when he doesn't, you pay a price."

"Well, he paid as well," Marietta declared. "Was the first to die, remember?"

"Doesn't ease the weight he bears to eternity," Martinson said, scowling. "If anything, makes it worse. Now we've got to find another man to lead us west, and how're we to do that way out here on this empty plain? Plenty of men in Independence to choose from, and I picked wrong."

"Well, I know for a fact there's a good man at hand," I told them. "Tom Shea. Best man there is."

"What?" Marietta asked.

"Three Fingers Shea," I explained. "Crossed in '43 with the Whitmans and Tom Fitzpatrick. Took my papa's company to Oregon in '48, another train in '50. Why, he's ridin' for Independence to sign on again. Seems maybe you could save him a ride."

"Shea's a scout?" Martinson asked, gazing around in an effort to find him. "You sure?"

"Wouldn't I know?" I asked. "We're partners, after all."

"And who would you be exactly?" Marietta demanded.

"Darby Prescott, sometimes known as Illinois on ac-

220

count of my being born there. Was down the trail myself in '48, then back through the mountains this past year and a half. Orphaned at sixteen, grown tall and strong now at eighteen."

"More bluster than anything else," Marietta grumbled.

"But Shea knew about the water," her father pointed out. "We could try 'em out, couldn't we?"

"Try us?" I cried, laughing to myself. "Mister, Tom Shea's apt to try *you* out."

"Wouldn't hurt to talk with the man," Mrs. Martinson suggested. "Jared?"

The captain nodded, then set off to locate Shea. I grinned and waited for Marietta to say something. She didn't, just glared angrily and stormed off toward her wagon.

"She's always that way around people she likes," Marty told me. "You figure you could show me how to shoot buffalo maybe?"

"Or how to wrestle grizzlies," I whispered. "They'd like you. Gobble you in one big gulp."

"Oh, hush," he said, shoving me away with a grin.

Shea soon appeared with Captain Martinson.

"Darby!" Shea called, waving me over. I turned and scrambled to his side.

"Yeah?" I asked.

"Hear you've been doin' a fine job of boastin'," he grumbled. "Sayin' how I'm top scout on the trail and such."

"You are," I said.

"You ready to put your wayfarin' behind you so fast? I figured to have another month on the trail."

"Well, you never know what's ahead, Tom. These folks need a guide, and they seem amiable enough."

"I'll meet your terms," Martinson added. "Pay you both."

"We'll speak of it," Shea said, leading me aside.

"Well?" I asked.

"You really sure?"

221

"These are good people," I argued. "I got a family kind of feel for them already. Winter's one thing, but I want more'n a fire to warm me in springtime."

"This is a job you could do yourself, Illinois," he replied. "You've got the smarts and the gumption, and what you may not remember's scratched in those journals of yours."

"Not everything," I insisted.

"What counts. Shoot, boy, I've taught you what I know. The rest is for you to figure out as you ride. You will, too."

"It's true I know the trail, Tom, but I've never ridden it on my own. If I'm good company as you've said, why not partner up and herd these folks to Oregon?"

"You've done your growin', son. Time you stood on your own."

"I am," I told him. "Have been awhile now. But riding alone, well, that's bitter hard. I've been alone, and so have you. Can't tell me there's a worse way to be."

"No, it's a cold trail."

"Then partners?"

He grinned and gripped my hand. We then sat down with Martinson and agreed on terms.

Epilogue

So it was that on the first bright morning in May, 1852, Tom Shea and I stood at the head of a long line of wagons heading west. We'd been there before, had ridden that same ground. Now we were set to lead the way again, pathfinders for a company of pilgrims.

"Feels like familiar ground," he told me.

"Yes," I agreed.

And as I gazed upon the faces of the men and women, the boys and girls of the Martinson company, I knew I'd found, for a time at least, that elusive sense of belonging, a temporary home. It might prove to be fleeting, of course, but such is the fate of wanderers, of wayfarers.

"Ready?" Shea called.

"Ready," I replied.

And on we rode—westward.